JAGGED EDGE HORIZON

P.G. Baumstarck

JAGGED EDGE HORIZON

DOUBLE DRAGON

A DOUBLE DRAGON PAPERBACK

ISBN 978-1-78695-523-4

Double Dragon
is an imprint of
Fiction4All

This Edition Published 2021
Fiction4All
www.fiction4all.com

Cover art by Deron Douglas

ACKNOWLEDGEMENTS

This book is dedicated to my lovely wife, Emma, and to my parents.

I would also like to thank those who read and critiqued early versions of this book and my other stories, in particular Adam S. Rowell, Adam Smith, Anne Mashimo, Brent Robinson, and Brent Smith.

Chapter 1 - The Ambassador

Admiral Lene Willoch smoothed over her uniform and adjusted her cap as she stepped up outside of the Lontan Ambassador's office. She had been meeting with him for years, but she always liked to be perfectly arrayed before proceeding in. She was conscious of being a representative for her species, especially because the Ambassador wore his own Lontan body, not a synthetic Human one as most aliens did. Willoch suspected the Lontans showcased their true form this way in order to allay suspicion: wearing 'Human clothing' might make them easier to talk to, she thought, but we still find it inherently sinister. We want to know that the strangers will always show themselves unmasked.

The door opened onto the Ambassador's office, showing off its high ceiling and gaping rear window that offered a feast of starlight. While the Earth was never visible from these levels—hidden in Gateway Station's nadir—, a full moon hung brightly in view.

Despite this being the abode of an alien, the Ambassador had decorated solely with antiques that had been gifted to him by Terran governments. There was European portraiture, Asian screens and calligraphy, and a grand piano. The Ambassador himself was seated on a chaise longue—with the Lontans' size they found Human chairs uncomfortably narrow. His four arms rested at his sides while his hands were clasped meditatively in his lap. He wore an unadorned, single-piece suit that covered all but his head and hands. His face was a

Picassoesque jumble of features, only some of whose organs could be paired with Human cognates.

"Good afternoon, my dear Admiral. I trust you've been well?" the Ambassador greeted her.

Since he was wearing a Lontan body, he had spoken in his native language. Willoch's implanted body computers had transcribed all these warbles and hisses, translated them to Norwegian Bokmål, then ticker-taped the lines of text to her over her Ocular Heads-Up Display—her OHUD, the computer interface painted into her vision.

While his greeting was simple in principle, most of the Norwegian words pulsed with caveats to show all the translation's imprecisions. The 'Good afternoon' was tagged to show that the original Lontan phrase had been more exact, specifying a time closer to the 'second dog watch' in nautical terms. And the word 'dear' wore an entire paragraph describing the exact breed of Platonic attachment the Ambassador was implying. But Willoch disregarded most of these and responded only:

"Very well, Ambassador. And yourself?"

"Occupied with preparations. I have just received my next assignment."

"Oh?" Willoch was genuinely puzzled that he would be moving on. The Ambassador had been 'the Ambassador' ever since the beginning of Earth's first contact. Ever since she had been a little girl.

As if sensing her exact confusion, the Ambassador answered, "Fifty years may seem to presage an eternal commitment to your people, but for us Lontans it is merely a passing engagement. Time to move on."

"I see. And your next posting is to ... "

"The Xaccus Ringsystem."

"... Oh."

Willoch was impressed. Xaccus was the only extraterrestrial place that most Humans knew of, as apparently it was to the Milky Way what Tokyo, New York, and Beijing would be to the Earth if they were all combined. This made it an obvious step up from being ambassador to a world barely past first contact.

"Congratulations," Willoch said.

"It is only a *deputy* position ... " the Ambassador stipulated.

"But any posting to Xaccus is prestigious," Willoch countered for him.

The Ambassador nodded thanks—the Lontan nod, which consisted of pursing the over-shoulders. The gesture was also tagged in Willoch's OHUD by her translator, which could decipher alien body language. Though by now Willoch could recognize even subtle Lontan gestures herself.

"You must be excited at the prospect of getting back to ... well, *civilization*," she said.

"It's a lot less civilized than you'd think," he replied while making a Lontan grin. "Though I shall miss the provincial charm of your Earth, every day breaking new ground, reliving the first steps to the stars ... I plan to come back and visit after a century or so, to see the progress that's been made."

"I'm humbled," said Willoch.

Though privately she suspected that the Ambassador was not telling her the whole truth about his sudden reassignment. It might really be due to the Singularity. The worldwide depression was now five years old and every day brought new anti-alien and anti-technology protests. Perhaps the Lontans were sacking their Ambassador as an act of *mea culpa*, hoping it would relieve some pressure.

The Ambassador joined his over-hands in front of him, steepling the fingers—a symbol of change in topic. "But then we have urgent business to discuss," he said. "The piracy."

"Oh. Yes, indeed." Willoch had forgotten the original purpose of this meeting. Earth maintained a low tempo of imports from the nearest Lontan system, but the last freighters that were scheduled to arrive had all been hijacked. Willoch was here as the liaison of Earth's navies to the Lontans, as she was one of only eight admirals who commanded a black-water fleet. It was a lofty position, but she always felt like a mere pupil who handed in homework and wrote down whatever the Ambassador said.

She opened a notepad and the latest reports in her OHUD. She used eye gestures to set these documents off to the side in her vision so that she still had a full view of the Ambassador. "Do you have any new information for us?" she asked.

"No, it is still just the three freighters missing, all intercepted around six parsecs out from your system while on their way in. And we have no more details on those who are responsible."

Willoch subvocalized some notes, then started working down a list of prepared questions: "Do you have any idea how the pirates discovered our trade route with you? We thought the Lontans were keeping Earth's location a secret to guard against occurrences such as this."

"Oh, yes—in fact, we protect the locations of *all* first contact planets. Yet that does not change the eventuality of their being discovered. There has not been one first contact in the last millennium where we have revealed the planet's location on schedule versus it being discovered prematurely. —And then typically by pirates.

"In Earth's case, we were only expecting to be able to keep you hidden for a hundred to a hundred and twenty years. So of course fifty—as it has turned out to be—was on the low side of our expectations, but it is still nothing exceptional. Pirating bands are only too eager to be the first to burn a virgin trade route—they collect them like titles. And it does not take much to discover the economic footprint of a first contact planet out here in the hinterland."

This piqued Willoch. She was aware that the Earth was on the fringes of Milky Way civilization, but it was still no trailer home.

"And what response is the Lontan Governate planning to this piracy?" was her next question.

"Oh, we have already made our response: we have put a temporary hold on trade to your system to prevent further seizures."

Willoch was puzzled. "I meant, what actions is the Governate planning to *resolve* the piracy?"

11

"Oh, none whatsoever."

Willoch was now stupefied. Yet how to show that diplomatically ... "I'm sorry, 'nothing'?"

The Ambassador performed a flourish with his hands. "Our role as the stewards of your first contact is twofold. We are to empower your people by accelerating your development, and we are to guide you along that altered course. But you must always remain independent and capable of making your own decisions. If you became reliant on us now, you would never recover.

"As an example of this policy, the Lontan Governate maintains no military forces in your system, nor do we allow any other species to do so. But meanwhile we have sold you a fleet of our own warships, and those are *your* ships operated at *your* discretion. You yourself are an admiral in your country's navy. You could even turn those ships against us, should you wish, and—though we would advise against that—," he joked, "that is the power of decision we have not deprived you of.

"So you have asked me how the Lontan Governate will handle the appearance of this pirate threat. But I should ask you how Humanity will handle it, as you're the only ones with a fleet around here."

Willoch now understood, but she had still not expected this abrupt washing-of-hands from the Lontans. A pirate blockade was an interstellar issue, yet Humanity had never taken the helm on that stage. While they did fly around in the spaceships the Lontans had sold them, and tended the colonies on Mars and Venus the Lontans had helped them establish, they had never done anything without the sanction of their stewards. It seemed almost reckless to suddenly give them the lead here.

Luckily Willoch was not caught completely unprepared, as she and the other fleet admirals had sketched out a response to this pirate threat. Although they had done so merely as an exercise, thinking this would be thrown out in preference for whatever the Lontans dictated as the optimal course of action. Now that the Ambassador was actually asking for this, Willoch felt as if a bluff had been called.

She cleared her throat. "Well ... what we *planned*"—she began tepidly, already on the defensive and stressing the past tense—"was to send a small task force ... out to investigate the ... the missing ships." She was skimming the plan in her OHUD, looking ahead for any glaring errors. "We need to gauge the strength of whoever did this. And it will also serve as a ... fitting martial response to their actions. They've challenged our sovereignty by raiding our commerce, so we have to show some muscle.

"Of course none of our military officers has seen a real battle yet. We're all drills and exercises. So we would still like some ... direction from the Governate," she looked up. "Whatever you feel appropriate to provide. And who better for that than yourself, Mister Ambassador: you did spend three hundred years as an admiral in the Imperiate, I believe." She smiled ingratiatingly.

The Ambassador bowed. "I am happy to be of assistance. And your plan lies in the right direction.

13

Might I ask what size task force you were considering sending?"

"We'd planned for thirty-five ships. That's a large number for a reconnaissance mission, but that many ships will be able to hold its own against even a significant force. And it still leaves nearly a hundred ships back here to defend the system."

"Which ships are you sending?"

An odd question, Willoch thought. He must not be asking her to recite names and hull numbers ... Then she realized:

"At first we considered sending just one of the large, single-nation fleets like the States's or China's—that way the fleet would be best at functioning as a single unit. But then we thought that, since this might turn into a search for the pirate vessels, it might be best to send a few ships from each fleet. That way they'll be able to break up quickly into small groups along national lines and still operate effectively. And, after the mission, we'll have given field experience to officers from all eight national navies."

"Yes, an excellent idea. And a sound plan."

Willoch was increasingly surprised. Praise from the gods.

"How soon do you plan to launch?" he asked.

"... Within two days." She had just made that figure up, but without flinching.

"You appear to have the tactical situation well in hand, Admiral."

"Thank you, sir." She shifted in her seat. "So would you have any advice for us? ... Any hint of what we'll face out there?"

14

"Oh, I can tell you exactly what is going to happen."

Willoch edged forward in her seat, proffering eager attention.

"What these pirates have done so far is drawn your attention, and you are rightly sending an expeditionary force. But your fleet will find nothing. Instead, the pirates will come find *you*. They will send some ships out to meet yours, and appear in numbers roughly equal to your own. They will allow you to survey them and gauge their capabilities, without making a hostile move. And afterwards your fleet will be allowed to return home unchallenged.

"Now comes the part you will find distasteful. After this, your leaders should immediately restart interstellar trade without attempting to circumvent the pirates in any way. And then, after a few weeks, what you will find is that the pirates are intercepting one out of every ... eight or ten cargo vessels while letting the rest through. This will be their 'tithe.'"

Willoch recoiled. "Excuse me, I'm puzzled. You want us to ... *pay* these pirates?"

"To pay a 'tithe,' yes," the Ambassador corrected.

"I don't understand. A minute ago you approved of our plan to send our fleets out to disperse them. But now you want us to ... subsidize them?"

"Ah, then I did not make myself clear. You could never have actually 'dispersed' them with such an action. These pirates are not like those on Earth—ill-equipped outlaws who will flee from any real power. These are mercenaries with modern starships and weapons. And they would not have made their appearance unless they were able to overpower you."

Willoch balked. This situation was turning out far different from her preconceptions. "Then why don't they just ... overpower us? Attack and get it over with."

"Because it's wasteful. Your system has no valuable technologies that would make it worth sacking. Just some natural resources—which pirates can find in any of a dozen uninhabited systems. What they're interested in is your trade route with us. Tithing it will bring them more benefit in the long run than any wasteful bloodshed would right now."

Willoch was growing increasingly agitated. "So you just want us to ... give in."

"I know, I know, this must be surprising. You are a proud people, and this is your first real challenge. I have laid full power of action in your hands, and yet I have just told you to practice appeasement—repugnant, yes. But you must trust that this is by far the easiest way."

She almost scoffed. "Do even the Lontans make such deals with pirates?"

"At times, yes. And, if even we must compromise ... "

Willoch looked off. While she had been right that there was an 'optimal Lontan response' to this blockade, she had never imagined that it would be something so craven. The Lontans were a truly god-like species, and one expected dazzling displays of omnipotence from gods, not puling compromises.

"If you try a military solution," the Ambassador continued, "these pirates will fight you to exhaustion. Finally you will be forced to accept a tithe, but by then they will exact a far greater tribute than they would have at first.

"And please know that tithing is not completely one-sided. Once the pirates pick a tithe, they will stick to it. You will have to 'renegotiate' every five to ten years, but otherwise they will never provoke you to military action. And they will even protect your trade route from rival pirates who may try to stake their own claim.

"In all of this I am speaking empirically, of course. As a first contact ambassador I have studied thousands of cases of piracy to fledgling systems. It always comes, and this is always the easiest way of dealing with it."

Willoch was looking down, hands folded in her lap. "I see," she said, by way of holding back anything less tactful. "I wonder ... what is the probability that these pirates are bluffing? If this type of business is done galaxy-wide, then there must be pirates who are extorting a tithe when they have no ability to back it up."

"That is possible, but it is a question that will be answered by your reconnaissance mission. If they are bluffing then you will encounter only a paucity of ships, either antiquated or in disrepair. But if they are not ... "

"I see," she said again. She was closing and minimizing windows in her OHUD, clearing her desktop. "Well, thank you for your input,

17

Ambassador. I will indeed pass your recommendations along."

"Thank you, Admiral. I am only trying to save you time and trouble in the long run."

Willoch nodded with begrudging respect and departed. She headed back towards her office where she would write up a brief on her meeting. She did not know how she would present the Ambassador's advice to the other admirals—she still had to sort through her own feelings on it first ...

But in a moment she strayed to a halt. She realized that this was the first time she had left the Ambassador's office with not just another homework assignment. This time they had been given a mandate: 'Deal with the pirates yourselves.' At first she had been stunned and unready, but now she was warming to the challenge, thrilled at the power and freedom it represented. The Lontans were treating them as equals.

... Though soon resurfaced her old fear of whether or not they were ready to act on their own. This was a long-standing concern with Willoch. She had often considered how, when the Lontans made first contact, that had effectively chosen the nations and leaders that would take Humanity to the stars. Appearing in the 1990's seemed to have gone well so far; but, if they had come only sixty years earlier, they would have cemented Hitler, Stalin, and Tojo as the statesmen of the stellar age. What a ludicrous dice roll it was. So how much better could Willoch trust her own leaders—and herself—were?

But I won't shy away, she thought, spurring back on her path. She did not know whether she and her leaders were Caesars or Neros, Solomons or Caligulas, but they were what Humanity had. She could only trust that the Lontans had known what they were doing when they looked at the whirlwind waltz of Human history and said, 'Let's cut in here ...'

Chapter 2 - The Mannequin

Arriving at work in the morning, ISSO Special Agent Townsend was surprised by a meeting announcement popping up in his OHUD: he was needed in the Big Room—immediately. Despite being caught off guard, Townsend was optimistic. He had been due for a new assignment, and, typically, the less warning they gave of one, the more important it was.

Once at the Big Room, Townsend saw that this was not just a 'new assignment' but a 'genuine ordeal' that was afoot. In attendance were thirty field agents, their sector Chief, and another man wearing a suit six pay grades above everyone else's. Townsend recognized most of the other agents, but he queried for this last man's identity over his OHUD. When an ID card appeared over him, all it read was:

?

Townsend squinted in disbelief. This was glaring. The ISSO headquarters was a secure building. Everyone should be able to query for everyone else's ID, and everyone should be *known*. ... Although, if this meeting were being attended by a truly nameless power, then this might not just be a 'genuine ordeal' that they had on their hands but an 'honest cataclysm.'

After the last agent arrived, the doors were sealed and all were sent the mission package. The

OHUD document blossomed before him—
'Operation Mal Voisin'—and the Chief took the
rostrum. It was 0900 and the man had an
unmistakable all-nighter mien: there were fresh dark
circles around his eyes, his collar was undone, and
his tie was hanging as a slack noose down his shirt.

"Good morning? ... " the Chief opened, as if
guessing at the time, and it could really be
Christmas in China for all he knew. "So what I hope
you're all aware of—because you at least read
CWN—is the day's headline. That twelve hours ago
a hostile alien fleet began raiding our interstellar
commerce with the Lontans."

Oh—Townsend was surprised. He had been
late getting in that morning and so had not yet
caught up with Classified World News. But an act
of interstellar piracy—their planet's first—was news
indeed. The fact that it had happened last night also
explained the Chief's disheveled state. Though
Townsend did not immediately see how this
concerned their agency. For all the things the
International Special Security Office did, it dabbled
little in space.

"Right now it's only three Lontan freighters
missing," the Chief continued, "all seized
simultaneously around six parsecs out. From the
data cast back over the freighters' autopilots, we
know that each was hijacked by a three-ship team.
Observe ... "

He motioned upwards, and a sensor
reconstruction of the hijacking appeared in
holoprojection overhead. And it was dry and
unnecessary—just some multi-colored dots flying

around. But Townsend knew the real purpose of this display was to show how the ISSO was privy to data that could only have come from the Lontan Governate.

"We're trying to identify the pirate ships and who was flying them," said the Chief, "but the sensor readings aren't detailed enough.

"Nowww ... what I hope you all *don't* know—because you certainly weren't cleared to—is the version of events you won't get from CWN. We're keeping this information sealed even within the intelligence community because, if *this* were leaked, it could conceivably start a worldwide panic.

"Just minutes after those freighters were seized, the pirate ships responsible broadcast a single hypercomm message into our system. It consisted of around three thousand bits. And then someone *responded*." The Chief paused dramatically. "A hypercomm somewhere on Earth cast back its own three-kilobit response."

Townsend did not understand the gravity of this, but he acted like he did—the same as the rest of the agents. He glanced at the unidentified man up front—'Question Mark,' he thought of him—to see if he made any telling response, but he had stayed looking intently forward.

"Before this we believed there were no unregistered hypercomms in the system," the Chief continued. "Any Human-operated ones were strictly licensed, and the alien ones were even more tightly controlled. All of these have since been checked, but none of them was used to broadcast the terrestrial signal. Which means someone has smuggled a hypercomm down to the planet."

Townsend still did not see the significance of this. Granted the ISSO was charged with cleaning up restricted alien technology, but the last time they had thrown thirty agents at something was when a watch-sized nuclear weapon had been smuggled down to Turkey. But a hypercomm was just an FTL communication device.

"Sir," an agent asked, "have we tried to decode the contents of the pirate messages?"

"Yes, we have. Though strangely they don't seem to be encoded. On the surface it looks like the first message was just a set of sequential Mersenne primes, and then the response contained the first seventeen terms from something called the 'Dashouk ensemble.' The IONI thinks that these math sequences might have been used as carriers for some hidden data, but they're still running the numbers on that."

"Do we have a point of origin for the broadcast, sir?" another agent asked.

"Indeed. If you look into the materials you've received, you'll see that our own equipment up on Gateway Station recorded the signal, localized its point of origin, and came up with this."

The main holo now showed a large, shaded region representing a three-dimensional probability distribution, sloping off on all axes as a bell shape. It took Townsend a while to locate the two dots in the display labeled 'Earth' and 'Moon.' So the best Human estimates had the signal coming from

23

somewhere within eight million kilometers. Informative.

"Not very precise," commented the Chief. "But they tell me there was some advanced scrambling put on this signal to make it nearly impossible to trace, so we weren't meant to do any better.

"But the Lontans have taken an interest in this signal—along with the whole pirate blockade, obviously. And they will be sharing their intel on this one. Their equipment is, of course, much better than ours, and they can verify that the signal came from a planetary source. In fact they narrowed it down to this."

The holo turned into a map of Europe. It was overlaid with an oval trace that stretched in its major axis from Morocco up to Novaya Zemlya, and encompassed most of the Continent along its minor axis. This at least explained to Townsend why the European branch of the ISSO had landed this assignment.

"Obviously much better, but it still doesn't narrow down our search too much. It turns out that this signal was from a modern hypercomm with up-to-date scrambling abilities, so it can befuddle even the Lontans.

"What all this means is that these pirates, whoever they are, already have some agents down on the planet. When their fleet moved into position and started picking off our shipping, they sent a code to their planetary operatives. And these operatives responded.

"Now, we could speculate about what these agents are up to. It could be to gather intelligence, to conduct sabotage, to perform some black ops—we don't know. But what we *do* know is that you don't need boots on the ground if all you're planning to do is to raid commerce from twenty light-years away."

Now Townsend finally understood this mission's importance, but, since he had already pretended to have gotten it a minute ago, he had to stifle his reaction now.

"Hence your current assignment, Mal Voisin. Our objectives are to find and secure the pirate hypercomm, and to capture its operators."

Townsend looked around at the other agents, and he saw mirrored satisfaction in their eyes. Here finally was a real assignment.

Townsend had joined the ISSO two years ago with typically James Bond–like aspirations. And then getting his posting to 'Special Field Ops' had seemed like a martini shaken to perfect agitation. But soon afterwards had come bitter disillusionment. The ISSO—the *International* Special Security Office—had been formed solely because the Lontans would only work with agencies that bore that vague, 'international' seal of approval. But the Kumbaya moment at the ISSO's ribbon-cutting had been short-lived. The veins of intra-Human distrust ran too deep, and it was soon clear that the ISSO, instead of an intelligence *agency*, was really an intelligence *router*, full of moles leaking everything they could back to the old, *national* intelligence agencies—CIA, FSB, MI6. Half of what the ISSO did was finding and purging its own spies—an obviously 'special' job that thus fell to 'Special Field Ops.' Townsend would have moved on long ago, were it not for the depression and the fact that there was nowhere to move on to.

The Chief proceeded, "And the Lontans will be doing more than just furnishing intelligence on this mission. They've volunteered some of their own personnel and resources to assist us, and we've agreed."

This announcement was jarring. Granted the Lontans were supposed to be their allies, but, the way Townsend saw it, when the gods themselves stooped down to meddle in the battlefield, some serious shit was about to go down.

"Each of you will be given a Lontan agent to work with as your partner."

"Uhhh, a Lontan, sir?" an agent joked. "Won't that be kind of conspicuous?"

"No, I don't think so."

At this Question Mark stood and turned to the assembly.

"Gentlemen, allow me to introduce, um ... " In lieu of a name, the Chief forwarded them a jot of curvy Lontanscript over their OHUDs. "Of course his Lontan name is unpronounceable, but for our purposes you can address him by his cover name: Inspector Bryant. The Inspector is a celebrated Lontan investigator and currently serving as the Chief of Security up on their Embassy."

So the unidentified man was really a Lontan wearing a Human mannequin. And Townsend realized that that was how all their new partners would be 'disguised,' as well.

26

"Thank you, Chief," the Lontan answered in a highbrow British accent. "Yes, as you might have guessed, this is the most important assignment yet in the ISSO's history. Someone has smuggled a hypercomm down onto the planet and is using it to maintain communications with a hostile alien force. Because of the possible global repercussions of this, and because of the technologically advanced level of your adversaries, the Governate has authorized direct Lontan involvement. Luckily this is just what the ISSO was designed for: to be the interface in any serious Human–Lontan collaboration."

"Pardon me, Inspector," interjected an agent, "but just to be clear, you came all the way down here from the Embassy—and so did thirty other Lontans—just to work with us?"

"Yes and no," he answered.

Typical Lontan sophistry, scoffed Townsend.

"This consciousness," he explained, "is merely a partial of my prime—the true Inspector—who yet remains invested up on the Embassy. And all of your Lontan partners will simply be more mannequins containing extra copies of myself. So please do not think of it as any more serious an investment of personnel than that."

Townsend took a moment to shiver in his outmoded Human sensibilities.

"So let me fill you in on your specific assignments ... " the Chief reasserted himself.

The room's holo now became a map of Africa. Ever since the twenties the Sahara had become the crossroads of the world's black market. Hastily built trading posts dotted the desert, invisible to all but the most fastidious satellite reconnaissance. Illegal goods and alien contraband were sold out of every tent from the Ivory Coast to the Nile Delta.

"A hypercomm is a substantial piece of alien hardware that can't be produced natively, so it must have been smuggled down. We're going to be kicking over some of the rocks where that might have happened. One hundred and fifty-four of them to be exact."

As promised, the map became stippled with 154 red dots clustered in the Eastern Sahara.

"To hit these camps we're assembling strike groups from European, US, and Chinese troops in the region. Some of you will be riding along with them to conduct our on-site investigation and intel collection. But you'll only have time to do a quick once-through at each scene. These camps are close-knit to sound the alarm in case someone tries an *en masse* raid just like this, so we'll be hitting them all within eight hours."

"Pardon me, sirs," said Townsend, "but I don't see what we're going to accomplish with this raid. You know that none of those camps is ever there for more than a few days at a time. Every hundred hours, they pack everything up and the hovers skip out. The location is quickly buried under the sand. If a hypercomm was smuggled down there, the actual camp used surely doesn't exist anymore. And the evidence will have been buried or broken up into pieces too small to detect."

"To detect with *Human* technology," corrected the Inspector, "but not with ours."

Townsend found it odd to see a Human body saying 'ours' and not meaning 'Human.' A sinister reminder that there was an alien unknown pacing behind those eyes.

"And the periodic relocations you mentioned will actually aid us. With the evidence of the hypercomm being now dispersed over many camps, our chances of finding something are that much higher. In fact, we did not pick these camps because they are specifically likely to yield intelligence, but because they will provide us with an even sampling of all the camps. This will maximize our chances of finding evidence of the hypercomm."

Townsend shrugged in concession.

"So that covers the bottom of the smuggling pyramid," the Chief stepped back in, "but we're going to be working all of its levels. So, while most of you are shipping down to Africa, some of you will start running down leads around Europe. Details of your individual assignments are in your folders. But some of you have places to be in half an hour, so we'll have to cut this short. Are there any closing questions?"

The room was silent. Townsend knew they were all anxious to see this assignment started.

"Very well," said the Chief. "—But just out in the hall you'll meet up with your Lontan partners. Like the Inspector said, they're all him inside, so they're all experts on everything. If you have any questions, just ask them. —Him."

Outside was waiting the promised mass of thirty agents. They may all have had the same consciousness inside, but every mannequin had a unique appearance drawn randomly from the ISSO's own distribution of races and genders. As each 'real' ISSO agent stepped out of the conference room, one of the pack of mannequins stepped forward to intercept them. Townsend briefly hoped he would be paired with one of the comely female variants— before reconsidering. There was a great deal of awkwardness possible when one's partner was a belle dame on the outside but an androgynous alien geezer within.

In the end his partner was a man of Sino-Caucasian features, above-average height, and average build. Townsend extended his hand to shake—before remembering that this was an alien who probably did not shake hands. Yet the mannequin reached forward and caught his grip firmly.

"It's all right, Special Agent Townsend," he said, "I have had Human customs grafted into my personality for this mission. They are second nature to me."

Townsend cocked his head and studied the mannequin's face, having never seen one this close before. The detail was flawless. He wondered whether this were a purely synthetic mannequin—a 'plastic'—or one where a natural Human body had been cloned and installed with a brain pan to host its alien mind—a 'skinjob.'

"Right, well ... " Townsend at last replied. "Pleased to meet you. ... Again. ... Inspector."

"Actually each of me has an individual cover," the man said, gesturing at his other mannequin-selves. He forwarded Townsend his own credentials: 'Special Agent Hector Zhang–Moseby.'

"Well, pleased to meet you, 'Zhang.'"

Zhang steered them out of the traffic jam of agents and mannequins. "We're one of the teams going down to Africa," he said over his shoulder. "We must depart straightaway for the airbase."

"Lead the way."

Meanwhile Townsend hung back to study Zhang from behind. He watched the perfection of it, the naturalness of its gait, the swinging of the arms, the turns of its head ... If this were some random person, Townsend would not have thought twice about him. But the very knowledge that this was an imitation cast his impression into the uncanny valley.

Zhang walked on wordlessly. He seemed to expect Townsend to accept him as his new partner as casually as they had shaken hands, but he was terribly far from that. Of course Townsend respected the Lontans, but he respected them as a vague ideal. It was a far different bargain to put his life into the hands of one of their 'units.' Was this Zhang an actual person whom he could trust, or merely a sentient set of algorithms and optimization objectives that would download back to the mothership the instant a fight started?

Though he thought of one way he could pry beneath this mannequin's exterior, if only slightly. It came from how the Inspector had used the politically correct word 'mannequins' to refer to himselves, since 'skinjobs' was somewhat regarded as a racial slur. Yet it was common in the ISSO, and

31

Townsend was bound to let the word slip some time. He wondered if Zhang would take offense, and he decided to find out:

"So, Zhang, these pirate agents down here ... I assume they're all wearing *skinjobs* like yours, hm?"

"Of course," Zhang chirped, as if immune to irritation. "And you needn't worry about offending me, Agent Townsend; you can be as free with your language as you wish."

"Ah. Well then, 'Fucking skinjobs.'"

"Indeed. Illegal mannequins tarnish the image of the rest of us."

"The rest of us? ... Say, how many skinjobs are there on the planet anyway?"

"Only three hundred legitimate ones, but several times more of the unregistered variety."

Townsend was stunned by this forthright answer. He had once tried to get a figure for the number of mannequins planet-side himself, but his request had been denied—it was not in his 'need to know.' Yet, now that he was working with a Lontan, all he had to do was ask and so many doors were opened ...

"So, Zhang—*quick*, does God exist?—yes or no?" Townsend blurted out.

Zhang paused. Then replied, "Meh." Bright but noncommittal.

Townsend stared. "I expected you to say something official like, 'I can neither confirm nor deny the existence of any deity posited by Human theology.' But 'meh'?"

"Meh," Zhang repeated.

32

A very Human response, that, Townsend thought. Perhaps there was more to this mannequin than just a robotic personality loaded Human Etiquette 1.0.

And suddenly he was looking forward to this partnership.

Chapter 3 - Lindon

"Corporate pig!"

A bottle smashed into his window and Peder Kjaerstad jerked backwards. His limousine had been driving him to an appointment in Stockholm, but it had suddenly pulled abreast of a mob of protestors.

After the bottle came a wave of litter and rocks. Then the protestors swarmed in to hammer their fists on his car, shrieking and spitting on his windows. Peder was briefly worried, but reminded himself that his limousine was a diplomat-class courier vehicle, with enough armor to survive being hit by an old groundtank.

But then his car stopped. The road was clear, so the autodriver should have kept going. Peder logged in to take manual control—but the crowd had already taken advantage of the pause and surged around him. They got in front of the limousine and blocked his way.

"Fucking driver ... " Peder muttered. Why had his car stopped here?

In seconds every window was filled with screaming faces. The protesters were all blind rage, unshaven, and disheveled. Peder got ready to hit the throttle and cowcatcher his way out of this jam.

Suddenly policemen and corporate security rushed into view. They were wearing a mix of riot gear and muscle suits that allowed them to easily herd the crowd. They pulled the protesters away from Peder's car and cleared a space. From the insignia on their uniforms Peder realized that he had arrived at his destination, Lindon Securities Corporate Headquarters. This explained why his limousine had stopped. —And it also explained the presence of the mob. Peder dimly remembered there being a citywide protest scheduled for today, and such organizers never failed to allocate a sizable horde for the Spire's entrance.

A guard opened his door for him, and Peder moved down a gauntlet of uniformed men. He glanced around and saw that the protesters numbered in the hundreds. Many of them had a virtual poster, slogan, or vid rendered above them in public augspace. Combined these were putting out a pulsing vitriol of anti-capitalism, anti-technology, and anti-alien slogans.

Security walked him to the edge of the Spire's pavilion. When he passed the fence line, the barrier's sonic dampening made the crowd seem to recede to a great distance.

Peder was relieved by this open, uncrowded space. The pavilion was dotted with fountains and box gardens, and there were only a few dozen people about, all civilized specimens wearing trim suits. The corporate arcology sat back from the street, bathed in sunlight and lording over the protest.

Approaching the arcology's facade, Peder saw a woman standing before the doors, her gaze fixed upon him.

"Mister Kjaerstad, good morning," she said crisply as he neared. "Secily Grundt," she introduced herself.

"Mizz Grundt," he replied.

She led him inside.

The Spire's decor was becoming more austere every time Peder visited. Years ago it had been as cluttered with designer furniture and abstract art as any corporate headquarters, but now it looked conspicuously as if it had been stripped for a liquidation sale. Grundt led him to the building's central lift trunk where a car awaited him. Peder entered alone and was ferried up to the CEO's penthouse suite.

Exiting the car he saw Olof Lindon seated at his desk. His back was to an array of floor-to-ceiling windows, which were breathing confidently over the arcojungle of Stockholm's business district. The light made Lindon's silver hair seem nearly incandescent, and it accentuated the wrinkles on his face into grave lines. Lindon was one of the few people Peder knew who had abstained from all cosmetic surgery. Despite its near outpatient ease nowadays, perhaps men of Lindon's age were still old enough to disdain it. But Peder, being a generation younger, had had no such compunctions.

"Good morning, Peder," said Lindon. He stayed seated and kept his hands joined on the desk, thus negating the possibility of a handshake.

"Good morning, sir," Peder replied, taking his own seat.

"We hope your ride in through the protest wasn't too eventful."

"No, sir. ... Just that little tussle at the end."

Lindon grinned slightly. "You don't mind that we used you for some fishing?"

"... 'Fishing'?"

"'Fishing for prosecutions'—it's a hobby of ours."

Lindon placed a vid into augspace between them. It was a security cam's view of Peder's car being mobbed. The vid looped, each time showing the scene from a different angle.

"These demonstrations are so unsightly," Lindon continued, watching the vid. "We've tried to keep them away from the Spire, but the law restrains us. Still, if *we* have to play by the rules, then *they* have to play by them, too. And look at all this ... " He pointed into the vid as he called out, "That's assault ... trespassing ... assault with a deadly weapon ... and the boy yelling 'corporate pig'—that's hate speech."

"... Really, sir?" asked Peder, surprised that the hate speech laws had grown so broad.

"Of course! 'Corporate pig,' that's ... disparaging someone based on their economic beliefs."

Peder squinted. "I thought hate speech dealt mostly with religious beliefs and such."

"Well, economics is the only religion that most of the world has left."

Peder admitted to that.

Lindon made the vid disappear. "Well! Shall we proceed with the authorization handover?" He gestured to a palm scanner on his desk.

Simultaneously a cascade of legal documents flooded Peder's vision in his OHUD. Each was primed for his signature.

Peder cleared his throat. This handover was the reason Lindon had called him here, but it still startled him.

"Of course, sir ... " he said, stalling while he used eye gestures to move the new documents off to the side on his desktop. "Though might I have a word with you first?"

Lindon acted as if Peder had not spoken and kept his hand pointing to the scanner.

"Just to reiterate some of the conditions we had agreed upon?"

Lindon waited several more seconds. Then he pointedly retracted his hand and straightened up, showing what an imposition Peder was making on him.

"We had thought we had already made you ample assurances," Lindon replied coldly, making liberal use of the Corporate 'we.' "The language in the contract has been approved by both sides. We have gone through all the trouble of calling you here, and yet you still insist on delay."

Peder looked down, admitting he was being difficult. He stretched forward his hand and placed it on the scanner, letting it confirm his identity. Then he flipped through the OHUD documents and appended his digital signature to each.

This handover could have been done remotely, but Lindon had insisted Peder come in. —And on a day when his headquarters would be besieged by protesters. Peder suspected that this was a power play. After his long resistance, Lindon wanted to impress upon him who it was between them who had the corporate arcology, the penthouse office, and the army of muscle suit'ed security guards. And it also explained why Lindon had made such a point of his 'fishing' with the protesters: it illustrated the lengths he would go to in order to punish disobedience, however minor.

Once Peder was finished signing the documents, Lindon relaxed his posture. It was only slightly, but enough to betray that he was relieved. A minute ago Peder was the CEO of a corporate security firm under contract to Lindon. Now he was completely subjugated. Only another one of the minor, sidelined bureaucrats in the man's 'corporate army.'

"Of course you needn't worry about your future with us, Peder," Lindon said melodiously. "This is but the start of a new phase in our relationship. Your company has been with us from the beginning, and you will continue to be invaluable in performing your crucial administrative role."

Peder translated: 'You'll still own your car and get to pay for all the gas, maintenance, insurance, et cetera. I'll just be the only one who gets to drive it now.'

He knew he was supposed to reply with a cowed 'Thank you, sir.' But after all of Lindon's pompous regal flourishes, and after having just signed away his self-respect, he could not help himself:

"*Ah*," was his reply—a syllable was spiked with sarcasm.

Lindon's gaze sharpened. "Oh?" he challenged.

But, "Hm?" Peder returned innocently, playing dumb that he had committed any offense.

39

Lindon frowned. Now he could either push on—and turn this into another one of his and Peder's famous arguments—, or he could let the man's insolence pass. He glowered while he thought it over ...

Though in the end he let it go. Lindon looked off into a window behind Peder while he swallowed his ire.

Seeing this, Peder became almost angry that he had not played the bigger man himself. A person could tolerate almost any flaw in their enemies, aside from the unforgivable one of being better men than them. —But Lindon was *not* the better man, which made these lapses all the more painful.

Lindon's frown gradually relaxed, but he stayed looking off as he said, "Well, you must be anxious to get back to your office. Secily will show you out." He motioned behind Peder where the lev car had suddenly reappeared, standing open with Ms. Grundt inside.

Peder looked back to Lindon, who was already bent down in other work. Peder nodded and left.

The lift carried him down to a subterranean garage where his limousine awaited—having parked there after dropping him off. He climbed in and the car set off on a winding path upwards. Eventually it surfaced into daylight, turning back out onto regular Stockholm streets. But Peder looked around, not recognizing the locale. The garage exit his car had used lay between a dry cleaners and a coffee shop, with no Lindon company insignia anywhere. Nor any protesters ... He checked his location over the car's maps and found that he was already two blocks away from the Spire. This had to be a secret exit.

... He realized the lesson Lindon was trying to teach him. Before today, the two of them had been enemies. But with those protesters out front Lindon was showing Peder that he already had plenty of those, and that they were powerless against him. Peder could count himself in their camp, but they would not accept him, and what could he even accomplish? However, once Peder had submitted and signed the handover, he was restored the privileges of trust. The Spire would stand up to the rising anarchy out front while Peder was made benefit of all the company's power and protection.

Too bad that the next thing he was going to do was to ruin that arrangement.

Chapter 4 - Märtha

Lieutenant Colonel Hanssen was staring out the cockpit watching the sea treadmill past. A radar blip distracted him.

"Huh ... " chirped his pilot, Lieutenant Erlend. "Odd set of contacts here. One looks like a fishing trawler, but the other's definitely a hovertank. They're nestled up close together. ... And both at elevation zero. The tank must be floating on its pontoons. Ten klicks out."

Hanssen checked the contacts himself in his augspace dashboard. "Another hovertank? I thought we were the only flight out in this sector."

"Me, too. Should I hail them?"

"—No," Hanssen realized something. "It might be a drug transfer."

"Ahhh, that makes sense," said Erlend. "An ANP hovertank moving cargo over to an innocent-looking fishing trawler. Only ... " he turned skeptical, "why would they be doing it in the middle of the day? Hardly subtle." He panned his head around demonstratively at the bright sky.

"Who knows. But let's surprise them. Drop down and close on stealth. We'll hail only once we're on top of them."

Erlend brought their hovertank down to wave top levels. They would lose their radar sighting while this low, but they could close the distance in only minutes.

As they waited, Hanssen wondered whether or not they should have called back to home base in

Leknes before charging in. The Home Guard was almost in a state of war with the drug runners of the paramilitary Army of Norwegian Patriots. He did not want to risk dying in a confrontation without leaving his people some idea of where to start looking for their corpses.

A black speck resolved ahead out of the scintillating ocean horizon. Erlend accelerated and gained altitude, intending to do a shock-and-awe flyover at attack speeds.

They watched feeds from the tank's ventral cameras as they crossed overhead. They saw the fishing trawler—which was Norwegian-flagged—and a hovertank sitting in the water off to its keel. There were four people on the ship, all looking up at them with surprise. Two of them were uniformed men, but the others were an old man and a teenage girl, perhaps sixteen or seventeen.

After their flyover, Hanssen looked back through the recorded cam feeds to examine them in detail. He isolated an image of the hovertank. While the ANP had no strict marking system for its vehicles, one could usually identify them just from the gaudy decals and spray-painted names they wore. This tank, however, was clean, and wore an insignia that was not the ANP's. Hanssen knew the symbol, but this was the first time he had seen it in person: the Lindon Securities corporate army.

"Lindon Securities—well, there goes our drug drop theory," said Erlend. On the comms he hailed in English, "Home Guard Flight to unidentified hovertank in Norwegian waters, come back." He

43

was circling back around to the scene and slowing in preparation for coming to a hover.

Over the cams they saw the uniformed men on the boat—the corporate army officers—arguing with each other. One looked up and spoke, and they heard him over the comms:

"Corporate Army Flight to Home Guard," the man's English wore a heavy German accent. "There is nothing happening here. Uh ... Over and out."

Erlend turned around to flash a suspicious glance at Hanssen. This was not easy with the seating configuration of the hovertank, but Erlend thought it worthwhile to make the look explicit. Hanssen motioned for him to set down.

They deployed their pontoons and landed in the water beside the ship. Popping their cockpit, the old Norwegian man on the ship threw them a line. They reeled their tank in, and Hanssen hopped over onto the deck.

"Thank God you came!" the old man exclaimed. "These men here—these *robbers*—" he gestured at the corporate army officers, "were stealing fish out of my catch."

The teenage girl next to him chimed in with her own part of the story, and added that the soldiers were 'perverts.'

A box full of iced fish sat next to the corporate army soldiers and the cargo door on their tank was open. They were both looking down wryly shamefaced. Obviously the fisherman was telling the truth.

"Huh," replied Hanssen. "You guys do this often?" he asked the soldiers.

When they said nothing, the fisherman exclaimed, "All the time! Boats everywhere across the bay, and all down the coast get stopped by the corporate army. They take whatever they want back to their base. Must be cheaper than buying at the markets," he huffed. "It's hard enough making a living without having to deal with this!"

"Look, we'll just go, all right?" interjected one of the soldiers. He spoke German now, so all the Norwegians had to glance down to read the translation that had appeared like subtitles in their OHUDs.

Hanssen stared at the man intently.

"Okay, get out of here," he said. "But tell your army buddies that these are Leknes waters. And that the Home Guard patrols them."

The men turned to go.

But the girl suddenly yelled, "Yeah, get out of here!" and charged one of them. The man easily pushed her away, but it made him lose his balance. The boat was also rocking, so he started to fall backwards. His friend reached out to steady him.

The girl charged him next and swatted at him. Both men were already unsteady, and the girl's assault bent them farther over the boat edge. The second man grabbed the girl's fists, but she climbed up onto the edge of the boat behind him for leverage. Now towering above she had the power to push them both over the side. But the man still had a grip on her arms, so as they fell overboard she went sailing over them in a somersault.

While all the splashes played out, Hanssen glanced at the old man. His look said he was

45

wondering what such a hotheaded girl was doing on a fishing boat.

The old man shrugged. "She's my granddaughter," he explained. "Orphaned by the Singularity."

'Ah,' Hanssen mouthed.

"Not too suited to a fishing life," the man added.

They stepped over to the side of the boat. The corporate army officers were swimming back to their tank, and the girl was splashing around and yelling. Hanssen and the man caught her arms and lifted her back aboard.

As soon as they set her down on the deck, she spun around and hugged Hanssen tightly.

"Oh, thank you, sir!" she exclaimed.

Hanssen held his arms out away from her. "Uh ... it's ... Colonel," he replied. Giving her his rank was the only personal distance he was willing to give up at the moment.

She released him and stood back, glowing and panting and dripping. Hanssen avoided her effusive look.

"Eiver Velding," the old man introduced himself, shaking hands. Hanssen was thankful to have someone else to pay attention to. "And this is Märtha."

Hanssen introduced himself and shook their hands. Looking around at their boat he asked, "Do you ... need a tow?"

"No, we'll be fine. But ... if you could follow that tank and see that it leaves the bay without harassing anyone else, I would be much obliged."

By now the two corporate army soldiers had climbed back into their tank and started its engines. With a loud exertion they lifted up and headed southeast, back towards the Norwegian mainland.

Hanssen jerked a thumb at them. "Does that happen a lot?" he asked Velding.

The old man had been looking at him thankfully before, but now his brow furrowed. "Are you serious?"

Hanssen put his thumb down.

"... You've heard of the corporate army, but you don't know about all the trouble they cause?"

Hanssen shrugged. "I'd ... heard of it, yes. But this is the first time I've actually seen them. And this far north. I thought they were concentrated around Oslo."

"Yes, *were*," the man huffed. "But they've been spreading for three years. There's no government stopping them from taking as much land as they want, eh? And then everywhere they go are more perks—like this bay — all the free fish they want!" He threw up his hands.

Hanssen kept an eye on the corporate army tank as it receded.

***

Back at the Home Guard base that night, Hanssen was returning from the mess when Erlend called to him from a recreation room.

"Haze! Check it out," he said, and forwarded him a video link. It was on VizPlay, the top sharing site for OHUD captures. The title was 'Corporate Army Shakedown Shaken Up.'

47

"It's from the old man on that ship we saved today," Erlend explained. "I guess he started recording everything in his viz as soon as he saw the corporate army coming. Usually the soldiers will erase shit like that, but they didn't get to this time 'cause we showed up. Now it's on the web."

Hanssen watched the video, which showed the incident from the man's perspective. It started with the corporate army soldiers boarding his ship and pushing him around arrogantly. Then there was the appearance of the Home Guard tank and their own intervention.

The highlight of the video, though, was when the manic teenage Märtha charged the heavily armed soldiers and manhandled them into the water. The full vid was seven minutes, but this eight-second clip had been spliced out and received hundreds of thousands of views on its own. And there were many edited versions that had mixed the vid with the memes *du jour*.

When he was done watching it, Hanssen sighed.

"'Course the whole vid itself is nothing new— I've seen dozens of others like this," Erlend continued. "But it's the *girl* that makes this one." He chuckled as he watched another variation of the eight-second attack sequence. "So I just thought I should warn you: this is gonna be *big*."

Hanssen clutched the bridge of his nose as if biting back a headache. He was a private man who dreaded any attention to his life. His policy towards the world was to just leave it alone to do what it always did, so why couldn't it simply return him the favor?

Chapter 5 - Zuzanna

After arriving home from his meeting with Lindon, Peder went to the entrance to his As-Secure-As-Possible Room. The matte gray door was unassuming and spotless to an atomic level. It sat in front of what used to be his study, but what was now an hermetic information chamber. This was where Peder spent most of his time at home; so much so that his house was really only a gaudy decoy for this one functional compartment.

He had placed a wet bar right next to the entrance, from which he poured himself a glass of wine. Then he opened the door and stepped into the ASAPR's vestibule. A slight breeze enveloped him as the compartment breathed millions of friendly nanomachines onto him. These scrounged for any hitchhikers or spammachines that had attached to him over the course of the day, and dismantled them into micrograms of scrap. He sipped from the wine while he waited out this minute-long procedure.

Next all of his body computers and internal systems allowed themselves to be taken over by the ASAPR's systems. The room's purpose was to make sure that nothing could be recorded—no information stolen—from inside of it, so it needed control over the dozens of pinpoint body mics and cams he had implanted in his skin. It switched these off and locked down their I/O.

Once the scan finished, a message appeared in his OHUD. Everything showed green, and it also announced the tally of foreign objects that had been purged from him. Today it was over six million. That was higher than usual, but not bad considering the huge protest he had walked through.

The inner door slid open and admitted him to the room proper. The ASAPR was small to limit expense, but it was fully decorated, including a kitchenette and a stasis chamber pot. Since it was round, Peder fancied it looked like the interior of an opulent flying saucer.

He sat down at his comp and pulled up Zuzanna Mukhina's information. He checked the time before placing a call to her, which he brought up on the large screen. She soon appeared seated at her own desk, in her own ASAPR, somewhere across Stockholm. She was dressed smartly as always, with only the lightest accents in jewelry and makeup. It was a modest but fetching look that well complimented her thirty-four years.

"Peder!" she opened warmly. "You're three minutes late. Something wrong?"

"No, no. I was just accosted a little on my way in to Lindon today."

"I saw, yes ... " Zuzanna spliced a vid feed into the comm channel. It showed Peder's car being mobbed by the protestors that morning.

Peder understood: she was showing off a bit of the Mafia's abilities, and how they could steal same-day security vidage from a company as powerful as Lindon. Zuzanna was Peder's connection to an intelligence services firm run by the Russian Mafia. Consorting with such illicit organizations was something he had never done before the depression—too pricey. But since then even the Mafia had been operating at closeout prices.

"Yes, very cute," he said.

Zuzanna grinned. "So! You have a job for us?"

"Yes, should be a simple one."

"Kind?"

"Blackmail fodder."

Zuzanna's lips quivered as she sub-vocalized notes into her OHUD.

"In my invite I told you about the meeting I was heading into today," Peder continued. "And it happened just like I said: I had to sign over control of everything to Lindon. Now I'm cut out like all the others. And all I know is he's bringing in some ringer named Reeser Atkins to run the corporate army for him."

"And this Atkins is the one you want dirt on?"

"Exactly. If I can get leverage over him, I can put myself back in the loop. Though ... before we continue, I do have a small confession to make. I didn't come to you first with this job. I ac—"

"You went to Georgiev's organization, yes, we know," Zuzanna said admonishingly. "Why did you use those amateurs, Peder?"

He shrugged. "They're cheap."

"And you got what you paid for. That now you're coming to us anyway, but you're already fifty k in the hole."

He was impressed that Zuzanna's people knew not only whom he had gone to beforehand but also how much he had paid. ... Then again, Zuzanna— being his Mafia handler—would know things about

52

him that his doctor, lawyer, priest, and mother all put together did not.

"And, honestly, Peder, why would you risk half-assing this?" she continued. "Lindon Securities isn't just another corporation. They're one of the few still growing during the depression—and it takes a special kind of evil to accomplish that. Their capabilities are enormous. And don't even get me started on that corporate army your boss is running ... "

"Corporate militaries are nothing new," Peder downplayed this.

"On Lindon's scale? Yes, they are. And then to go and build it all on top of the Oslo ruins ... " Her vision drifted off as she became absorbed in her OHUD.

"Don't tell me the Mafia's actually intimidated by Lindon," Peder challenged. All of Zuzanna's showing off told him that he could poke at her ego.

Zuzanna's eyes snapped back to him and she frowned. "*We* are not. But Georgiev is—that's my point. You hired him for something way over his pay grade, so he just took your money, pussy-footed around, and invoiced you for lunch."

Peder shrugged. "Granted. I should have come to you first."

Zuzanna nodded thanks. "Now, getting on with this Atkins job, you must know that blackmailing operations are never sure things. Someone like Atkins will have exceptional security around him, and, even if we breach all of it, he may come out as clean as Sunday."

"I understand that. And I'm willing to bet that there's something there to find." In fact, Peder had a rule of thumb that every powerful person had something sinister in their past. It was only a matter of finding the right secrets and applying the proper torque—just as the right leverage could move the world, so could it destroy a man.

"Is there any time limit you're looking at?" Zuzanna asked.

"No. Even if you got me something tomorrow, I'd have to wait for the right time to use it. That could be a few months or even a year at the outside."

Zuzanna nodded. "All right. We'll take the job. —On one condition. Normally we wouldn't ask this, but your flirtation with another organization has made us jealous. So, if we take this contract, we want exclusivity. For a year."

Peder mumbled favorably. "Agreed."

He did not need any threats about how it would be suicide for him to try and go behind their backs later. Zuzanna had advertised the Mafia's meticulous knowledge of him just to show how closely they could watch him going forward.

"Then our price is one fifty."

Peder flinched slightly. "Don't I get a discount for taking the exclusivity deal?"

"In fact, you did."

He grinned wryly. "Fine, fine."

"It's a pleasure doing business with you again, Peder."

"Likewise, Zizi."

They both leaned back slightly now that a formal deal had been concluded.

"Though ... we'll have to proceed a little differently this time," said Zuzanna. "We'll be meeting face-to-face from now on. We'll do all of our business inside of a single ASAPR."

Peder looked off. "Why is that?"

"You and I are old acquaintances from school, so we can meet in person without arousing suspicion. Then we can discuss the job in private, in person, which is a lot safer than making *sub rosa* calls between our ASAPRs."

"Really?" Peder squinted. "But I thought even *sub rosas* were as secure as possible. ... I mean, it's a call from one 'As-Secure-As-Possible Room' to another 'As-Secure-As-Possible Room' ... Doesn't that pretty much spell it out?"

"You'd *think*, but actually no, they're not that secure." Zuzanna reached out of the shot and picked up her own wine glass to sip from. "An ASAPR prevents anybody from recording what's going on inside of it, and that guarantee is based on physical laws. Cracking into it should be impossible no matter how much computing power you have. But the call we're making right now is still going out over the infostructure, and that's only as secure as the cryptography. Eavesdropping then just becomes a question of beating the encryption the data is using."

"But even our worst crypto is worth a few decades of security. That's not good enough for the Mafia?"

"Well, there are reasons. We're actually in a ... a high-security mode right now," she said delicately.

"Oh?" Peder raised his eyebrows. He looked down and traced a finger around the rim of his own wine glass. "Anything you can share?" he asked unassumingly. "—It's just that, if there's something's going on that could set even the Mafia on edge, I'd hate to be left in the dark."

Zuzanna gave him a pensive look. She was weighing whether to tell him anything or not. Indeed, her saying that they were in a high-security mode had probably been a slip.

"And I am a trustworthy 'old acquaintance,' after all," Peder added, feigning a disingenuous smile.

Zuzanna gave him a sarcastic grin, but decided to humor him. "Well, there's nothing concrete ... Mostly just rumors."

"Oh, if it's only a rumor, then—"

"Err, 'rumor' is much too weak a word for it," Zuzanna interrupted. She now felt she had to say something, if only to impress him. Peder knew how to push her buttons. "But the gist is that the alert has something to do with the ISSO."

Peder sat forward.

"The boss who ordered this heightened posture has a lot of connections in the FSB, including some operatives who went over to the ISSO. Whenever something big goes down there, they drop him a line. And these are real sources, not rumors. This same boss has dropped several alerts before, and they all coincided with large-scale ISSO operations."

At first Peder was surprised that Zuzanna would be telling him all this. But then it really contained nothing specific or damaging that he could pass along. Even if he went to the ISSO and told them 'There's a Mafia boss with connections to ex-FSB moles serving in your organization,' their response would be, 'Yeah, and the sky was blue today, too.'

"And ... " Zuzanna continued, "there's even a hint that this may not be *just* about the ISSO this time. That the Lontans could actually be involved."

Peder set his wine glass aside. "That's exceptionally bad news."

"And also why we suddenly trust our cryptography much less. If the Lontans are involved, then all assumptions are off the table. And only things that happen strictly inside of an ASAPR have even a prayer of being secure."

Peder nodded. "Thank you for all the precautions you've taken." He cleared his throat. "So, we'll be meeting in person ... What are we supposed to make it look like? That we're dating again?"

"Whatever you care to," Zuzanna waved her hand. "I'll message you when we're ready for a meeting, then schedule an outing within a few days. And afterwards we'll head back to my place or yours to talk in an ASAPR."

"Good. Well, I ... look forward to seeing you again." Peder smiled succinctly.

Zuzanna made a small smile herself. Then disappeared.

Chapter 6 - Cause Celebre

Hanssen was seated at his usual booth in Lutefisk's, eating breakfast with Kristin Kitano, another Home Guard officer. The door chime rang and Erlend entered, who walked straight to their table.

"Have you guys seen this shit?" Erlend said while sliding into their booth. He forwarded them a vidstream that showed a paused newscast. The headline at the bottom read 'Interstellar Incident?' Playing it, the anchorwoman said:

"Information is scanty at this point, but what is known is that Lontan trade into the system has apparently ceased, with the last five Lontan freighters scheduled to dock at Gateway Station now long overdue.

"As yet the Lontan Governate has made no statement as to the fate of the ships, whether they were recalled purposefully or met with some incident in transit. Lontan cargo ships are unmanned and piloted by computer, so at present no personnel are missing.

"While no governments have yet acknowledged the shipping stoppage, naval activity from the Eyes has ramped up noticeably. Speculation runs rampant as to the cause of the trade stoppage and the martial response by Terran governments. Analysts are positing everything from a break in Human–Lontan relations to the intervention of a hostile alien—"

Erlend paused the vid and interjected a, "Weird, huh?"

"Nah, it's just an exercise," suggested Kitano, shrugging complacently.

"Oh yeah? Then why'd they lower the DEFCON, genius?"

"Wha—They lowered the DEFCON?"

"Yup, the Space DEFCON's down to three now."

"That's serious ... " she set down her coffee. "How'd you find that out?"

"I got an ex-girlfriend on board the *Jotunheim*."

"The *Jotunheim* ... " Kitano repeated blankly. "Which is?"

"One of the ships in the Norwegian Navy ... " Erlend was incredulous.

"Oh, okay."

"We only have seven of them up there. It shouldn't be that hard for you to remember their names."

"Yeah, whatever—you were saying?"

"Anyway, their ship left Gateway Station early this morning. And Sonja shot me a message just before."

"Why'd they lower the DEFCON? Did she say?"

"Nah, didn't have time. Whole message was like, 'Shit—DEFCON 3—I gotta go.'"

"What about the other DEFCONs?"

"For all I know those haven't budged—Planetary at five, Infostructure at three ... So yeah, 'morning, all," he said, belatedly servicing the pleasantries. He nodded to them as he pawned remnants of food from their plates.

Tatia Quisling, Lutefisk's owner, approached and set a cup of coffee down in front of him.

"Thanks, Mama," Erlend acknowledged her. He called her 'mama' not by any dint of biology but because that was what everyone called her. Hanssen suspected it was to offset the historical infamy of her surname: Vidkun Quisling had run Norway for the Nazis during World War II.

"But the thing that gets me, Haze," Erlend said to Hanssen, "is shouldn't the Home Guard have gotten some word when the DEFCON changed? I mean, Norway was in the Eyes, and yet I had to hear about this under the table from someone who works on a destroyer. Where are the proper channels now?"

"They were all in Oslo," Kitano answered grimly. "'Norway' doesn't officially exist from the Eyes' point of view anymore."

"Granted, but we still have a navy up there. And the Home Guard is like the army now. So together we're a *de facto* military for a *de facto* Norway ... "

Hanssen spoke—in long-coming answer to Erlend's question—, "They did let us know, just unofficially. You heard about it from your contacts; I heard about it from mine. Those are our 'proper channels' now."

Erlend shrugged. "Still ... " and he sipped at his coffee.

Shortly Hanssen stood. This was the announcement that it was time for work. They left Lutefisk's in a carpool and headed west out of the city.

They crossed the bridge from Vestvågøy over to the adjacent island, where the Leknes Home Guard's main base was located. The craggy islands of the Lofoten archipelago would traditionally have been poor sites for military bases, but Leknes's Home Guard installation was a recent addition, having been constructed in the boom years of the thirties. Nanoconstruction had been at its cheapest then, so the entire base had been carved out of rock for almost no cost in Human labor. Most of its facilities were buried under a hundred meters of stone, yet its hangars and garages were still as capacious as an aircraft carrier's.

After passing outer security, they drove into the base through a long tunnel. They left their car in one of the civilian garages, whose ceiling held large fans that continually circulated the air.

Once they had logged onto the base's secure network, they received their latest messages.

"Oh, what's this—the Brigadier wants us," said Erlend, seeing one message CC'd to them all. They headed towards their commander's office.

When they entered, Brigadier Krohg was seated at his desk, drumming his fingers and staring into the vidwindow. This was a vidscreen, portrait-sized and mounted on the wall, which was displaying a live simulated view of downtown Leknes. With the entire base underground, false windows like these were instrumental in staving off claustrophobia. Also present was Major Cassandra Steffens, who was third in command after the Brigadier and Hanssen.

"Colonel, come in," said Krohg, bidding them to sit down. He ran a hand through his gray hair, which was long and straggly. The Brigadier had let his hair grow out after the Singularity and Norway's dissolution. Finally being his own boss meant he could do what he liked. But, when other Home Guardsmen had tried to follow suit and dress casually, the Brigadier had clamped down. Most of the men liked this mix: here was a commander who could be at ease in an apocalypse, but who could also still run a tight military operation.

"Bad news," the Brigadier began. "The City Council's going to pass a directive soon. They're going to order us to take action against the Lindon Securities corporate army."

His audience exchanged worried glances.

"A military campaign, sir?" balked Steffens.

The Brigadier shrugged. "Let me just read you part of this mandate they've cooked up for us ... " He brought the document up in his OHUD. "We're supposed to, quote, 'take any and all action necessary, feasible, and commensurate to the curtailing of Lindon Securities' corporate army's expansion into Nordland,' unquote."

Steffens scoffed. "'Necessary, feasible, and commensurate' ... Sounds like a vague way of passing the buck."

"Exactly. And it's all because of this damned Märtha Velding incident—though no offense to you, Colonel," he looked at Hanssen. "You were just doing your duty out there. You shooed some corporate mercenaries off of our citizens. But the way this has since blown up in the press ... " he

62

shook his head and raked his hand through his hair again. "The girl and her grandfather have been interviewed by every Leknes plug and cast, and even by a few others as far away as Trondheim. The public around here is raving about the corporate army. But the City Council has no idea what to do, so they came up with the perfect alternative: just tell *us*—the Home Guard—to 'do something,' as vaguely as they can, and then it all becomes our problem."

"I see, sir," said Steffens. "But isn't a military action against Lindon a little precipitate?"

There was a communal pause while everyone looked up the word 'precipitate' in their OHUD dictionaries. Steffens was asking if they were being 'hasty.'

"The Council actually did try some diplomacy first," said Krohg. "When this all started a few weeks ago, they sent some communiques to Lindon, trying to set up a dialogue about his forces. His replies were hilarious. He said he believed that he had the tacit consent of the Norwegian government to operate as he was—since he'd never received any notice from them to cease and desist. And, until he sees something like that from a proper national agency, he won't listen."

Erlend huffed. "Cocky bastard," he muttered.

Krohg looked at the man. He might have been annoyed at this coarse intrusion from a mere lieutenant, but then 'Cocky bastard' was exactly what Krohg had been thinking. He let it slide. For now.

"Right, well," Krohg continued, "this directive is still going to land in our lap soon. So, Hanssen, what do you think of going after the corporate army?"

"Tactically?" Hanssen asked.

Krohg nodded.

Hanssen took a second to think. "Suicide."

This was a typically succinct Hanssen answer.

"Please elaborate."

"They out-number and out-gun the Leknes Home Guard by a wide margin. And they're much closer to the first-tier military technologies coming down the space elevators. The only advantage we have is that their men in Nordland are operating far from their home base in Oslo, so a conflict here would put them under more of a logistical strain than us. But still, Lindon has far more money, and if he dedicated enough to fight us, he'd win."

Krohg nodded. "Exactly the conclusion I came to. Which means that, sooner or later, we'll have to abandon the idea of a military action."

"If those are the facts, sir," said Steffens, "then just tell the City Council. They'll have to come up with some other course of action then."

"I wish it worked that way, Major, but that's exactly what the Council is counting on. No one can do anything about the corporate army, but someone will have to take the blame. And, if the Council tells us to fight a hopeless battle that's doomed to fail, then—in the court of public opinion—it'll still look like *they* did something while *we're* the ones who couldn't deliver. We'll be the scapegoats. And the scapegoats are the ones who have to tender resignations," he looked between Hanssen and Steffens.

Steffens mouthed a small 'Oh.'

"But the reason I've called you here ... " Krohg turned slyly, "is another idea I have. The Council's game is all about scoring publicity points. So I've been thinking about how we can rack up some of those for ourselves."

He brought up a news vid in augspace over his desk. Muted, it showed one of Märtha and Eivar Velding's interviews with a Leknes caster.

"Märtha Velding," said Krohg. "She's the focal point. It was those vids of her that started all this, so I figure the key to riding out this storm isn't to do something *against* the corporate army—like the Council thinks—it's just to do something *for* this girl."

His audience looked between each other, warily this time.

"What did you have in mind, sir?" asked Steffens.

"Bring her on board. She and her grandfather are still staying around Leknes, so we invite her to come work with us—an internship, call it. Nothing elaborate, just give her some things to do, get some photos taken, we'll build up a portfolio. Then, when we have to scrap this ridiculous military campaign against Lindon, we can say, 'What do you mean we didn't get anything done? Here are all the pics of us taking this poor country girl and giving her a job and some experience. Isn't that more than the City Council's done?' ... That's our ammunition."

His guests gave him specious looks.

"I don't ... think that's wise, sir," said Kitano. Though she heard too late what an abrupt thing this was to say to her CO.

Krohg looked at her. Rebuke time. "When I was speaking just now? That wasn't me asking for opinions. That was a general telling his junior officers how it's going to be."

Kitano skewed her mouth contritely. "Of course, sir. I only meant ... that we might be putting her in danger. Working with the Home Guard isn't exactly risk-free—it's the military. If this Velding girl got hurt, that'd be catastrophic PR."

"I'm not talking about giving this girl the stick in a hovertank," Krohg became a little exasperated. "Just something around the base—yeoman's work. And ... " he looked towards Hanssen, "I was thinking of having her attached to your team, Colonel."

"Ahhh," said Erlend, "I was wondering why you had called us both here, sir," looking between himself and Kitano. Hanssen and Steffens were senior staff, but Erlend and Kitano were only Hanssen's pilot and backup pilot, respectively. They otherwise had no reason to meet with the Brigadier.

"I want this Velding girl close, but not in my hair," said Krohg. "And the best way I can see for that is to put her with your team. Handled right, I don't see her being much of a burden. Are you on board?"

Erlend and Kitano looked at Hanssen. They both expected him to veto this idea immediately. Märtha Velding was a living conduit for publicity, so Hanssen would loathe any proximity to her.

Except his reply turned out to be:

"Of course, sir."

The others all glanced at him. Then at each other.

"Good!" said Krohg, sitting back. "I trust you'll see to it all. But get her in here as soon as possible. Dismissed."

Out in the hall, Hanssen and Steffens split off in one direction while Kitano and Erlend stayed behind. After they were out of earshot, Kitano asked Erlend,

"All right, so what the hell was that?"

Erlend was still looking after Hanssen when he replied, "That's exactly what I'll be trying to figure out for the next few hours ... "

Chapter 7 - Xenoklavier

Willoch was at her vanity applying makeup when the door chime rang. "Come!" she announced.

Admiral Arkady Suvorov entered wearing a smart tuxedo. "Lene," he greeted her.

"Arkady," she replied, looking at him in her mirror. "Thank you for accompanying me on such short notice," she added in Russian.

Willoch had picked up the language early in her career when working in an exchange program with the Russian Navy—back before OHUD translation had made the rote learning of other languages obsolete. Consequently she had come away with a nautical-heavy vocabulary, but this worked perfectly with Suvorov. Here, for example, she had approximated what she had wanted to say with, 'Thank you for sortieing an escort with such a short scramble time.'

"Have a seat, I'm almost done."

"You women are always 'almost done' ... " Suvorov grumbled as he sat in an armchair.

"Thinking of your wife?" Willoch said over her shoulder. Here she had used the word 'support carrier' when she stumbled for 'wife.' "But actually I only got this invitation at the last minute."

"What's so special about this concert, anyway?"

"It's not the concert. It's whom the invitation came from."

"Oh?"

"... The Zaichi Ambassador."

"Ohhh ... " Suvorov cooed.

The significance of this was not in being invited by the 'Zaichi' Ambassador but just by the 'Alien-Sounding-Name-of-Anything' Ambassador. Had she said 'the Body Snatcher Ambassador' Suvorov would have been just as excited.

A scant fifty years after First Contact, aliens remained enigmas. Most of them stayed aloof on the Alien Embassy—a space station hidden behind an opaque information shield—, and even those who wore mannequins and intermingled with the Humans were inscrutable. Yet they held all the keys and guarded all the doors; so, when an alien made any request, all Human governments gladly tripped over themselves complying.

"I just wish the damn concert had been at some other time ... " she protested.

"Oh?"

"You know, the recon mission to find the pirates. It's going to be coming on station during the concert."

"Oh, that," said Suvorov lightly. He was Willoch's opposite number on the Russian side, commander of his nation's black-water fleet. "I wouldn't worry. The fleet will only be arriving at the place where the freighters disappeared from, and I doubt the pirates are still lingering around there. The search will take days. ... I guarantee you, when anything does happen, you and I will have been sitting in the situation room for hours, bored to tears."

"I hope so ... "

Willoch finished her prinking, snatched up her purse, and was out the door on Suvorov's arm. They took a lift from her quarters and made their way to Gateway's Green Wing, the alien-run section. Aside from its name, there was nothing special about this section of the station, not even the decor. As always the aliens sought to blend in.

They arrived at the concert hall and surveyed the moderate crowd of several score. While a significant number of the guests were aliens, they always wore Human mannequins to these formal functions. Willoch's first glance around the room was thus deceptively homogeneous, offering nothing more exotic than several dashikis.

"See our host yet?" Suvorov asked her.

"He didn't say what mannequin he'd be wearing ... " said Willoch. "I'm pinging people's info cards, but I haven't seen a Zaichi yet."

Suvorov joined her, using eye gestures and subvocalized commands to pick people out in his OHUD and ask for their identification cards. The Humans they found were mostly ambassadors, ministers, or generals, and the aliens were all identified as either 'attaches' or 'consultants.' The alien personae were also tagged by what degree of partial was operating the mannequin, which signified how much of the alien's attention span was invested in them. Most of those present were secondaries—as was typical—, although a few were primaries or tertiaries.

Willoch wondered, of all the mannequins she was seeing, how many were for real aliens. Not just for vertebrates or bipeds—like the Lontans—but for aliens that slithered, or swarmed, or even oozed. The aliens' info cards listed their native species, but gave no portrait or likeness. But Willoch was curious so she started looking up encyclopedia entries for each species over her OHUD.

Willoch and Suvorov were soon approached by a formal European mannequin who was identified as a secondary of the Lontan Ambassador. He greeted Willoch and she introduced him to Suvorov. Black-water admirals often worked closely with the Ambassador, but Suvorov was new to his post and had not been formally presented yet.

"Admiral Suvorov, a pleasure to meet you," the Ambassador said. Being in a Human body, he had to speak a Human language, and he had chosen English as apparently the most neutral option for speaking to a Russian and a Norwegian. "I heard that the Zaichi Ambassador had invited you at the last minute," he said to Willoch. "I'm glad you could make it."

"Thank you. Though ... do you know where your colleague is?" Willoch asked. "Or what he may be dressed like?"

"I'm afraid not," the Ambassador answered while glancing over the room. "And I don't know what the Zaichi Ambassador plans to wear, either. He often checks out a random mannequin and refashions it as he wishes."

"... He checks out a random mannequin?" Willoch repeated wonderingly. "But ... don't you always wear the same one to these functions?"

"Yes, though only because I think it polite to maintain the same appearance. Humans cannot change their bodies at will, so I would not want to seem to be flaunting something. ... But I'm afraid I must see to the other guests. It was a pleasure speaking to you both."

They let him depart, though Willoch was disappointed to have lost his ear—he possessed so much tantalizing knowledge. And it was much easier to speak to him when he was in a Human body. Aside from not having to read everything he said, a mannequin was far less intimidating.

Soon after Suvorov split off for solo reconnoitering, leaving Willoch alone.

In the interim she browsed the concert programme. This was arranged with the typical Embassy dichotomy: the first half contained Human works adapted for the Lontan piano (here *Kindertotenlieder*—the Lontans loved Mahler), and the second contained native Lontan pieces. Willoch generally enjoyed the first halves of these concerts, but she had yet to find Lontan music anything but ... odd.

Though she had recently discovered that there was a scientific basis for this. It turned out that the structure of a species' music was greatly influenced by its biology. Bipeds, for instance, favored the walking rhythm of 4/4 time (or at least four-measure structural units, as in the case of waltzes); tripeds favored true triple time; and pseudopodal aliens were meter-agnostic. In this respect Humans and Lontans were at least on the same page, with them both being bipedal.

But there was another manner in which Humans and Lontans differed entirely: their manner of copulation. While the mechanics of Human sex explained why so much of their music was

72

structured around extended build-ups to loud and rhythmic climaxes, Lontan sex was rather characterized by an initial, hurried coupling followed by an extended erotic plateau while the full congress played itself out to gradual remission. Hence why Human and Lontan music were largely immiscible. And so Willoch had come to understand that these concerts were made half Human/half Lontan not to provide 'exposure' to either side but only 'fairness.' At least everyone heard something they enjoyed part of the time.

Willoch was suddenly approached by a middle-aged man. Before she could read his identification card in her OHUD, he said in rush,

"Admiral, I'm so pleased you could make it! Allow me to introduce myself: the Zaichi Ambassador, Laiidjokun."

"Ah ... pleased to meet you," Willoch managed while offering her hand. So this was the ambassador who had invited her. Though she almost cringed at the name 'Laiidjokun.' While she found it ridiculous for aliens to adopt Human names like 'Hans Dorchester' or 'Tiffany Xu,' these names that sounded like attempted transliterations were even more awkward.

"Though I'm afraid my prime won't be able to stay for the concert itself," Laiidjokun continued. "I must meet for negotiations with the Nusantarian Ambassador."

On hearing the word 'negotiations,' Willoch pulled down the latest copy of 'the War Matrix' in her OHUD. It was a spreadsheet where the rows and columns were labeled with faction and species names, and the grid spaces were color-coded to show the relations that existed between them. Scanning along the Zaichi's row, Willoch saw it populated with many yellow marks that designated 'border warfare.' And for the Nusantarians there was an orange mark that meant 'sector-level warfare.' Feeling up to speed, she commented:

"Peace negotiations, I take it?"

"Quite," answered Laiidjokun. "We are winning, so it is time to cash in the chips."

Willoch looked curiously. "Quitting while you're ahead? That's ... magnanimous."

"It's because of the Lontans," Laiidjokun grinned. "They see us all as their children, and so they take it as their duty to maintain a balance of power—a sense of 'fairness'—between us. Much like these half-and-half concerts."

Willoch's brow furrowed. Laiidjokun had chosen words too closely mirroring her own thoughts on the programme. She even suspected that he may have been eavesdropping on her mind—'thoughtdropping' alien technologies did exist. The Lontans were supposed to severely restrict their use, but Willoch still felt that Laiidjokun was peering on her thoughts.

"Whenever one species starts a war," Laiidjokun continued—oblivious to the qualms he had aroused in Willoch—, "the Lontans let it run to exercise the bad blood out of the situation. Then, once they decide it has gone far enough, they step in to aid the losing side. The trick for the aggressor is to anticipate where that point lies and stop *just* short of it."

Willoch nodded. "And you're conducting the peace negotiations here on Earth. To what do we owe this honor?"

"Oh, we and the Nusantarians have already ejected all of our ambassadors from the usual places. Your first contact planet is one of the few neutral spots where we both maintain a presence. ... Though we shall actually not be conducting the negotiations on Earth. They'll be out at Mars—on Haven Station."

"Oh? Why is that?" Willoch asked out of simple curiosity.

"Well ... 'Mars,' of course!" he exclaimed, as if that answered everything.

Willoch only stared.

"Is not the planet named after some ancient Human war god?"

"Oh! Yes it is ... "

"I just hope my little dramatic touch will not be lost on the Nusantarian Ambassador," Laiidjokun cocked his head. "Now, if I may ... " he said oddly.

Suddenly they were both surrounded by a slight refraction, as if they were insects trapped in a jar.

"Pardon the imposition," said Laiidjokun, "but this horizon shield will prevent eavesdropping on the next part of our conversation."

'Eavesdropping'—he's one to talk, Willoch thought.

"An horizon shield?" she asked. "Isn't that the same type of device that conceals the Alien Embassy?"

He grinned. "Oh, that is but a cudgeling application of the technology. All that Lontan shield

75

does is conceal the Embassy and make it a black void in the sky. But look around us ... "

He motioned to the crowd, which seemed unaffected. If this were like the Lontans' horizon shield, then she and Laiidjokun should have been swallowed in a black bubble. But no one was paying them notice ...

"Why isn't everyone staring at us?" she asked.

"The Lontans' horizon shield merely prevents information from escaping the barrier, but ours is actually publishing false light and sound to the outside. It is simulating the two of us standing here as everyone last saw us, and that pair is engaged in a conversation as a cover. You can view the animation, if you wish."

Laiidjokun forwarded her a vidwindow showing a simulated pair of the two of them:

"Why is it," asked alter-Willoch, "that you all wear mannequins to these concerts?"

"The seating arrangements," beamed alter-Laiidjokun, as if this were a clever barb. "A front row packed with two-meter Lontans and slug-like Wilusans would prove quite irritating to the Humans seated behind them."

Alter-Willoch laughed wittily. "Are the Zaichi also so physically obstructing?"

"Us, no," he grinned. "We are wide and stocky, but only yea high," he held his hand to his abdomen—a graduated height.

"Forgive me if you think unfitting the words we have put in your mouth," said the real Laiidjokun. "We thought them innocuous enough."

76

"Oh, yes, of course," Willoch offered pardon. Though this also added fuel to her fears that Laiidjokun had been listening to her thoughts. The lines for her alter ego seemed to have been inspired by how she had been looking up the alien species' appearances on the web earlier. Had Laiidjokun been monitoring her net activity, as well?

"But now I must tell you why such security measures are necessary. I wish to discuss with you the pirate blockade of your system."

Willoch was now paying grave attention.

"You must be tired of hearing nothing but vague recommendations from the other ambassadors on how to deal with this crisis. So let me ask only if you know how the pirates uncovered your system's location and its trade route?"

Willoch considered her response carefully, fearful of revealing any classified—or worse: Lontan—information.

"No, we don't. ... Only that it was no small undertaking," she said.

"True. But aren't you anxious that it has not been sufficiently explained? The Lontans thought they could keep your system secret for a hundred to a hundred and twenty years, yet here you are at only fifty and already compromised."

Willoch was unnerved. Laiidjokun had quoted the exact numbers that the Lontan Ambassador had. Yet, whereas the Lontan Ambassador had meant those numbers to assuage her fears, Laiidjokun was using them to contrary effect. It made her take him seriously.

"But let us consider how the pirates might have discovered you," he continued. "The easiest way would have been by bribing someone who already had the information. That means there are only two species to go to: the Lontans and the Eththelnt—the two who originally discovered your world. Meanwhile, did you know that the Lontan Ambassador has been reassigned?"

"Yes. To—" She was about to say, 'to the Xaccus System,' but stopped herself, wary that this was not common knowledge. "Yes."

"And to the Xaccus System, even."

Okay, no worries.

"A very prestigious post considering that the Ambassador is being sent from his post here in disgrace."

"He is? I thought he was merely ... moving on." In truth Willoch already suspected the reason behind the Ambassador's reassignment, but by feigning ignorance she was hoping to get more information out of Laiidjokun.

"Oh, no no no no no," he shook his head. "Under the Lontan system, first contact ambassadors usually serve three or four terms, but yours is leaving after only one. That would be understandable only if he had done a poor job ... " he hinted.

Willoch understood his implication: the Singularity.

"Many of the Lontan Governate's major officials are being reassigned at the end of their current terms. And yet, from out of this sweeping house cleaning, your disgraced Ambassador

78

emerges with a post to Xaccus. Hardly a logical chain of events.

"Of course there are explanations. Might I say that bribery is still very much a thriving enterprise. And your Ambassador, even while steeped in opprobrium, could still secure a position on Xaccus with a large enough payout. The trick, however, is not to simply dole out bribes, since the draw on his finances would be noticeable. But it's to procure money secretly, and then dispense of it in kind. Interesting, is it not?"

The refraction field around them disappeared and Willoch knew the horizon shield was gone. Laiidjokun's countenance had turned from its clandestine seriousness to a warm smile.

"Well, it was a pleasure speaking to you, Admiral," he said, extending a hand. "Enjoy the concert."

Willoch took his hand. "I'm ... obliged for the invitation, Ambassador," she played along. "And thank you for the chance to receive such ... enlightenment."

Laiidjokun bowed and withdrew.

Willoch stood behind, subtly awestruck. Laiidjokun's implication was clear: the Lontan Ambassador had sold out the Earth's location to the pirates, then funneled all the proceeds into his Buy the Xaccan Ambassadorship Fund.

At first it was impossible to believe. Willoch had met with the Ambassador a hundred times, had spoken to him just minutes ago, and never had she imagined him capable of such corruption.

... And yet, why not? she posed to herself. The galaxy at large had not come to them as a utopia. From what they knew, there were still wars, strife, and suffering out there, and on a galactic scale. With all those inveterate ills, why not corrupt public officials, as well? Indeed, that particular ill would probably be the last to go.

Suvorov was approaching her, shaking his head. "Lene, Lene, Lene," he spoke as to a naughty child. "You're the first person the Zaichi Ambassador talks to in weeks, and you spend the entire time blithering about seating arrangements and— ... "

He trailed off when he caught how Willoch was staying awed and silent. He looked back and forth between her and the Zaichi Ambassador, who was yet retreating through the crowd. Double takes upon double takes ...

At last realizing that something secret and groundbreaking had taken place between them, he uttered a seething, "*Shit*."

Chapter 8 - Dichotomy

Kitano and Erlend were in one of the base's lounges waiting for Hanssen to arrive with the Velding girl. It was not long before they appeared turning the corner, walking side by side. And, when Erlend saw them, he could read the state of affairs in only a glance. From the way the girl was looking longingly at Hanssen, while he was glowering off and away, it was clear that the girl was in love, and Hanssen was regretting ever thinking of bringing her on board.

Erlend smirked. Of course he had known long ago that those would be the facts of the case. The formula had been obvious back when he had first seen her out on the boat: take impressionable girl, A; put her in tense, maidenhood-threatening situation, B; have her saved by hunky, taciturn guy, C; and doomed, unreciprocated love, D, must follow in short order.

The two of them approached. Hanssen introduced the girl directly, "Märtha, this is Erlend and Kitano." And, while Märtha was still shaking hands, Hanssen waved good-bye behind her back and left.

Erlend grinned again—Hanssen had dropped the girl in only six words and two seconds.

"Pleased to meet you, Kitano," said Märtha.

"Kristin," Kitano answered, offering her given name.

"Oh, that's pretty."

Erlend jumped in, "And 'Kristin' is one of the few Norwegian names that doesn't die a bloody death in katakana, so it cross-translates with Japanese well."

Märtha smiled, but she meanwhile did an OHUD search to figure out what 'katakana' was.

Looking around, she at last noticed that Hanssen was gone. "Wait—Where'd Hanssen go?" she asked.

"Work," Erlend answered. "The Colonel's a busy man."

Märtha squinted with innocent unbelief. "But ... he still had time to pick me up, didn't he?"

Erlend would have to make a little more elaborate excuse for his boss. "Well ... he only had that little time to spare. He's gotta get back to gearing up for the campaign against the corporate army, you know."

"Oh, right!" Märtha was quickly distracted. "I saw something about that on the news. So Leknes is actually going to do something about the corporate army?"

"That's the plan."

Erlend and Kitano started walking and Märtha followed along.

"I ... didn't think anything big like that would happen from just that thing out on the boat," Märtha spoke up from behind. "Still, I'm glad you guys are doing something."

Erlend cast an eye on her and tabulated all of his reactions. First, he was annoyed by her teenage ineloquence: 'like that thing that happened with that stuff that one time ... ' Second, when she said 'glad you guys are doing something' it made the Home Guard sound like some slack-asses who were finally getting around to doing their jobs. In reality they were stretching their mission considerably to help a great many people—and all out of the goodness of their hearts. But third, she had also spoken plainly and unpretentiously. For all the publicity she had recently endured, she appeared unspoiled by it. Summing it all up, Erlend decided not to immediately hate her.

"Well, it wasn't just that 'thing' out on the boat that started all this," he answered her. "There have been anti-corporate army groups springing up all over the country for years. So you guys would have just been another 'citizens groups plus-equals one.' But for some reason all the publicity blew that little thing up into a whole *casus belli*, so now here we are."

"Oh," said Märtha. While she had followed the gist of what Erlend had said, the phrases 'plus-equals one' and '*casus belli*' were total gaps. She had resolved 'katakana,' however, and so she started new OHUD searches down those branches.

They had been on the move for a minute before she thought to ask, "By the way, where are we going?"

"Taking you to the doctor's," said Erlend.

The answer startled her.

They walked to one of the base's civilian garages and drove out in a groundcar. They headed for the bridge leading back to Vestvågøy, Leknes's main island. When they were halfway over the bridge, Märtha ventured,

"I thought you said you were taking me to the doctor's."

"We are."

"But ... doesn't the base back there have an infirmary?"

"Yeah, but not for technical medicine anymore."

"Oh! tech medicine," Märtha made a relieved exclamation. So this was not a date with the kind of medicine that dealt with scalpels and specula. "But why are you taking me to a TMD? My OHUD works fine, and I haven't had any comp problems ... "

"Still, we gotta get you up to snuff in all departments," said Erlend.

"What?" Märtha asked. She was now feeding 'snuff' into her dictionary.

"And seriously, it's called a 'viz.'"

"What?" Märtha was now typing in 'viz.'

"'OHUD' is like what you would call it in scientific papers, but actually *saying that* is like calling it 'the TV box.'"

"Wha—okay ... "

Märtha wondered whether Erlend was not purposefully trying to confuse her with all of his scattershot jargon. It seemed a motley of terms from both ten years ahead of her and a hundred behind.

After crossing the bridge, they steered not for the Leknes city center but towards the grittier northern enclaves. They exited the expressways and were soon navigating the stoplight stutter of the city grid. Märtha became unnerved as each new block brought in sight more disrepair, more refuse and dilapidation. At first she tried to accept this—she knew that there was a depression on, after all. — And that Leknes had been riding a few bubbles of its own that had burst with all the others back in 2040.

But Märtha had spent the years since the Singularity with her grandfather in Steigen, which was a small, vocational village. Everyone knew everyone else; no one was rich, no one was poor; and the only law was the Jante Law. The town had had very few ambitions before First Contact, and it had sat out the Colony Years and the Second Roaring Twenties with a chaperone's detachment. When the Singularity and the depression hit—all with little direct effect to them—, these just became more reasons for the Steigeners to shake their heads and mutter in aphorism.

Which was why this one drive through outer Leknes was the showcase of more horrid, inhuman squalor than Märtha had ever seen. The lone street they finally stopped on was the worst of them all. Märtha had seen abandoned buildings before, but the ones on this street had been necrotized: walls punched through, roofs toppling, all the wiring and plumbing removed ... And the homeless were everywhere lining the street, cast in death-lank poses and crumpled in the gutters. Half of them had skin either waxy and translucent with malnutrition, or stained the steely sallow of nanodrug addiction.

But most shocking to Märtha was the perfect obliviousness with which Erlend and Kitano parked their car, stepped out, and proceeded about their business. She wanted to stop them and say, 'Wait—

wait—wait—What the hell?' But she followed their lead. Maybe they simply knew there was no real danger.

They started towards a building that, at first glance, looked a sooty ramshackle like all the others. But Märtha noticed that all of its windows and doors were intact and that the structure looked sound. In the central window hung a faded sign:

NorCarePrime
Sigrid Giske, MD
Per Östbye, TMD
Walk-ins welcome

Another sign hung below, hand-drawn in black marker:

Drugs kept in auto-destruct anti-tamper vault

Märtha figured that the building was camouflaging itself to blend in with all of the other dead edifices. There were even some homeless sitting to either side of its entrance to complete the illusion. They looked asleep, though one of them was an obvious 'vizhuffer'—someone who used their OHUD to indulge in endless pornography sims. The telltale was the splotches of semen stains running down his pant leg.

Erlend suddenly jumped between Märtha's eyes and the sight of that man.

"Sorry, dear—just a second and we'll be inside ... " he said self-effacingly. He opened the door and the three of them scurried through. Märtha, more than shocked, was actually thankful that someone had at last shown some basic alertness.

The doctor's office inside appeared laughably commonplace compared to the apocalypse conditions outside. There was a reception nook behind plaz, a ring of chairs around the walls, a coffee table covered with carefully arrayed pads, and a few toys for occupying the children—though Märtha could not imagine what family would venture out into this Stalingrad district for medical care. The windows were frosted over, permitting the outside world to leak in as only a sanitized radiance.

Erlend walked up to the receptionist. "Hey therrre, Benedicte," he said in an interrogative leer.

"Howdy, soldier," the woman looked up warmly.

"Is Per busy? I've got a new patient for him."

"I'll check." The woman looked off to the side and spoke over a comm, "Per, Erlend's here with someone."

Per, a doctor in his early thirties, emerged quickly from the inner door. Märtha found him an incongruous figure. On the one hand he wore a pristine lab coat and his chest shone with a TMD's holographic ID, but on the other hand his hair was spiky and multi-colored and there were holo-tattoos poking out from his sleeves. Overall he gave the impression of honest medical care augmented with some amount of narcotic quackery.

"Erlend! Kitano!" he greeted them warmly. Then his gaze came to rest on Märtha. After Erlend had introduced her, Per gave her a pert and antiseptic smile. "Ms. Velding."

"Pleased to meet you—you can call me Märtha."

"No, it's a little rule of mine. I'm afraid that while we're in here on business it's 'Ms. Velding' and 'Doctor.'"

"Okay. Doctor," Märtha managed. Per's manners obviously sided with the more conservative elements of his appearance.

He leaned in a little, saying, "You'll thank me one day when you have to come in and discuss some embarrassing problems, I promise."

Märtha wondered what could possibly be embarrassing to confess to a TMD. ... Maybe having one's OHUD hacked by a porn site?

Something hit the window with a loud *smack*. Everyone turned and saw a pantomime of dull shadows through the frosted plaz. Several of the homeless outside were beating against the windows with their emaciated arms.

"Ah, that reminds me," said Erlend, unfazed, "Per, you've got some addicts out on your stoop."

"Yes, sorry," said Per. "Tint," he commanded, and the office windows polarized, dimming the room as if a solar eclipse had struck. "I used to call the police and have them shooed away, but they always come back. I've given up."

"What are they doing out there?" asked Märtha.

"They're drug addicts—a mix of sledgers, loopers, vizhuffers ... Their brains are near-completely fried, but they know enough to hang around this medical center and comb through my garbage whenever I put it out. Rather like intelligent zombies. Though of course I'm careful never to

88

leave anything out that they could use. ... So!" he chirped, "what can I do for you?"

"Märtha's going to be sticking around with the HG for a while," Erlend answered, "so she needs a full technical. Latest software, hardware, the works."

"No problem. Bill going to the Ministry of Defence I assume?"

"Of course."

"Then, to give you a heads up, the cost is going to run a little higher."

"'Little' being ... five percent?"

"Mmmm—more like ten. The Russian nanofab I've been ordering from shut down, so now I have to go through the Confederation, and with their export tariffs ... "

Erlend shrugged. "Well, shit, it's not my money. At least not directly."

Per nodded. "Now, Ms. Velding, if you'd come this way ... "

Per led her through the inner door and into a domain of clean tiled floors. They entered a private examination room, and he motioned Märtha over to a dentistry-style chair. She took a seat while Per rolled over on a stool. Along with him he brought a tray stacked with swabs, depressors, and many individually wrapped objects. His eyes went into a frenetic dance as he became fully engaged in his OHUD.

After he had logged onto Märtha's comps in privileged mode, he asked, "So, Ms. Velding, have you ever been to a technical doctor before?"

"Well, probably to have my OHU—er, my *viz* installed, I guess ... "

"Nah, installing a viz can be done in a tattoo parlor nowadays."

Märtha glanced over his body art and thought, He would know ... In fact, 'tattooist' might even be Per's part-time job. It took most people several occupations to scrabble together a living nowadays—even doctors.

"Oh. Then ... probably not," she replied.

"No big deal. But, just to give you an idea of what we're about, the name 'technical doctor' means pretty much what it says. I specifically handle the care and side effects of all the technology you have inside your body.

"What I'm doing now is performing the tech equivalent of a physical. I'm looking at your bioware, your comp clusters, your viz, making sure everything's okay ... " His speech turned distant as he became more involved in his OHUD ministrations. "Oh wow, the first thing we need to do is get you an up-to-date operating system. Six years old is the one you have in here—*pre*-Singularity."

She winced slightly at this overt mention of the Singularity. Most Norwegians were still sheepish.

"A new OS?" she asked. "What will that change?"

"Well ... when you first got here, did you see a lot of messages in your viz that went, 'Unreadable data format: aborting rendering'?"

"Oh ... Yeah! actually."

"That's because your OS is too old for all of the modern codecs and augspace graphics, so it just threw up its hands and gave up."

Per performed some rapid-fire actions, and Märtha's OHUD downloaded a new OS and primed it for installation. When her body comps shut down, her OHUD interface also blinked away. Like most wired Humans, Märtha found this type of denuded vision discomfiting. She exercised her OHUD like a second master hand, and, now bereft of it, she was experiencing 'phantom virtual limb syndrome.'

She knew the OS install had started when she went blind. Then her vision snapped back, but it was in monochrome. Then it sizzled with noise and rotated through calibration patterns. Soon the back of her neck was tingling with heat. That was where her body computers were located subcutaneously— like everyone's—for ventilation. The new OS was putting her comps through a power test, and they were bleeding the waste heat out through her skin.

Finally a screen of tessellations blazed before her and her normal vision returned, though now it was framed by the veneer of a sleek, space-aged OS. Märtha cooed.

"Now that you're up to date," said Per, "I can take a proper look at your systems. Running diagnostics ... "

With this new OS, Märtha saw a window open in her lower-left vision that showed Per's activities as a guest user. It also displayed his verified medical credentials that allowed him privy access to her systems. Märtha realized that, just as medical doctors were some of the few, legitimate professionals for whom people would undress, apparently so would her body's technology only 'disrobe' with certified TMD credentials in evidence.

"Okay, your comp housings look okay; bio-heat sinks, fine; hookups fine ... " Per narrated. "It's all in good condition, but it could use some refurbishing. So I'm going to give you some nanites to sniff out your existing tech and fix it up." He picked up one of the white pouches from his tray and ripped it open, extracting a grey patch that he fixed to her arm.

"That will be home base for the nanites while they work. They're part biotech, so they'll pull most everything they need from your bloodstream as they go. But this'll deplete your blood sugar and nutrients, so stay off your feet a bit today and get lots of fluids.

"But the nanites will also need some more exotic elements—gold and tungsten, for instance— that they can't get from your body. So take these ... "

Per gave her another handful of patches from his tray. Märtha saw microprint on their surfaces detailing the elements they contained.

"You'll get a message in your viz whenever the nanites need more raw materials," said Per. "Then slap another one of those patches onto your arm and throw the old one away. You should go through all of those inside of the day. You may itch in some places while the nanites do their work, and there might be some light-headedness, but that's all."

"Okay."

"And one last thing: I see you don't have any hand chips."

"Hand chips?"

"Yeah, they're chips ... in your hands." Per became furtherly tautological by holding up his own hands and pointing at the skin in between the thumb and forefinger of each. "They're used for fast identification, file transfer, security, a little bit of everything. You should've gotten some when you started high school, but maybe because you were out of the cities. ... You want some, right?"

"Sure?" she shrugged.

Per spun away on his stool and retrieved a large plastic packet. Tearing it open divested a pair of objects the size of rice grains. He loaded these into a large injector and placed its muzzle against the skin pads of Märtha's hands. She winced in expectation of severe pain, but felt surprisingly little when he depressed the trigger. Each hand received an implant.

"Those'll take a few minutes to get wired into your system. But then they'll fire up and send your viz a, 'Hey there!' message. From then on they'll be self-explanatory. ... And with that I give you a clean bill of health."

***

Back outside, Märtha moved around uniquely entranced. Her new OHUD OS brought with it a novel set of skins and interfaces, and simply swapping out the electronic interface with which she beheld the world made her feel briefly as if she were on another planet.

Once they had driven a few blocks back towards civilization, though, her vision became flooded by hundreds of flashing ads.

"Ah! What's going on?!" she cried.

"Oh yeah," remarked Kitano, "with all those upgrades you would be getting the modern spam full-on now ... "

"Yes! That's it! What do I do?!"

"Go to your global preferences and—"

"Wha—I can't see my global preferences to—"

"Roll your eyes to the back of your head."

Märtha did so and the ad-occluded pane of her vision fell away, being replaced by a tinted, semi-transparent screen arrayed with icons. The din of the ads had also receded to a distance.

"And go find 'Preferences' ... 'Connections' something ... " Kitano continued. "Or you can just search for 'Smart Spam Filtering.'"

"Ah. Got it."

Märtha inferred that she could get back to her normal desktop by looking far downwards, reversing the rolls-back maneuver she had performed to get to the preferences screen. When her main desktop returned, it was almost clear, and she only had to manually kill a few ads. Once those were gone, she made a joyous exclamation at what she beheld.

"Not getting any more 'failed to render' messages, huh?" asked Erlend.

Märtha was overwhelmed.

When she had first come to Leknes, she had been disappointed. The city was supposed to be the 'Tokyo of the Arctic Circle,' yet, aside for the lone arcology and some avant-garde architecture, she had found it mundane: spartan shop fronts, bland districts, and only a slim augspace presence—not to mention the appalling squalor. It had all belied her assumption that Norway was still a first-tier country.

But now she realized that that was only because her OHUD had been severely behind the times. No one was publishing augspace data in such outmoded formats anymore. Now that she had been updated, every business had its own glistening virtual facade; entire districts were arrayed with special skins and unifying aesthetics; half the people on the streets were either bedizened with augments or replaced entirely with avatars. Augspace links were everywhere uncountable, with people wearing VizPlay or MiddleDreaming vids, and taxis and catering vans spooling out brochures like electronic exhaust. For the first time Märtha understood the gulf between the two halves of the world: the base, physical substrate, and the neon-shining virtual veneer.

"Awesome ... " she remarked.

She soon noticed that the streets and sidewalks were all tiled with many copies of a single link. Following it delivered her to a list of 'City Beautification Augments,' which were available free from the Leknes government. Märtha selected one of these called 'Street Sweeper.' When she added it to her augspace, it altered what she was seeing to draw black panels over the roads and grey ones over the sidewalks. The city suddenly seemed much cleaner with no more tar seams, litter, or potholes.

Pleased, Märtha returned to the list and browsed for what else she could activate. There were augments to cover up the graffiti, to hide the abandoned shop fronts, to remove the homeless ...

—Suddenly she realized. If Erlend and Kitano were running these same augments, it would explain why they had been unaffected by the neighborhood around Per's office. The street could only have looked half bad with the full force of these Beautification Augments weighing down on it, erasing the litter, the homeless, and the carcasses of buildings. Maybe that was why Erlend had only noticed that vizhuffer at the last moment. When they had finally approached close enough that the man had broken through the veil of augments painted over his sight.

Having first seen the city un-augmented, Märtha knew what a pernicious effect this was having. With the ease of simply airbrushing over everything in augspace, the government must have first delayed making essential structural repairs, and by now it had put them on indefinite hold. But the rots, left unchecked, had turned chronic. And, the worse conditions became, the less incentive the Erlends and the Kitanos had to turn the augments off, and the more the Märthas were pressed to turn them on and become addicted to the illusion themselves.

"Hey," Märtha asked, "are you guys running these 'Beautification Augments'?"

"Ha! Wouldn't look at the world without them," said Erlend, cavalier as always.

Märtha smirked. That answered too much.

96

Chapter 9 - Biological Dither

The ISSO attack formation was skimming over the dune tops, slaloming up and down with the fold of the desert. Agent Townsend was riding in a dropper along with a dozen US Delta soldiers. He had his sunglasses turned up to their highest level of tint, but he still could not look out into the sand sea without squinting.

On the other side of the dropper he heard Zhang slap a fresh magazine into his automatic rifle. The Lontan was staying as inconspicuous as possible: Human body, Human cover, Human weapons. In their entire, fifty-man assault team, Townsend was the only one who knew they had an alien batting for them.

Major Lufthaus said on the comms, "Two minutes out from the next camp. Attack plan Golf Niner."

When Townsend looked out he saw nothing but sand treadmilling past, dunes replacing dunes. They could be stuck in a wraparound universe where all they did was fly past the same couple of dunes every ten seconds, and Townsend would never know.

... Of course Zhang probably would, he thought, glancing over at him. Townsend did not pretend to know what a mannequin's superhuman abilities were, but he figured they lived in some half organic, half computational world, possessing all the intuitive abilities of a Human, yet also able to instantaneously distill the world into floating-point numbers. Right now Zhang was probably building a mental dune-by-dune map of the Sahara, while still fully aesthetically digesting every curve that streaked past.

"Deploy," Lufthaus croaked on the comms. Townsend's tactical map showed the other droppers splitting up to diversify their angles of attack.

He sighted the camp ahead on the external cams. It looked the same as all the others they had hit that day: a pond of sand-colored tarps breaking out of the dunescape with their juts and angles. As their strike team cinched in, dozens of hovers and microlights began scrambling out in retreat. It looked as if some of them might escape just by the sheer confusion of their numbers, but the area had already been encircled by ISSO hovers and UAVs, which would chase down and disable the fleeing vehicles.

The droppers reached the camp and set down, and the assault teams hopped off from each ship. Gunfire funneled in at them, but the droppers' powerful static shields pinged away the bullets. Yet they had to secure the camp before the hostiles started firing back with things that were hulking, explosive-tipped, and recoilless.

The tarp camp was nearly transparent to Townsend's advanced sensors. Panning across the scene in his tactical view, he could see every gun-wielding body as clearly as if they were using open air for cover. He simply picked out one of the highlighted forms, swiveled his weapon around, and placed his OHUD crosshairs over them. The barrel's auto-aim took over from there and adjusted for a perfect shot. Townsend squeezed the trigger and a non-lethal round took his target down.

His OHUD also showed him the crosshairs from the weapons of the others in their team, which were all darting around and flashing red as they fired. These special forces men were firing much faster than Townsend, such that there was soon nothing left to shoot at.

As they moved out into the camp they found almost all of the inhabitants had already surrendered. Only a few of them had been foolish enough to take up arms against a first-tier military, but the others had all laid down, knitted their hands over the backs of their heads, and waited for processing. In three minutes all 92 bodies in the camp were gel-cuffed and arrayed kneeling in the sand.

Collecting evidence never took long. As Zhang had explained to Townsend beforehand, on arrival he would release a team of Lontan micromachines that would take a molecule-for-molecule snapshot of the entire camp. Then the Alien Embassy's forensic AIs could pick over that at leisure.

But, to put on a show for the troops and the prisoners, they still went snooping about manually. Most of what they found fell into the usual catalogue: small arms, not-so-small arms, advanced electronics, alien contraband a few years ahead of the allowed technologies. Data intelligence was what they were truly interested in, but almost everyone in the camp had been cognizant enough to wipe their drives once the raid began. Every storage device they recovered would either have been purged with random numbers or written over with repeated Unicode strings of 'FUCK USA FUCK CONFED FUCK ISSO' in a kaleidoscope of languages.

Strolling through the camp, Townsend found Zhang in one tent, squatting down to look at the edge of a table. "Look at this," the mannequin said.

Townsend saw he was examining a series of notches cut into the table's edge with a sharp blade. Zhang forwarded him a vidstream with a magnified view coming from his own eyes.

"So?" Townsend took it lightly. "Someone was getting edgy with a knife. Cut some notches into a table."

"But look at the spacing between the cuts," said Zhang. "One point five millimeters each, with a maximum deviation only in microns."

Townsend looked again. To him they just appeared evenly spaced, but calculating the exact spacing—as Zhang had done—revealed the conspicuous precision. No biological arm could have cut such laser-fine marks. Only a robotic one. Or, as was more likely:

"A mannequin," concluded Townsend.

"Specifically a plastic," stipulated Zhang. "That is, a mannequin with a robotic body that has been made to appear Human with artificial skin and organs."

"I know what a plastic is," Townsend said, a little annoyed. "Aren't plastics cheaper than fully biological mannequins?—'skinjobs' like the one you're wearing?"

"Yes."

100

"Does that mean that we're dealing with second-rate aliens here?"

"Not necessarily. The aliens might have only used plastics because of the danger involved in coming here to this camp. And they probably did not want to compromise the identities of their more expensive skinjobs."

"Ah, so it was like they were ... renting a car? They had some errands to run down here, so they got some cheap and disposable bodies to do them in?"

"More or less."

Townsend looked again at the cuts. "Okay, so we're saying that a mannequin was sitting here and cutting notches into the table. That part I'll buy—it's just a simple nervous tick. But, if the mannequin's going to cut some notches, then why does it make the cuts so precisely spaced? It's like leaving a signature behind."

"It was probably unintentional," said Zhang. "The way a plastic's body works is different from the way yours—or mine—does. Your brain is wired directly into your nervous system, and, since neither your brain nor your muscles are exact instruments, you cannot make such precise cuts as these.

"But, in a plastic's body, the consciousness is not directly in control. The mannequin's computers are always scanning the consciousness's thoughts, identifying the physical actions it wants to perform, and executing them. This happens so quickly that the consciousness is typically not aware of the delay, so its actions appear like natural biological

101

locomotion to it. But the computers are actually effecting everything.

"So, when the computer finds that the host mind wants to 'cut some notches into a table,' it estimates how closely it wants them and starts repeating the action. But the consciousness is never directly in control, so it can never add that 'biological dither.' And, since the computer does not naturally randomize its host's actions, the result is that the notches come out precisely spaced."

"Huh ... So this was a mistake?" Townsend asked. "They unwittingly left this evidence behind?"

"Most likely."

Townsend was piqued. "I'd thought that being a mannequin would be universally better than being Human—nothing but advantages. But apparently that's not the case."

Zhang glanced at him, but refrained from commenting.

Townsend grinned and turned back to the table. "Okay, so mannequins are confirmed. And, whether they were wearing plastics or not, that still makes them pretty highbrow visitors for a camp like this."

"True," said Zhang. "And also look at the grooves of the cuts." He zoomed in his mag window appropriately. "These weren't just made by any sharp instrument. This was something even sharper than a greymatter scalpel."

Townsend squinted. "The only weapon I know of like that is a ... a nanokatana?"

"Exactly."

"So we've got mannequins with nanokatanas. One plus one equals 'Yakuza.'"

Among the many varieties of illegal mannequins on Earth, those who had inserted themselves into the Japanese underworld were the rarest of all.

"Definitely too highbrow for this camp," said Townsend.

"And a sign that we're on the right path," added Zhang.

Chapter 10 - Overtures

"Okay, Liev, we haven't got long," said Hanssen. He was walking down the hall with Major Lievgarten. "What can you tell me before we get to the Brigadier's office?"

"That's simple: we're fucked."

Hanssen groaned. "We still can't get any surveillance on the corporate army bases?"

Lievgarten shook his head. "Up until this morning it actually looked like we had something for once. It was our latest attempt. My division put together all the best tech they could—as close to first-tier as we're gonna get. Microscopic surveillance robots that communicate over an ultra-quiet tightbeam radio mesh. It's like having a million ants that can crawl anywhere and stream you back stereo and HD.

"We put a hive of them together and dusted one of Lindon's bases with them. And it was working overnight—the longest we'd ever gotten. But then the bots all started going dark. The feeds were winking out as they were getting shut down. In five more minutes the base's defensive nanotech had gobbled them all up. Nothing."

Hanssen sighed. "So what's the next step?"

"There isn't one. That was our moon shot. And, even if that had worked, it was still too expensive to deploy to support the entire campaign. It was our best and it got shot down. It's like trying to crack the Carbon Curtain out there ... "

They arrived outside of the Brigadier's office.

"Well ... " Hanssen stopped. "Just play it cool."

Stepping inside they found Krohg at his desk and Major Steffens already present. Once Hanssen and Lievgarten were seated, Krohg began:

"So we have two problems. First, the Major tells me," he motioned to Lievgarten, "that we're still shut down on intel. Which means that the campaign is dead in the water—like we always thought."

Hanssen realized that this was the long-awaited 'admission of defeat' meeting. The campaign was a non-starter, the announcement would have to come soon, and the Home Guard would be going to war with the city government.

"But the second problem," Krohg leaned forward, "is we've received an offer that might change all that."

He brought up a holo over the desk. It showed a square kilometer of topography with a large camp atop a hill. It held a grid of Quonset huts, a large communications tower, and several hovercars and tanks parked off to one side. Point defenses drew a perimeter around this, and a fence delineated the ground farther out. The feed switched between dozens of spectral views, flaunting the breadth of coverage.

"Looks like a corporate army camp," Steffens observed.

Lievgarten squinted. "Actually ... I recognize this. It's the camp we sent our surveillance mission against today. It looks ... exactly the same. Even has the cars parked in the same spots."

"But this data isn't from you?" Steffens asked.

"No, this came in yesterday," said the Brigadier. "Along with a note."

A short message appeared on the holo. It contained a contact IP and a time—that day, only an hour from then. And it was signed, 'General Arnst Roscher, ANP.'

"The ANP?" said Steffens, voicing the name with distaste.

"What is the 'Army of Norwegian Patriots'"— Lievgarten spelled out the full name bombastically—"doing watching corporate army bases?"

"Unclear," said Krohg. "But they're apparently doing very well. They probably saw us try and launch our own surveillance missions and stake a claim. —And they saw us fail. Now they send us this sample from their own network. And it's everything we need to run our campaign."

His audience looked between each other.

"You mean the ANP ... " said Steffens, "is ... *advertising* their intelligence net?"

"They want us to *buy* it?" said Lievgarten.

Krohg leaned back and entreated, "Thoughts?"

Steffens and Lievgarten burst out:

"Whatever price they'll ask, it's too high!"

"Ridiculous! As if we'd be reduced to bargaining with them!"

"—like we could trust anything they have to offer—"

"—if they can do it that only proves how easy it should be for us to—"

"—preposterous that we could go into battle with such a compromise—"

106

"—we just knuckle-under and find some way to get it done!"

The Brigadier raised his hand, and the two officers fell silent. "As I expected," he replied. Then he looked at Hanssen. "Colonel, your thoughts?"

Internally Hanssen had tabulated all of the pros and cons of the bargain. Steffens and Lievgarten had already blurted out the obvious ones, but tops for Hanssen was the one pro that, if they moved forward with the military campaign, it would stave off their showdown with the city government. No salvos of press conferences, no stockpiles of publicity points, and no bureaucratic bloodletting. He liked that.

Of course he realized that fighting an actual war would mean that real people would be getting hurt and killed. Most people would have chosen the safe path—and so would he, once upon a time. But that had changed with the Singularity. Seeing a million people die all at once had shown him how meaningless life was. Nowadays the way he saw it was, if the universe could snuff out 10^6 Humans on a whim, then why can't we kill each other a few hundred at a time—and for actually valid malicious reasons.

His response was: "Without the ANP's help this campaign is already over. We have nothing to lose by listening to their deal."

"Except our *dignity* ... " said Steffens.

The Brigadier ignored her and nodded. "We make the call."

Chapter 11 - The 'General'

The party left Brigadier Krohg's office and reconvened in a conference room. This room was at the top of the Home Guard base, and so was one of the few with real windows. The view breathed out over the bay that separated the island from Vestvågøy. But Major Steffens commanded the windows to tint opaque, as if she wanted to hide what was about to transpire within.

The room's main holo held the image of a Leknes police detective. Lievgarten was asking him, "And you have all the tracing routines set up?"

"Yes ... " said the detective evasively. "Though tracing the ANP is ... rather hopeless, sirs. They've got such a technological lead on us that I'd say *we're* more at risk to a counter-infiltration than they are to us actually tracking them down."

Lievgarten grunted sympathetically. Then he put the man on a sidechannel.

A minute later they placed the call to Roscher. The channel stuttered more than a standard comm did in connecting—the side effects of the multiple scrambler layers the ANP was routing it through, and the Leknes police's attempts to trace it. When a clear image appeared, it struck the Home Guardsmen as an alternate universe perversion of the image they were projecting.

Another conference table appeared in a dingy, ill-lit room. It was not precisely 'filthy' but looked like it had been hastily tidied up by filthy people who had an atrophied sense of cleanliness. At the head of the table sat 'General' Arnst Roscher. His dark clothes, dark demeanor, and straggly grey hair gave him a wolfish look. He was smoking a cigar, whose coal-bright end was bleeding smoke into a halo over his head.

For the Home Guard officers, suddenly seeing Roscher in a live image was unsettling. They had been hunting him for three years, and he was their foremost public enemy, so to be suddenly parleying with him could only mean a world gone mad. Even Hanssen, who had so quickly acceded to making this call, was repulsed by the reality of seeing the man before him.

Both parties silently appraised each other. This allowed an excruciating pause to build. After a while, the call's audio channel increased its gain, searching for any meaningful sound to transmit. Amplified white noise hummed from both rooms' speakers.

"—Well," broke in Roscher, if only to cause the audio gain to correct. "Good evening," he mumbled through his cigar.

The Home Guardsmen did not yet answer.

Roscher leaned forward and set his cigar down in an ashtray. "Oh, but come now. You must at least try to strike up a conversation. Even if you called me only to run a trace, you still have to keep me talking while your police muddle around, isn't that right?" His voice was tinged with the edgy calm of a psychopath who was only momentarily at rest.

The Brigadier cleared his throat.

"Introductions then?" the Brigadier finally offered. "This is my second, Colonel—"

"Oh, I already know them all—Colonel Hanssen, Majors Steffens and Lievgarten. Hello." He grinned.

There was some unspoken threat in Roscher's already knowing their names. It kept them from replying.

"Welllll, down to business," Roscher's voice slid. "That intel sample I sent you ... Interested?"

Lievgarten looked to the Brigadier to gather permission to proceed. "What you sent us ... " he started. "That was from an ANP surveillance network, yes?"

"Correct," said Roscher, clasping his hands before him. "A little system we set up to keep tabs on the corporates."

"... That's how you noticed us launch our own surveillance missions against them last week?"

Roscher nodded. "At first our boys were confused. 'Why's Lindon sending this shit against us? Do they just want us to garbage-collect it for them?' Some of our boys even thought it was a clever ploy—see if our net would ignore stuff that was too old to be a threat."

Lievgarten smothered a scowl.

"But once our system ripped the newcomers apart we saw where they'd come from. 'So Leknes is finally getting on board! Fancy that!'" The emotion in his voice seemed an eerily off approximation. "I mean, we all *claim* to be on the same side against the corporates. But, back when the scum first invaded our country, it was *you all* who sat back and did nothing," he struck a finger out at them. "The ones on the 'legitimate' side of military

110

power—with a mandate to defend the country—who couldn't be bothered. That left it up to the regular citizens like us to—"

"Cut the shit, please, 'General,'" Krohg interrupted.

Roscher stopped and stared, and the Home Guardsmen hung nervously. From the call's start they had taken Roscher for a short-fused maniac who could be upset by even a single syllable stepping out of line. This was just the challenge that could send him into a fury.

"What is this?" the Brigadier continued, waving a hand to encompass the whole affair. "This little speech, your posturing ... Are you playing this up so that you can put this vid on the nets later? Trying to score some points by buffing up the ANP's image?

"Well, we are not brothers in some anti–corporate army crusade," he asserted darkly. "What we are is law and outlaw. Never mind the cozy front you've built for yourself. The ANP is a drug cartel. And it's our job to take it down." He stared intently.

"But ... " he turned, "we're rather stalemated in that. And now it appears that you have something we need. That we're placed in the unfortunate position of being accommodating. So, if we're going to talk at all, let's have it be on that ground. The truth." He eased back a little.

Roscher stayed focused on the Brigadier for a long moment. They could all feel his tether being stretched ... threatening to snap into a wild display ...

"Oh, have it your way then," Roscher replied lightly, his menacing aura suddenly dissipating.

111

"'Law and outlaw' it is." He picked up his cigar and resumed puffing. "So, you're probably wondering how these 'outlaws' ended up with surveillance technologies that make yours look like eight-track cassettes."

After a delay, Lievgarten realized the man was waiting for a prompt. "... Yes?" he deigned.

"It's a simple answer. We didn't just start collecting intel last week on a whim. We've been doing this for three years. —For as long as you've been hunting me, in fact.

"See, back when we realized the corporates were here to stay, we knew we needed to keep an eye on them. So we rolled out basically the same package you did last week—and it worked. But, within a few days, the corporates ferreted out our bots and we were shut down. So we adapted to their countermeasures and got the up back on them. Then they hit back, so we hit back. And on and on. Competitive, evolutionary surveillance and counter-surveillance." He waved his cigar around in a circle. "Playing this game continuously, for the last three years."

The Home Guardsmen knew to reinterpret the history Roscher was relating. The ANP had formed in late 2040 after the Singularity, as armed citizens banded together, believing that the country's meltdown would soon go critical. But, once everything stabilized into the extant city–state paradigm, the ANP turned out to have placed a bet on an apocalypse that had not come to pass. Yet they were loath to simply disband; and so, as had

112

many disappointed doomsayers throughout history, they looked for a new *raison d'etre*.

Following public sentiment, they seized on the unpopular presence of the Lindon corporation's security forces. Thus the ANP's new mission became to oust the invaders from Norwegian soil—thereby preventing some other apocalypse that was envisioned to satisfy their dogma. But by then the ANP had achieved the position of having a stated purpose and public support, but no money. This opened the door for someone to come to the helm—Arnst Roscher—who had some novel ideas about how an aspiring army could pay its way. Only a year later the ANP had become the largest drug cartel in Scandinavian history.

Roscher continued, "Now, if you think all that work is something you can just duplicate overnight, then have at it. But not even top-grade, on-the-curve, just–off–the–space elevator surveillance gear is going to help you, because we and the corporates already went through that stuff months ago."

"Okay, this *one* example you sent us is impressive," interjected Lievgarten. "But does the ANP have this level of surveillance on ten corporate army bases? Twenty? Fifty? What?"

"Oh, all of them," Roscher answered easily. "Of course we have the best penetration on the smallest bases, but even the largest ones have few things they can hide. ... —Well, all except for the main base in Oslo."

The Home Guardsmen could not fault him there: the corporate army's Oslo superbase was probably as secure as an ASAPR.

"But what we sent you was only the coarsest view," Roscher resumed boasting. "We're not just recording vidage and throwing it away, you understand. Every time a corporate base test-fires a weapon, we record the firings rate, the ironside bearings, and the heat curves. Every time they run a drill, we record the festivities and infer the men's response times and aptitudes. Hell, any time they have a hooker on base, sometimes we can tell you exactly how long she was ridden by every jockey in that joint and which STDs were exchanged. Don't believe me?"

Roscher sent them portal access to a program through the comm channel. It offered itself to each of the Home Guard officers in their OHUDs. Hanssen opened it in a quarantined workspace. After a proud, ANP splash screen, a 3-D geophysical map of Norway appeared infested with detail glyphs and info portals.

"Oh, try it out, try it out," said Roscher hammily. "This is an interface program that turns all of our live-wire surveillance into a picture of what every corporate army base and unit is doing across the country. And it does a few nifty things with all of the backlogged data, too. This is only a snapshot from last year, though—I'm not showing you all our cards."

Hanssen eyed the program suspiciously ... before allowing himself to be overwhelmingly impressed.

All of the nearly hundred and fifty corporate army bases were covered, and zooming in on each gave its establishment date, a flipbook of its

114

construction, an analysis for possible security deficiencies, hardware upgrade schedules, the history of how many people had been deployed there, topographic imaging of the surrounding terrain, overlay traces of the most common routes taken in and out of the base by vehicular traffic, logistics routes, reinforcements routes, killing vectors for the defense systems, the weather recorded hourly for years, what kind of foods were eaten by base personnel and in what quantities, how quickly medical supplies had been consumed, standard patrol vectors, the current staff manifest, links to the service records of everyone who had ever been stationed there, psychological makeups and preliminary background checks on all of them, their sleep cycles deconstructed into Markov chains, records of all their visits to the head—and the data went endlessly on.

Hanssen was awed by the depth of pinpoint tactical planning that this level of detail enabled. Imagine attacking a camp when the platoon sergeant was having a bitter disagreement with his bowels, or was in just the wrong phase of their sleep cycle. Simply having the right person in the wrong place—or wrong mood—at a certain time could mean the difference between a unit that would fight to the bitter end and one that would wave the white flag as an opening maneuver.

—Then Roscher revoked the portal and it all blinked away. The effect was jarring. One instant they were all possessed of omniscience—replete with spreadsheets—and the next they were blind.

Krohg looked narrowly between his officers. It was obvious that this system was exactly what they needed, so their looks said nothing about that. Rather they were all bracing for the unstomachable price the ANP would ask.

"Then, 'General,'" Krohg said coolly, "I would like to know your terms."

"Oh, 'terms' is such an adversarial word," Roscher said. "All I'm asking for is a little *quid pro quo*. We share this system with you, and in return we want only two simple things."

Guaranteeing to be anything but 'simple,' the Home Guardsmen knew.

"First," Roscher proceeded, "you guys are going to be fighting the corporates. A fight the ANP's been waiting for for years. We could never take them on by ourselves, so you can imagine how frustrating it's been. Our surveillance lets us read the corporates' mail, but we've never had the muscle to act on it. ... Until now. Our first term is to be partners in that fight. To form our own squadrons to fight alongside yours."

The Home Guardsmen were stupefied. This had to be a mistake—Roscher must have lapsed back into playing for the cameras. To pay service to the ANP's anti–corporate army facade, he had blithely volunteered its participation in a war.

"And second?" asked Krohg warily. Indeed, Roscher's first term had been so innocuous that they all imagined true, Faustian horrors to come in the second.

"Second ... we both know that the ANP relies on certain ... diverse sources of income," Roscher began delicately. "And it has recently come to my attention that some of our members have pursued ... unorthodox methods in tandem to these. We'll not go quibbling into details, and I trust you'll accept my personal guarantee that all such activities will be stopped. And any 'crackdown' will only be facilitated by our association with the Leknes Home Guard, of course. So my second term is ... immunity. Blanket for the whole ANP."

There it was.

"And that's all?" asked the Brigadier.

Roscher nodded disinterestedly. It was as if he had made a sales pitch that he did not expect to succeed, nor even cared whether it did.

"All right, I believe we understand your offer, 'General,'" said Krohg. "Though of course we'll have to consider it carefully. And the ultimate okay will have to come from the city government. But you'll hear from us soon."

"Oh, call us at any time on this channel," Roscher replied, spreading his arms in greeting. On that the call disconnected.

The Leknes detective was brought back up immediately after. "How'd the trace go?" asked Lievgarten.

"Oh, the *trace* ... " the detective said, as if recalling ancient details. "We were on the defensive against an ANP attack the whole time. Never had a chance to run a trace."

Lievgarten humphed—that was exactly what he had expected. The Brigadier thanked the detective and closed the channel, leaving his party to deliberate.

"I said before that any price would be too high," Steffens immediately led off, "and now they just asked the highest price they could. —And you noticed how he said, 'blanket for the whole ANP'? Making sure he included himself in that clemency package ... "

"Well, to be fair," Lievgarten stepped in, "granting them immunity doesn't cost us much. We may make a lot of noise about a 'three-year investigation,' but in reality we can't touch the ANP. That debacle just now with having the police attempt to trace their call? That was typical. They're out of our league. We could have mountains of evidence stacked up, but it's all worthless because we can't track them down or bring them in."

Steffens crossed her arms over her chest. "But then ... why do they have such a good surveillance network covering the corporate army bases?" she asked suspiciously. "Is it just to keep up their image? But, even today, most people have heard about the ANP and drugs, but they don't know that they're one and the same. The average Lekneser might even *like it* if they heard we'd teamed up with the ANP to fight Lindon's men. Their cover is secure, so why go through all the trouble of building a first-rate surveillance network on the corporates that no one even knew they had?"

"Probably for the same reason that they keep tabs on the police and on us:" answered Lievgarten, "to watch anyone with the firepower to challenge them. They probably even sell drugs to the men at the corporate army bases themselves, so they have to have them staked out well enough to make a clean drop."

Steffens sunk back, routed again.

"But what *I* don't understand," Lievgarten turned—offering his own doubts to mollify Steffens—"is why he offered to fight alongside us. What good is it to get immunity if he only sends his forces in to get blown up?"

"I considered that, too," said Krohg. "But there are plenty of ways he could volunteer to help while still keeping his own forces out of danger. Especially if he's controlling all the intelligence we'll be seeing. He could send us to the real danger spots but put his own men on the milk runs."

Steffens sprang up. "Or maybe ... that's not what he wants at all. Maybe asking to help on the campaign is only a ploy—what gets him in the door. So that he gets his forces showing up in Leknes, mixing with our own. He might even be planning on making contacts inside the Home Guard to expand his business ...

"Wait—*Yes*," she seized on that thread. "We all thought that his first term—about joining us on the offensive—was a smokescreen for the second term. But what if it's the other way around? Liev said it: our evidence on them is worthless, so blanket immunity for them is worthless. But consider what letting them let inside the Home Guard gets them ... Inside the last military defense the country has left ... To twist it like he did the ANP ... " she lilted off.

The possibility she struck chilled them all. Five years ago Norway had pulled back from anarchy, but that stability was built on the few organizations that had survived the collapse in public confidence after the Singularity, the Home Guard being one of them. But Roscher was a man famous for having taken one 'legitimate' enterprise—the ANP—and perverting it to his own ends. Now he was knocking on the Home Guard's door—and so on all of Norway's, in fact ...

Though the idea that this could even succeed was too outlandish. Granted there were plenty of small countries that were just money-laundering fronts for cartels—their populations mere Human camouflage, and their culture, history, and Wikipedia articles all just flavortext to add credence to the sham. But the idea that Norway—a first-tier European country—could join those ranks was preposterousness.

The Brigadier grumbled. "Though I fear this is our only option. The ANP has the intelligence we need. Without it, this campaign is over. Our only option beforehand required too much money, but now this one requires too much—what? Risk?" Krohg drew a long breath before at last entreating, "Hanssen, your thoughts?"

Hanssen cleared his throat—this being the first time he would speak in a long while. Indeed, Steffens and Lievgarten were surprised to remember that he was present.

"We accept their deal," he said, as plainly as if he were making the final call. "Let me worry about keeping the ANP under control."

Hanssen saw this as a prime example of his style of command. Steffens liked to enumerate all of the risks beforehand, and typically in front of the

Brigadier, as if she were saving up for a storm of 'I told you so's later on. But Hanssen rather knew that, no matter what the risks were, they would have to be dealt with by someone. So instead of wasting time cataloguing them he would step up and say, 'I'll take care of it.' Assume responsibility, and then they could fire him if he failed.

The Brigadier accepted this solidly. "Very well. I'll present Roscher's proposal to the Council. I'll be giving them *my* assurances based on *your* assurances, Hanssen, that we'll be able to handle the ANP, whatever else they have in mind."

Chapter 12 - The Hezokeen

When a meeting's attendees were situated all over the world, holding it at one time was usually just as inconvenient as any other, and so they were scheduled randomly. This was the case with a meeting for the Eyes ministers of defense that was convened at 2330 Zulu.

As each participant logged into the simulation, their appearance made it obvious what time zone they were operating from. Willoch and Gzowski were wired from being up late—they must be on European time. Lin was groggy from having been dragged out of bed early—east Asia. Arrillaga was alert but miffed at having had his dinner interrupted—he came from across the Atlantic. Only Owada and Bryant were bright-eyed—must be the western Pacific where it was morning. And poor Borodin and Prashnakhan were the worst off, looking vacant and zombie-like—the Asian steppe. But the fact that all of the MINDEFs had appeared without sending a deputy showed how serious this meeting was.

Admiral Stennis had found the pirates.

It had not taken his task force long since the pirate fleet had been waiting close around where they had seized the Lontan freighters. Once the encounter was over, Stennis had sent back a complete sensor record. A team with the International Office of Naval Intelligence had analyzed it and prepared a brief, which the MINDEFs were assembled to receive.

The meeting's IONI point man, Captain Surjeet, appeared as a pewter-sized holo in the middle of the table. Into the air above him he was conjuring a sea of graphics and plots. From the middle of his briefing:

"The pirate units kept considerable distance from Stennis's ships throughout contact, approaching no closer than as shown here."

The holo was showing a clip of sensor telemetry: a 3-D field of blue dots—friendly units—being shadowed to the port keel by a tangle of red dots—bogies. Willoch, as an admiral, had already been pouring over this data herself ever since it had come in. But the rest of the MINDEFs—being civilians—were getting their first looks.

"As the pirates only ever closed within mid-range sensors," Surjeet continued, "this made it difficult to pick out any distinguishing ship characteristics that might have determined their identity. But we pooled many weak observations of hull designs, hyperdrive characteristics, sensor profiles, and other fiducials ... " The holo flashed with a fireworks display of accompanying graphics: dissected ship keels, analyzed emission spectra, engine performance curves. "After feeding this data into the Lontans' Galactic Ship Registry, we derived an unequivocal match. Sirs, these are our pirates."

The holo now hosted the projection of a wiry, erect body. Its colorings and anatomical structures were so perturbed from Earth norms that Willoch had trouble deciphering it as a tripedal, bimanual species. The creature was over two meters in height, with glistening, serpentine skin, and an elongated head. Information at the bottom said that the species was asexual. So, from her knowledge of xenomusicology, Willoch imagined that these beings might enjoy light waltzes, but that their music would in general be lax and meandering—no rhythms or climaxes.

"The Hezokeen," said Surjeet. "Contact was made with this species by the Wilusans some thirteen thousand years ago. Hezokeen civilization expanded mostly peacefully, and now comprises four hundred star systems that are around twenty-five thousand light-years away from Earth.

"But a significant fraction of the Hezokeen have also taken to piracy. In this quadrant of the galaxy, they actually represent the second most populous species of pirates. Their fleets operate in groups of fifty to a hundred ships, raiding shipping on the fringes of galactic trade. They are not strong enough to challenge the larger powers, but they have made their living by preying on the softer targets prevalent on the rim. They have also been known to serve as mercenaries from time to time, and have made appearances in several wars."

The Hezokeen holo disappeared, being replaced with the old ship schematics.

"Returning to the specific fleet we face," said Surjeet, "our analysis shows that the Hezokeen's ships are built on mostly outdated military technologies, with hull designs suggestive of fifty-to one hundred–year–old designs. If their weapons systems are at the same level, then individually our ships—being modern Lontan hardware—would possess perhaps a fifty percent advantage in strength

124

and firepower, with a marginal three percent advantage in top speed.

"However, while we have the edge in quality, it appears the Hezokeen have it in quantity. Our task force encountered sixty-seven unique Hezokeen warships, and it was able to roughly scope out the size of their primary staging area. Given those observations, we estimate the entire Hezokeen fleet consists of three to five hundred warships. This constitutes a three-to-one superiority in raw numbers, and potentially greater than a two-to-one superiority in adjusted strength, even versus the combined Human fleets.

"The IONI report provides many further details, but if there are any questions I can now answer them."

Surjeet was finished, and the MINDEFs now performed all of the upkeeps of an audience that had just endured a long symphonic movement— coughing, clearing their throats, shifting in their seats. But the meeting's simspace was smart enough not to send each person's body noises over the channel to the others.

Australia's MINDEF, Connor Bryant, was the first to speak, "Thank you for your presentation, Captain. Now, you said *if* the Hezokeen's weapons are as old as their hull designs, then we possess a fifty percent advantage. Why the 'if'—why no hard data?"

"Because there was no fire exchanged between us and the Hezokeen ships. In the absence of that, we based our analysis on historical weapons systems that the Hezokeen would be most likely to have given their access to galactic trade, and as suggested by the general state of their ships."

Bryant nodded.

"Do the Hezokeen know where the Earth is?" asked Owada Hisashi. "Since our fleet found them waiting around where they intercepted the freighters, does that suggest they don't know where we are?"

Lin Deming interjected, "And I'm told that the Lontan freighters' courses are always randomized going to and from our system. So, no matter where the pirates intercepted them, it still wouldn't have necessarily pointed them the way to us, yes?"

"Actually, sirs, they must know where we are," replied Surjeet. "Granted the freighters' courses were randomized, but the Hezokeen still intercepted them twenty-two light-years out. At that range, the Earth is visible by dint of its 2023 EM signature, which is strong enough that the Hezokeen could have discovered us after a brief all-sky search."

"Ah, like the old SETI project?" asked the US SECDEF, Charles Arrillaga.

Surjeet paused while he looked up 'settee,' 'setee,' and several other permutation spellings in his OHUD. Shortly he had resolved the reference: "Ah, you mean the Search for Extraterrestrial Intelligence project ... " He lightning-skimmed an encyclopedia article and said, "Yes, sir, exactly the same methodology."

Willoch approved of these questions, but she would have preferred to read through this section of the meeting transcript later rather than watch it happen live. So she slipped into her OHUD and began viz surfing. She skimmed more of the IONI report, did some background reading on the Hezokeen, fielded her mail ... She could not imagine what people had done—what she herself had done—back in the days before OHUDs when there had been no polite way to stop paying attention during a meeting and go put a dent in actual work. They must have never gotten anything done at all.

Willoch tuned back in once Captain Surjeet was dismissed. Now would begin the strategy portion of the meeting.

"Now that we've verified the threat," said Arrillaga, "we have to consider our response. And broadly I see three options.

"One, we head out and meet the Hezokeen full force to kick them off our trade route. That's simple, but, with the estimates we've just seen of their strength, I'm sure that's out of the question. Four hundred Hezokeen ships against only a hundred and thirty of ours isn't exactly betting odds—even with some supposed ship-for-ship advantage.

"Second option, we try and maintain trade with the Lontans by sending our cargo ships on eccentric routes, far out of range of the pirates, and with military escorts. But that's not viable if we want to restore trade to its previous levels. It would also put us in open conflict with the Hezokeen, and the draw on our resources would double or triple the effective price of imported goods.

"The third option is we do nothing. We keep tabs on the Hezokeen, patrol the system, but we otherwise live with the embargo."

The other MINDEFs nodded in agreement. Their own staffs would have generated the same three options for them beforehand.

Miklan Gzowski, the European Confederation MINDEF, leaned forward: "I believe we should all find option three preferable by far. Cost is determining the factor. Alien imports were already expensive, and now, with the depression, many of our economies no longer have the leeway to continue them. How then can we justify a military action to restore them?

"But, if we simply ignore the pirates, then we incur no extra costs. And the cessation of trade itself becomes immediate savings—with this incursion giving us a convenient way of explaining it to the public."

"I wouldn't be so ready to simply drop our Lontan imports," said Bryant. "Granted cost is a factor, but so is consistency, and many of our governments have made it a sticking point to keep up the tempo of alien trade. We want the public to know that the depression hasn't changed things so drastically. But stopping the imports ... " he lilted off in worry. "That would make it look like we've been completely cut off from the galaxy."

"We already *have* been cut off ... " said Gzowski.

"Whether we have or not, public perception is the key. And allowing alien trade to lapse would be a negative shock—even with such a plausible excuse for it."

Owada entered: "And I would urge caution on another point. Using this pirate intervention as an excuse to stop trade may seem a good option now, but think of the long term. Once it sets in that we have a hostile fleet besieging our planet, how will the public take it that their leaders simply accepted that fact? Even *welcomed* it as a 'cost-saving measure.'"

"I'll grant you that," said Arrillaga. "I know my government is of the mind to do *something* about these pirates. President McAdams specifically told me that option three is 'no option at all.' I just don't think there's anything better I can offer him."

There was a pause ... One just long enough as Willoch had been waiting for.

"Pardon me," she stepped in delicately. "But I believe there's a fourth option."

Everyone turned to Willoch, and Gzowski looked at her with particular displeasure. She knew the line she had crossed by speaking.

She was not truly the Norwegian Minister of Defence. The reality was that the last, proper Norwegian MINDEF had died in the Singularity, along with most of the other top brass. Only then–two-star Admiral Willoch—head of the Norwegian Navy and up on Gateway Station at the time—had survived. With all of her superiors deceased, she had not been 'appointed' Minister of Defence but rather had the title lapse to her by default.

After she had met with the MINDEFs for a year, her country had splintered and her inherited post no longer existed. When Gzowski became the new Confederation MINDEF, he had moved to have Willoch excluded from the meetings. Yet, however practical this was, the other MINDEFs were against it. Dissolving Norway's international posts would be a further admission of the Singularity's impact, and just when the depression was proving so dire that the only logical response to it was abject denial. They implored Gzowski, and he had only withdrawn his objections after he had been given the assurance that Willoch would serve as a mute figurehead. Thus, if she so much as said 'Good morning,' Gzowski already regarded it as an impertinence, and her actually participating in discussions was rank effrontery.

Willoch waited to see if anyone recognized—and legitimized—her interruption.

Arrillaga grunted. "Well, if there's another option besides giving up or spending billions, I'll hear it."

Willoch nodded gratefully. That gave her a few sentences of leeway.

"I know you've all reviewed my meetings with the Lontan Ambassador concerning these pirates—the Hezokeen," she corrected herself now that they had a name. "You may recall that he mentioned something a week ago called 'tithing.' The idea is that the Hezokeen only want to 'wet their beaks.' If we restart trade as normal, they'll grab only one out of every eight or ten of our cargo ships for their own."

Some sighs escaped the table.

"I know, I know," said Willoch. "But, if it works, we'll be able to get trade back up to its previous levels immediately. And the relative increase in cost will only be ten to fifteen percent—proportional to the rate that the Hezokeen seize

130

ships. That's much better than the doubling or tripling in price that would come from providing military escorts. And this is a bloodless solution that restores trade immediately."

"Well, thank you, *Admiral* Willoch," said Gzowski, cutting her off, "but now—"

"Just a moment," Owada interrupted him. "I don't think there's any harm in discussing this tithing option."

Owada looked between Willoch and Gzowski. Their silent test of wills played out for a few seconds ... Gzowski soured even more acutely, but he ultimately looked away. Owada continued:

"And I should first say," she turned to Willoch, "that, even though this tithing option looks beneficial, we have no guarantee that the Hezokeen are the kind of 'professional,' 'business-like' pirates that the Ambassador described to you. If we attempt this tithe, the Hezokeen might simply seize every ship we send their way. Then we're back to an embargo—and only after having aided and abetted our besiegers."

"That concerned me, too," said Willoch, "but I have a few points. First, Minister Owada, you noted how the Hezokeen were still holding position around where they intercepted our freighters. But why stay there? They know where the Earth is, so why not send their ships closer in? Easier to maintain a blockade, then. There was no reason for them to hold position.

"Unless they expected us to send a recon. The Lontan Ambassador said the pirates would wish to

131

'introduce' themselves to us. So they stayed in a place where it would be easy for us to find them.

"And second, let's look more closely at Stennis's sensor logs." She took over the main holo and brought up a snippet of telemetry—she had prepared this while viz surfing. "Watch the motion of the two fleets as I play this at ten times speed."

They saw a tiny cluster of friendly blue dots soldiering through the darkness—Stennis's recon. A set of red bogies appeared at their periphery, at first closing in, but then maintaining a steady distance. The bogies would rotate around and inspect the Human fleet, but they never approached closer than mid-range sensors. And, whenever a new Hezokeen ship arrived, one of the existing ones would depart.

"See how disciplined it is?" said Willoch. "These pirates are very composed. Once our groups came in contact, they could have played it confrontationally—pressing inwards, jockeying for position, seeing how close we let them get before responding ... But instead they kept their distance. And note how, whenever one ship arrives, another one leaves. Which means they never brought enough ships together at one time to threaten us, even though they clearly had the numbers to do so. If *I* were running the pirate fleet, and were trying to open up a 'mutual business transaction,' this is how I would manage it. Coolly, patiently."

She paused the replay, causing everyone to focus on her next words:

"They were doing just what the Ambassador said they would: showing themselves and letting us evaluate their ships. Our fleets were like ... two

132

knights lifting their visors as they approached each other on the field. And, once this introduction was complete, the Hezokeen let us retire.

"So this 'tithing option' is not just some random proposal from the Ambassador," she concluded. "It's something that the Hezokeen have offered to us. And it's our loss to reject it. We don't have to go on an all-out campaign. Just a marginal increase in cost and we will have completely restored alien trade. That'll be a political victory for every government at this table."

By the end of her speech, Gzowski's expression had pickled viciously, but the other MINDEFs seemed to be countenancing her argument. There would doubtless be more debate, but Willoch knew she had made an impression. And, given that tithing was their only feasible option, that was all she had needed to do.

Chapter 13 - Merger

Erlend was standing in front of a score of Home Guard officers in one of the base's underground garages. The launchways were open and the long tunnels glowed with daylight peeking in at their distant ends. The Leknes City government had approved the Home Guard's collaboration with the ANP, and the first of their corps were arriving that morning. Erlend's men were assembled to serve as a welcoming committee.

Kitano ventured curious onto the scene. Approaching Erlend's party from across the tarmac, she asked him, "So I heard you had something going on to—"

"Yeah, meeting the ANP," Erlend interrupted, and with a tone that made her realize there was something clandestine afoot.

She switched to secure-texting and asked, ">What's the lowdown?"

">We *are* meeting the ANP," Erlend texted back, ">but there's something else on the agenda, too. / We're going to start our search for ways into their organization."

Kitano was puzzled. ">How's that?"

">Informants. / The ANP's gonna be trying to screw us from minute one. / Our only defense is counter-infiltration."

Kitano looked at the other officers assembled behind Erlend. ">Won't that be a little conspicuous? / If you're all trying to recruit sources into the ANP as soon as their guys step off the transports?"

">Well, I'm not asking these idiots to bring me gift-wrapped defectors," he used body language to indicate his men—and to add some exasperation. ">We're running background checks on all these ANPers / looking for anyone promising to approach. / But another important factor will be man-to-man impressions, / which is what my guys are here for. / You can help us if you want."

">Really? How?"

">Nothing too involved. / Just, for every ANP jackass you talk to, jot down whether he's an 'asshole' or 'not an asshole' in your viz. / Then at the end of the day mail it to me and I'll tally all the votes."

Kitano bridled at this. ">How about I just vote with 'thumbs up'/'thumbs down'?"

">Whatever you want." "Okay, looks like we're all set," he said to his group.

Shortly the first set of ANP vehicles arrived: three dots appeared at the mouth of the launchway, hovering in the bath of sunlight. They swept into the garage and excited the space with the roar of their engines. The two ANP transports and one tank landed in gridded-off spaces. Leknes deck hands scurried out to attend them, and the ANP crews started deplaning. As they stepped down inside the Home Guard base, many of the men made animated gestures and exclamations. They panned their heads around and hard-blinked to save OHUD captures of what they were seeing as if they were touring the Sistine Chapel.

The new arrivals were mostly men in their twenties, with their hair longer and their dress more

135

unkempt than what a true military enforced. Their most distinctive feature was their uniforms, which were not 'uniforms' *per se* but rather absurd, costume-like pastiches of clothing and insignia assembled with vainglorious haphazard. Each man had lavished himself with honor cords, epaulets, and sashes as busily as if he had been decorating a cake. The only common facet of their ensembles was the patches on their sleeves that bore three red letters: 'ANP'—'Arme av Norsk Patrioter.'

The ANP and Home Guard officers drifted towards each other, as tense as if they were making first contact with an alien species. The two organizations had yet to swap facebook applications, so no one's OHUD could label the new people with standard identification cards. Instead they performed introductions manually. Erlend, at the prow of the Home Guard formation, met and introduced himself to the man at the head of the ANP's, who proved to be:

"Captain Toresson, sir," the man replied.

It had taken a great deal of diplomacy to resolve the question of ANP–Home Guard rank equivalence. Even though they both used the same ranks, the two systems were hardly miscible. Ranks in the ANP were awarded self-indulgently, and on the basis of ego rather than merit. As a result their 'rank inflation' was so horrendous that one had to be a colonel in the ANP before one exercised the same powers as a sergeant in the Home Guard. So it had been decided that all Home Guard officers would outrank all ANP officers, and similarly for all enlisted men (so an ANP major would still say 'sir'

136

to a Home Guard lieutenant). The one exception was 'General' Roscher, who was allowed to outrank all Home Guard officers.

Erlend took Toresson's hand and shook it solidly. The man reciprocated solidly. Erlend squeezed tighter. Toresson did the same. And they continued throttling each other as Erlend said nonchalantly,

"Glad to have you and your men on board, 'Captain' Toresson." Erlend was determined never to say an ANPer's rank without scare quotes.

"I—uh—yes—thanks—" the man managed. He was losing the handshake contest.

"If you'll just log onto the net, you'll find where you've been assigned quarters. All of you have been given guest access to our system." Erlend finally released the man's hand, and he jotted down in his OHUD: 'Toresson – cupcake.'

A man at Toresson's side stepped forward and placed himself in front of Kitano. "Why hellooo ... " he smarmed, and reached for her hand as to kiss it. "And who might you be?"

Erlend intervened and roped the man's hand into his own grasp and squeezed.

"Wouldn't it be more polite to introduce yourself to the lady first?" said Erlend.

The man struggled to keep from wincing. "... I'm—Lieutenant Lambrechts," he managed. "—*Sir*," he added after a prompting squeeze from Erlend.

"Nice to meet you, Lambrechts," Erlend finally released him. In his OHUD he wrote, 'Lambrechts – ultra-asshole.' "Like I told Toresson, just check for your bunk assignment over the net."

137

In like kind the rest of the ANP arrivals were introduced to the Home Guard. The talk was sparse, and even then perfunctory, but it accomplished what modest ice breaking could have been expected. The two organizations had at least acknowledged each other's existence and begun the long, glacial thaw towards detente.

Shortly Hanssen and Roscher appeared at the entrance of the garage. It had been expected that the brass would be present for at least part of the ANP arrivals, and so Hanssen and Roscher coming after the first group was equivalent to being fashionably late.

Roscher was only telepresenting, however, and was being rendered as a full-sized figure in all their OHUDs. While the ANP and Home Guard had agreed to a ceasefire, Roscher was not foolish enough to physically expose himself. Where the man's actual body was located remained just as much a mystery as before.

Hanssen and Roscher walked up to Erlend's party.

"'General,'" Erlend greeted Roscher.

Hanssen was amazed how Erlend could make his scare quotes stand out even in single-word sentences.

"Lieutenant," Roscher acknowledged him. "Well, what do you think of my troops so far?"

Erlend was surprised at this question, which seemed almost a direct invite for an insult. Well, if you insist, he thought ... —But, *No*, he stopped himself. I'll play it cool.

"They're very ... varied," he replied.

Roscher wondered. "Oh—you mean their clothes!" he realized, chuckling. "Ah, yes, their fashion sense is a bit scattershot ... "

"Ah, yes," Erlend echoed, chuckling along. "Though ... it might do for them to button up around here. Trim down a little bit. ... I'm only thinking of our laundromat. Our machines only have one setting, but all your men's *sashes* and *silks* probably have to be washed on 'delicate.' Sir."

"Oh, it'll be fine—this place could use a little color," Roscher said amiably. "And, with all the crucial intelligence the ANP is bringing to this campaign, we should be excused the normal military pedantry."

They locked eyes.

"Hm. I didn't know not having lice was considered 'military pedantry.'"

"Ah, lice, very good ... " Roscher laughed this off..

">Cool it," Hanssen texted to Erlend.

Erlend frowned, but muzzled himself.

The second group of ANP vehicles soon entered the garage: two tanks and three transports. As this tide of officers deplaned, they made the same tourist-like displays on seeing the base as the first had. Though Roscher quickly sent them a secure text ordering them to behave with more decorum. They straightened up and began issuing salutes.

As some men were passing by, Roscher called out, "Ah, Ingstad! Ingstad!"

A man looked up and approached, bringing two other officers behind him. Roscher put his simulated arm on the man's shoulder and presented him to the Home Guardsmen.

"Colonel Hanssen," he said, "allow me to introduce Captain Ingstad. And his leftenants, Waage and Kvaerner. One of the ANP's finest tank crews," he rattled off with mock pride.

Erlend shook hands with them, and—as before—aggrandized each of his shakes into a small wrestling match. Here he easily routed Waage, but Ingstad managed a draw. When he reached for Kvaerner's hand, though, the man seemed not to notice him. He was twitching fiercely, and sweat was beading off his scalp so quickly as to raise concerns of dehydration.

"Hi, uh ... " Erlend said to him. "You ... you doin' alright there, pal-y?"

"He's fine, he's fine," said Roscher, simu-patting Kvaerner on the back.

"... —Yeah. —Yeah," the man made a stalled reply. He sounded as if he spoke no Norwegian and had been coached only to say 'Yeah' in response to any challenge.

"Uh-huh," observed Erlend. "Well, 'Captain' Ingstad, looks like you and your crew are set up down in C deck—just check the comps for directions."

Ingstad nodded demurely, and he led Kvaerner off.

To Erlend it seemed that Ingstad was rightly shamed by his man's behavior. And there also seemed another reticence about him ... To his notes he added, 'Kvaerner, Waage – pansy; Ingstad – provisional possible non-asshole.'

Meanwhile he texted to the other Home Guardsmen, ">Well, that Kvaerner guy was our first major train wreck."

">Yeah," replied Kitano. ">Doing sledge, or chilt, or *something*."

">Maybe all three."

Roscher glanced at them in disapproval. He could not have read their secure texts, but he could have been alerted to the message traffic. And, since it was hardly difficult to guess what they were saying, he was displaying an *a priori*–allowed amount of umbrage.

After several more such strained introductions, Roscher drifted off to talk to some of his men. Hanssen texted Erlend, ">How are we on leads?"

">Got a few possibles ... / Looks like we'll tally the votes and crunch through the numbers like we planned. / Meet up tonight?"

Hanssen nodded, and offered a verbal, "Carry on." Then he departed—and carefully headed for whichever side of the base where Märtha wasn't.

141

Chapter 14 - Prototype

Peder arrived at Zuzanna's flat in Upper Norrmalm on a bright Saturday afternoon. Zuzanna had invited him over in an ebullient email that spoke of the weather and fashion but made no mention of their job. Thus Peder knew that the Mafia's heightened security measures were still in place. To keep up the pretense of this being a social visit, he brought flowers.

Zuzanna greeted him warmly at the door.

"Oh, flowers! Lovely!" she exclaimed. She grabbed his hand and pulled him inside. "We must find a place for them ... " she said, sweeping her gaze over her foyer and putting a finger to her chin.

This was indeed a challenge as Zuzanna's home was manic with plants. Vases on the floor, vases on stands, vases on windowsills, pots on the floor, pots on stands, pots hanging from the ceiling, and there was even a whole wall covered with an ivy-wrapped lattice. Peder had always known that Zuzanna had a plant fixation, but it was still 'moderate' the last time he had seen her place a year ago. What he saw now meant he had to raise his estimate a few notches.

"Still collecting plants, I see ... " he said in an 80%-friendly, 20%–expressing-genuine-concern voice.

"Yes!" Zuzanna smiled. "You can see how big the Adiantum capillus-veneris has grown since you were last here. Oh! and there's a Encyclia tampensis that I've just acquired ... And I've been trying my hand at Gesneriaceae cultivation ... "

While she rambled off details, Peder piped her voice through his OHUD search. It picked out the scientific names of the plants, did web searches, and gave him reference images so that he could follow along as well as a seasoned botanist.

"Well, there's no room in the foyer ... " Zuzanna said casually. She led him to the kitchen and cleared a space for the flowers on her table.

She poured them drinks and they chatted for a while about old classmates and current events. This smalltalk was necessary. If Zuzanna were under surveillance by the police, then this little masquerade would at least put it in doubt whether Peder was a client or not.

All the while Peder could sense some eager energy radiating from Zuzanna. She was anxious to get to business.

Soon they went and cycled into her ASAPR. Zuzanna's was slightly larger than Peder's, and it had been decorated with a feminine touch, including its own touch of verdure. Peder was impressed that Zuzanna had been able to cultivate living things inside of an hermetic information bubble.

Once they were safe inside, Zuzanna made the first serious comment of his visit with, "—Sorry for the delay getting back to you, Peder—I know two weeks is a little long." She sat at her workstation and logged on.

"Yeah, I noticed," he replied. "I was actually getting worried."

"Worried about me?" she looked at him with a mock pouting expression. "Awww, how cute."

Peder took his own seat. "Well ... you do work for the Mafia," he said casually. "It's not like you're that insulated from mortal danger."

"Don't be so dramatic. Working for the Mafia isn't a prison sentence. It's a job. Usually just eight-to-five, like everyone else's. There are a few strange twists to it, but every place has some of those. ... And I haven't had to kill anybody in months."

It took Peder a few seconds to realize the joke.

"*Well*," said Zuzanna, segueing as she stood before her main display, "what I have to show you today isn't actually about Reeser Atkins. We did start looking into him like you wanted, but this is about something else we uncovered during the course of that.

"What you asked us for was to dig up blackmail fodder on this man. In such investigations we have to get to know our target first, so we arranged for covert intrusions into his home, his office, his favorite restaurants, his gym—every place he frequents. And, since he's been to the Lindon Headquarters a few times, we tried to get some surveillance on him from inside the Spire. Here's a sample of what we recovered."

Her ASAPR's main display came alight with many security cam shots showing corridors, cubefarms, and stairways. The lack of decor and the employees' dress identified the shots as coming from inside the Lindon corporate headquarters. Side screens also flashed with plots of building statistics and secure data. As Peder took it in, his mouth began sliding open in astonishment.

Zuzanna narrated, "We have sparse security cam vidage from just over half the building's floors ... complete power and water consumption records ... time logs for the lifts ... locations and timestamps for thousands of personnel swipes—"

"*How* did you get all this?" Peder asked, agape. "Do you know how *secure* the Spire is? —I mean the whole company is tighter than a safe, but then the corporate headquarters itself is like an ASAPR. I can't imagine how you got all this so quickly ... "

Zuzanna struck a self-satisfied grin.

"We combed through this data," she ignored him and continued, "but it didn't seem to lead anywhere. Until we found something ... interesting." A new screen appeared. "This is a fraction of the lift time logs we recovered. It shows arrival and departure times for almost every lift trip in the building, accurate to the millisecond. And we also had the vidage from the security cams inside of the lift cars. So we fed these two components into a standard data-mining routine that calculates the mass of everyone in the building."

Peder held up a hand to stop her. "Sorry, I have to ask: *why* would you have a data-mining routine like that?"

"It's actually an industry standard. The paparazzi developed it a decade ago so that they could spy on celebrities. The way it came about was they were trying to get the room service records out of some Beverly Hills hotel—to see who was eating what. But their hackers could only get away with the lift data instead. But then they figured out how they could use that to measure the weight of

145

everyone in the building. Then they made a headline out of Syla D—"

"Oh, right, 'Syla Dalton Pushing 55 Kilos,' I remember that story now," said Peder.

"Exactly. It was the first time an article was published simultaneously as a scientific paper *and* as a tabloid entry. Anyway, the intelligence agencies adopted the methodology soon afterwards. They figured they could use it to track the weights of heads of state and ambassadors, which would help them gauge their health."

Peder nodded, and he also tipped his hat to Human ingenuity. The power of science and technology lay not just in inventing new things— like elevators or data mining individually—but in the exponential number of ways of fusing unrelated inventions together to achieve wholly unanticipated results—e.g., putting elevators and data mining together to yield 'weight surveillance.'

"This routine is ubiquitous now," said Zuzanna, "and it was just included in a standard battery we ran on the data. Let me explain how it works. First it uses the elapsed time between all of the lift stops to estimate the mass that was in the car on that trip. If we know the physics of the lift cars and the power consumption of their motors, with this data's accuracy we can estimate the load to within ten kilos. Then, once the program has those estimates, it takes the security cam stills and notes who was in the car on each trip. For every trip you write down an equation: the weight of persons A, B, and C equals one sixty kilos; on another trip persons B, C, and *D* equals one-eighty. Once you have enough

146

constraints, you can solve for everyone's mass using simple numerical methods. Here were our results."

The screen flashed him some large matrices: they had run the numbers on 15,000 people and 60,000 lift trips—plenty of constraints. This gave them a mass for everyone in the Spire, and, when they took the global average, it came out to 48 kilos.

"Wait a minute, that's too light," said Peder. "That would make them all petite women. ... Or it would mean that there were a lot of children inside. So either your data is off or your methods are."

"That's what we thought," said Zuzanna. "So we looked closer. And we saw that the average weight was really sixty-five kilos—as it should be. But only over people with *non-zero* mass. Meanwhile over a thousand people inside the Spire added no mass to the lift trips. The presence of all those zeros was what was dragging the average down to forty-eight kilos."

The security cam shots on the main screen were now augmented to show everyone's mass superimposed over them. Most of the results were reasonable: small women were massed 50 and 60, men 75 and up. Yet there were also those who obliviously wore a '0 kg' weight. Ghosts.

Peder was grasping for an explanation ... until he realized the obvious one:

"Your data was tampered with," he said. "When you raided Lindon's systems, the security trapped you into a honeypot. You thought you were grabbing real data, but they sent you this doctored junk to put you on a wild goose chase." And he had been so impressed up till now ...

147

"The data's real," Zuzanna stated.

Peder frowned.

"That was our first assumption, too. So we went back and asked where could Lindon have tampered with our exfiltration. But, with the methods we used, he *couldn't* have. So the data's genuine.

"But, even if you don't accept that, let's assume that this data was doctored. Then *how* could it have been doctored to get this result? Lindon could have done a thousand things to corrupt the data we were getting. He could have put some small noise on the lift timestamps, or shuffled the cam vidage. But these would have demolished our numerical approach. We would have gotten bogus solutions and degenerate systems. Yet instead we come up with a perfectly reasonable solution where it just so happens that some of his employees have zero mass? For us to get that result, the data would have to have been altered exactly to produce that result. But why would Lindon's security do that?"

Peder squirmed. "You do have a point ... " he grumbled. "You only ran this lift/body mass tool as part of a standard battery, so you never would have looked at the numbers unless something had been off. Which leaves the question of *why* would Lindon have prepared phony data specifically designed to draw attention to such a random test? ... Fine, I'll bite," he conceded. "So a thousand people inside the Spire are ghosts. How do you explain that?"

"Our theory is a massive vizhack."

Peder was crestfallen not to have thought of that himself. A vizhack was the act of gaining root access to someone's OHUD and using it to render

148

arbitrary sights and sounds into their senses. The most common types of vizhacks were used for spam and malware—drawing unkillable ads or phishing windows into the subject's vision. But vizhacks could also be used to simulate real-world objects and persons in the same manner as augmented reality. That was what Zuzanna was suggesting. Since the ghosts were not actually physically present—having zero mass—, but since the non-ghosts could see and interact with them, then the ghosts had to be simulations drawn into the OHUDs of all the non-ghosts.

"Of course there's not even a 'hack' component to this," Zuzanna continued. "Everyone in the Spire is already running company software in the highest privileged mode in their vizes, so Lindon has the power to tinker with everyone's augspace at liberty. All that remains is to simulate the presence of a thousand artificial people inside of a building to a fidelity that will fool the other nineteen thousand."

"—Which is impossible," Peder objected. "Augspace is good at rendering videos and effects, but it's impossible to get real-world fidelity on that scale. You can render a coffee cup that looks almost real, but not hundreds of Human beings at hundreds of FPS."

"Right. That would be 'nöo-realistic augspace.' 'Magical reality,'" Zuzanna threw out the buzz terms.

"Exactly. It takes so much computing power that even the largest simulation I've heard of only involved a handful of objects and a dozen onlookers. But this! Twenty thousand people and an entire corporate arcology ... " He shook his head.

"Oh, we agree. If there's a ghost walking down the hall, then the sight of them has to be customized for every real pair of eyes looking at them. If one person is far away, the ghost has to look blurry to them. If someone's crossing their eyes, the ghost has to appear in two half-images ... And it's not just graphics: if a ghost *says* something, the sound has to be propagated through a 3-D acoustics model and customized for everyone, too. If someone has bad hearing, the sound has to match that. If someone has a cold that day and their ears are stopped up, the sound has to match *that* ... There are a dozen super-scale problems that have to be solved to make such a system work. But what if they're not playing by Human rules ... "

Peder mouthed an 'Oh.' He was surprised how sluggish he was sometimes, thinking always in terms of what was 'Human-capable' as if that still subtended the entire universe.

"What if Lindon smuggled down some alien 'ultracomp' that he's using to backend this thing?" Zuzanna continued. "That would be the easiest way to explain where he suddenly got this phenomenal amount of computing power."

Peder was slowly nodding. "Now I see why you were excited upstairs. If Lindon's solved nöo-realistic augspace, then a system like this would be worth billions. —But only if it's legal. If he smuggled down the technology to make it possible, then he can't sell it."

"And, since he's keeping it under wraps, it might mean exactly that."

"Which puts his entire company on the blackmail hook ... "

"Precisely," she grinned. "You wanted us to blackmail Atkins, and we snare all of Lindon instead."

He gave her an impressed nod.

"Which is why we're going to pry deeper into this system," she said. "There are so many questions. For one, we're still only theorizing that this thing exists, so we want to confirm it. We also want to figure out as much of its backend as possible. Any technologies we can pull out of it will be golden. And even if Lindon catches us he won't be able to go to the police. We could just do a smash-and-grab if we wanted."

Peder saw the promise. Whatever this system was, it should at least yield some techs and devices a few years ahead of the established curves. The Mafia could auction those off to Lindon's rivals, or at least blackmail Lindon to keep them secret.

"Great," said Peder. "Only where do I come in ... "

"We want backers for the operation we're launching, and I thought you'd be interested."

Peder squinted. "Backers? The Mafia is shopping for VC now?"

"I know, yes ... " Zuzanna smirked self-effacingly. "Before the depression we would have just done this ourselves, but nowadays we have to play it safe. We expect a huge return, but we still have to spread the risk around in case something doesn't come through. So I'm asking you to invest in this job. Separately from your Atkins one. But I can offer you a senior partner position: first money out."

Peder took a deep breath. "How much were you thinking?"

"Two hundred thousand."

He waited a second. He could possibly be financing half the operation with that amount. "Okay."

"Great. We'll keep pressing on Atkins, of course, but meanwhile we steam ahead on this."

"—Oh, and speaking of Atkins ... " Peder had almost forgotten the reason he had come here. "Any update on him?"

"Nothing yet. We finished our first two passes on him and are starting the deeper dig. You know these operations usually take a month or two."

"Okay. ... Is he one of these 'ghosts' in the Spire?"

"Him? No. He weighs around seventy-eight kilos, if I recall."

"Ah. And what about Lindon?" Peder had remembered his last meeting with the man: the wide desk between them and no attempt at a handshake.

"He's a ghost, yes."

Peder nodded. "That makes sense. If I'd put my entire company at risk by building an alien augspace system, I'd want to try it out, too."

Peder also noted how Atkins had not yet been given permission to play around with this advanced augspace prototype. Peder's campaign against him might not be too late ...

Chapter 15 - The Contact

Once Peder had left her house, Zuzanna stayed in her ASAPR to relax. She laid back in her favorite chair and closed her eyes. The ASAPR was not an ideal place for napping—the air was stagnant and the silence was eerily pure. But it was the only private room in her house. The rest of it was under constant surveillance, but not from the ISSO or the Confederation Police. It was from her bosses.

This was a bargain Zuzanna had been forced to accept, the same as all Mafia employees. Before she had ever moved into her new apartment, the organization had sent in a team to wire it with cams and mics from every angle. The stated reason for this was to ensure security: if the Mafia were watching its own people with the same technologies—or even better ones—than law enforcement was using, then they would be the first to detect any weaknesses.

That was plausible, but Zuzanna knew that the real reason was distrust. Every boss suspected every employee of secretly plotting their downfall, and so their only defense was constant surveillance of them. That was why every crevice in her house was being recorded. —Except for the ASAPR. That was only safe because it was where Zuzanna did all of her lawbreaking on her bosses' behalf, so it would be foolish for them to record her there.

After ten minutes of lying down Zuzanna was close to dozing off, so she imagined she had wasted enough time. She sat back up and returned to her desk.

Over the last week she had been helping plan a raid on Lindon Securities to investigate their nöo-realistic augspace system. With Peder's investment, her organization finally had enough backers to proceed.

This would be a major operation. The surveillance vidage she had impressed Peder with had actually been easily obtained, but to crack into this prototype system would require much more than just some exfiltration parlor tricks. They had to take on the full security of the most unassailable corporation on the planet, and rout it. There were only six or seven people alive who could accomplish this. So naturally Zuzanna's organization had one of them in their rolodex.

**

Zuzanna had to get clearance from her boss's boss's boss to reach out to him. They gave her access to a hotline that the Contact had provided them, which churned out pseudo-randomly shifting IPs at 30-second intervals. She pulled the latest one down, routed her signal through the standard sterilizers, ping-ponged her way around the world several times, then sent over a pre-agreed key. And waited ...

A minute later came a reply:

•

Zuzanna was not sure how to read this. —Until her computer alerted her that it had received the

154

language 'Precio Lontanscript B' and that it was paging in a translator. She belatedly recalled her boss warning her that the Contact liked to communicate in obscure galactic tongues. — 'Obscure' to Humans, that was. Perhaps the man liked to make people think he was an alien.

Once the appropriate translator was online, it interpreted the dot as a 'Yes.' Zuzanna thought the translation might end there, but the dot had also been painted with a blue tinge, which in Precio Lontanscript meant that the word had been inflected as a question, so it was really a 'Yes?' And it was also blurred as if it had been flying to right, which indicated impatience. Thus the full Russian translation came out as, ">Yes, hurry up, get on with it." Compact, she thought.

">Greetings," Zuzanna replied, and she saw her transcribed reply sent back over the line.

A jot of intricate Lontanscript symbols returned, which became:

">Ah, Zuzanna Mukhina, nice to meet you. I've always wanted to work with your little department."

">And I'm honored to meet you ... "—she wondered how to address him ... ">Your Anonymousness."

Another burst of Lontanscript symbols arrived, which unfurled into the surprisingly lengthy, ">While I am always delighted to have a chance to work with the Mafia, I must say I found your organization's last several offers increasingly pedestrian. I am not a consultant to be hired via simply transacting a fee, but an artist whose priority is to be presented with a worthy commission. The

155

material compensation I vilipend as mere bookkeeping."

Zuzanna rolled her eyes. ">I fully understand. / And, while I am unfamiliar with the previous offers we made you, I am sure you'll find this one to your liking."

The response was several dots:

•••

This time they simpered with an orange tinge— for incredulity—, and the repetition meant sarcastic impatience. Thus the meaning this time was not, 'Hurry up,' but rather a sarcastic, "Yes, yes, yes, please continue; what glorious opportunity do you bring me now?"

Zuzanna proceeded, ">We're going after some info deep down in a top-tier corporate target. / We expect we'll need a huge raid to cover for the brain surgery we need to perform. / And purely electronic warfare won't cut it—most likely we'll need some physical operations to help expose soft targets. / Yet, even with all that, we may get a window of no more than five or six seconds to find what we're after. / The people we're going after are that good." She let him hang in suspense before she gave him the name: ">They're Lindon Securities."

The chat went dead while the Contact thought it over. The pause lasted ten seconds ... then twenty ... then a minute. Zuzanna was becoming anxious ...

Finally a single sigil came back over the line:

156

This dot was larger than the others, with no blurs or hues, but it did have embossed edges. Fully translated, this meant the Contact had looked at her directly, made a slight nod, and, with an expectant glint in his eye, said, "... Okay."

Chapter 16 - The Recruit

"All right, so we've narrowed it down to these three," said Erlend, waving his hand at the headshots on the wallscreen. The Home Guard had tallied their votes on the ANP arrivals—using Erlend's 'asshole'/'not an asshole' methodology—and had come up with a trio of candidates. Now they were considering to whom to make their overtures.

"Not many prospects ... " remarked Steffens.

Erlend looked at her. "'Not many'? You kidding? This is a gold rush. ... I mean, half the ANP is outright addicts, and the other half is plain mercenaries. So the fact that there's any middle ground with some partway decent guys in it is remarkable."

Steffens shrugged. "Still ... even though we've ended up with three, I don't have a strong feeling about any of them. I don't feel that these are the 'best' three we could come up with but just the 'least bad' three."

"Eh, you have a point there ... " Erlend cocked his head. He turned to Hanssen and asked, "Any input, Haze?"

Hanssen was in one of his moods where he was averse to speaking, texting, and any form of communication. So he picked up a stylus, aimed it as a dart, and tossed it at the holoscreen, hoping for a random outcome. It struck off the headshot of 'Nikulaus Ingstad.'

Steffens mouthed a sarcastic, 'Ah.'

But Erlend leaned back. "Actually, you make a good point, Haze ... " He stood and approached the screen. "You may not have any strong feeling about these guys, Steff, but there *is* one thing that sets this 'Captain' Ingstad apart."

Steffens looked back and forth between him and Hanssen. She was wondering whether this were some stretching inside joke on their part.

"Okay ... " she replied at length. "What's so special about this 'Ingstad'?"

"The way he dresses."

Steffens squinted. "I haven't watched him that closely myself."

Erlend frowned at her insinuation. "It's just something I noticed, okay? I mean, we all hate the way the ANP dresses—it's getting like a costume ball around here. But this 'Ingstad' ... I remember him being a little more demure than the others coming off the transport. And since then I think he's even trimmed down his ensemble a little, trying to look more normal."

Steffens shifted in her seat. "That's not much to go on."

"... Actually it kinda *is*," Erlend rebutted. "Think about it, it tells us that this guy doesn't really fit in with the ANP ... He's not 'died in the wool' ... He's even rebelling against it slightly now that he finds himself surrounded by adults again. He's trying to *fit in* with us—he already *wants* to work with the Home Guard ... "

Steffens grumbled, but made no definite objection.

159

Hanssen shrugged, and his silence said, 'Works for me.'

***

Erlend arranged things so that he would find Ingstad alone in his quarters. The man was cleaning up when he arrived. His own bunk was clear, but his crewmates had left behind unmade sheets and personal items cluttering the dressers and drawers. All of the walls had also been tiled with augspace pinups and porn vids. Erlend was disgusted by the level of squalor that the ANPers had achieved after only a day's habitation. But at least Ingstad cleaning up after them became another fuzzy point in his favor.

"... Lieutenant?" Ingstad said, noticing that Erlend had entered but said nothing.

Erlend had been distracted trying to filter out the room's porn augments.

"Er—like the accommodations?" Erlend managed to say neutrally.

"Fine. ... Just fine, sir." Ingstad went back to cleaning.

"Good." Erlend nodded. He tried to look around the room without actually having to see any of it. "Much different than the usual ANP racks?"

Ingstad shrugged. "These are more private. Back there we just had a barracks."

"Ah ..."

Well, that was all the skirting-the-issue Erlend had prepared, so he moved into his opening gambit: "So, Ingstad, if I looked around into these drawers, where would I find Kvaerner's stash?"

Ingstad looked up. "Heh, I ... wouldn't know, sir." He half-smiled, trying to take Erlend's comment as a joke.

"... So you're saying you're okay with having a man in your tank who's riding higher on sledge than any altitude you're ever at?"

Ingstad glanced back. "No," he answered seriously. "But both Waage and I are clean and we keep a close eye on Kvaerner. We don't even let him in the tank if we don't think he can handle himself. And yesterday ... I mean, he isn't nearly that bad *all* the time. It was just because Roscher wanted to parade the ANP before you guys, so he cut off the drugs and Kvaerner started going through withdrawal."

"A-ha."

Ingstad went back to straightening up.

"But *you're* clean, you say?" Erlend persisted.

"That's right." Ingstad showed irateness.

"But *how* clean? I mean, you may not do drugs, but when was the last time you did a run for Roscher? A week ago? Two weeks? What?"

"Never. Okay?" Ingstad at last turned around to face him.

"Looook, it's all right ... " Erlend said unctuously. "We had to give the ANP immunity going back to—shit—*10,000 BC* to get access to your intel system. You can talk about this stuff without worrying about jail time."

"It's not that I don't want to talk about it, I just *really don't* run any drugs."

"But I thought you were in the ANP: the *Army of Norwegian Pill-Heads*?"

161

Ingstad huffed. "We're not all like that. In fact most everybody's clean. The drug part is just the inner circle. Roscher has his guys and they're apart from the rest of us. There are still users everywhere—like Kvaerner—but that's all he does. Use."

Ingstad was surprised by how quickly he was vouchsafing these details to an outsider. But he was aware of how sullying his connection to the ANP was, and he felt his openness would show that he had nothing to hide.

"Roscher keeps it insulated like that because he needs the ANP's public image," Ingstad continued. "It's a nice setup for him: he keeps all the straight ones like me running the organization—fixing the vehicles, doing the maintenance. Then the waste-brains just check the equipment out once in a while to do the drug runs."

"And a nice setup for you guys, too," countered Erlend. "The drugs bring in the money, and you all look the other way."

"What is this about, sir?" Ingstad flashed. "You knew about all this beforehand, so what? Is this about me?"

"Actually, no. The Brigadier put me up to this."

Ingstad squinted. Until now he had thought Erlend was here simply to pick a fight—he looked the type. But this told him something else was going on.

"What are you here for? What do you want?"

"Let's talk about what *you* want. Do you want to keep going on as you have been, playing dumb to the whole drug racket? 'Cause let me tell you, we in

162

the HG were wondering just *why is it* that Roscher is throwing his lot in with us against the corporates ... " Erlend leaned against a chair and crossed his arms. "The obvious answer—the obviously *wrong* answer—is because the ANP claims its mission is to stop Lindon. So they can't sit out while the Home Guard does just that. There would go their credibility.

"But, honestly, if Roscher had wanted to keep the ANP out of this fight, there were a thousand ways he could have done it. He could have said he didn't agree with our tactics. Or that we couldn't run a war. Or that it's just not the right time. Then all he would have had to do was sit back and wait for us to suffer our first defeat before saying, 'I told you so.' —And, with the way our surveillance was putting out, that first defeat would've coincided with our first *anything*. So why's he still pitching in?" he posed condescendingly.

"We figure two things. One, he gets the chance to make direct connections inside the Home Guard. That expands not just his pool of users but his organization and contacts. Could be planning to move into whole new realms of business.

"And second ... since the ANP *will* be going into battle against the corporates, he gets to single out which men to put on the front line. Maybe the ones he doesn't trust. Could be planning to use this offensive as a convenient way to clean house without having to get his hands dirty. To shake up all the complacent ones who've stayed away from 'his guys.' ... That sound about right to you, 'Captain'?"

Erlend waited a beat.

"So, again, the question is do *you* think you can keep up the 'see no evil' bit and Roscher will leave you alone."

Ingstad had stayed staring defiantly at Erlend throughout this speech. Until the end, when his eyes sank downwards.

He had defended himself on the grounds of having 'stayed clean,' which he had perhaps done honestly. But Erlend's questions reminded him that it was a far different accomplishment to actually *feel* clean, and that, in the ANP, would have required a funambulist's feat of cognitive dissonance. Erlend had pegged it exactly: Ingstad had settled into a complacent rhythm of 'see no evil,' and consoled himself that he made only an innocuous contribution to the evil empire around him.

But Ingstad could remember back to when he had joined the ANP. At first he had thought it a noble enterprise. Only later had he gone behind the scenes and discovered all the people doing drugs—and running drugs—and *making* drugs ... He had first vowed a crusade to clean up the organization, but that had floundered. Then he had set his sights on fixing the excesses of the system, but that had proved futile. Until he had ended up quietly maintaining the whole apparatus.

He was appalled at where he had ended up. Roscher and the others on the drug side probably even held him up as one of their greatest victories. Here was a young crusader whom they had not had to kill, nor even oppose. Ingstad had simply set to work against their odious machinery, failed to make any headway, and ended up a part of it. That was perhaps why Roscher had presented him to Colonel Hanssen the day before. The General had never shown any interest in Ingstad, but subconsciously he must have always thought of him as proof that the ANP's corrupting system worked.

Then this partnership with the Home Guard had suddenly made it seem that the ANP was a legitimate enterprise all along. Briefly Ingstad could delude himself that he had failed at nothing. But Erlend's questioning instantly took that away. To the Home Guard they were all toxic waste.

Ingstad looked up, finally knowing what Erlend was here for. "Are you serious about this?" he asked darkly. "You really want to go up against Roscher?"

Erlend gave him a resolute stare.

"And you said the Brigadier is behind you?"

"Yup, the Brigadier and the Colonel," Erlend replied. "Consider me Hanssen's mouthpiece. He would have done this little chat himself, but, as you might have noticed, he's not exactly a talkative chap. They're behind me. So are *you* behind *us?*"

Ingstad bent his head down, but he was not considering his answer. He realized he was trapped. The Home Guard must have approached him because they sensed something sympathetic in him—that was obvious. But, if the Home Guard could get that impression within just minutes of meeting him, then whatever his 'scent' was must already reek to the ANP. Even if he turned Erlend down now, then, no matter what the Home Guard did next, the ANP's suspicions would fall on him. This choice from Erlend was really an illusion.

So he was instead wondering how much his life expectancy had just dropped. Surely it had plummeted down to just a few weeks—or even days, depending on how soon the Leknesers wanted to move. —Hours, in fact, if Roscher's men had already defeated the Home Guard's internal security and bugged these rooms.

"Let me ... think about it," Ingstad said, quietly but promisingly.

"Oh, sure," replied Erlend in a mock sympathetic tone. "Take all the time you need. Think it over. Get some beauty sleep. Talk to your priest. Listen to some Grieg. Make—"

"All right! Fine! I'll— ... I'll do it—I'll do *something*," Ingstad blurted out. "Just ... come to me when you have an idea. Something concrete."

Erlend nodded slightly. "Glad to hear it. Good day, Captain," he turned and left.

That was the first time he had said an ANPers' rank with a straight face.

Chapter 17 - Turnaround

When their transport arrived back at the London office, Townsend stepped off exhausted. It had only been two days since the start of Operation Mal Voisin, but he had already flown ten thousand kilometers, dropped into a dozen firefights, and been exposed to temperatures halfway to boiling. He was ecstatic.

Zhang dismounted from the transport just after him, moving as nimbly as a greener arriving for basic training. He hoisted his forty-kilo pack as if it were air, and pluckily jogged up alongside Townsend.

"As soon as you're ready, Agent Townsend," he said brightly, "the Embassy has some promising results from the Africa data."

"Is that right ... " said Townsend.

"We could begin following the leads immediately."

"'Immediately'?" Townsend looked at him. "You mean ... go to the locker room, change into our suits, head back to our desks—that level of 'immediately'?"

"If you desire. But I can see you are fatigued. Perhaps waiting till tomorrow would be better."

Townsend sighed. He wanted to rest ... but there were three dozen other agents working on this case. And all of them bucking for promotion.

"Okay, fuck it, what do we got?"

An hour later they were back in an ISSO jet and headed to Stockholm. Two other ISSO agents,

Mallors and Farrows—and their partner skinjobs—were accompanying them. Townsend was standing with the Humans over by a window, while Zhang and the other mannequins were sitting calmly in their chairs.

Farrows motioned over to the mannequins. "What do you think of that?" he asked.

"What?" asked Townsend.

"How natural they look."

Townsend glanced at them. "I hadn't really noticed."

"Exactly!" said Farrows. "They don't have anything to do right now. They're just waiting. So you might think they would be staring blankly into space. But instead they're looking around ... shifting positions ... scratching themselves. Just like we would be."

The agents all looked. One of the mannequins reached up to scratch his neck. Another brushed at his pant leg. The third rolled his fingers on the armrest. Suddenly it was odd how perfectly Human they were at killing time.

"You're right, that's ... an unsettling attention to detail," said Mallors.

"It's like their bodies are running a screensaver ... "

Townsend grunted. "Back at the briefing someone asked the Chief whether it wouldn't be conspicuous to have Lontans as our partners. At the time I thought the mannequins would always behave a little ... off. But I haven't seen anything I could call 'alien' from them at all. In fact, I don't think I ever would have noticed."

"Nope."

Zhang suddenly stood.

"We have reached altitude," he said, approaching the Human agents. "We can now discuss our assignment." He motioned to a booth of four seats facing each other.

The three Humans and Zhang sat down.

Farrows looked back at the other mannequins. "Won't they be joining us?" he asked.

"Why?" said Zhang. "They're just more me's on the inside."

"Oh. Right."

Then again there were times when the Lontans did not bother to hide their alien-ness at all.

"So first I should explain why we're headed to Stockholm," began Zhang. "In Africa we were looking for any trace of where the hypercomm had been smuggled down. And we discovered minute concentrations of some telltale chemicals across forty camps. But over approximately those same camps—with high spatial correlation—we also found ultra-trace amounts of DLPT, rezocanthic residue, and polyxercane half products. Of course you know what those mean."

"They're some of the chemicals used in arcology infrastructures," said Mallors confidently. "They typically only get released through deconstruction disasters."

Townsend knew this was only half the answer, so he picked up the slack: "... The worst of such disasters being the Singularity, which explains why we're going to Scandinavia."

"Err, right," said Mallors.

169

Farrows said, "But I thought those chemicals dissipated quickly. How could we detect them?"

Zhang was about to answer, but Townsend cut in:

"—The sheer scale of the Oslo disaster means that anyone who visits the city—even today—will still come out wearing the stuff." He wanted to show Zhang that the Humans did not have to go to him for all the answers.

"Well, that's a break," said Farrows. "My scanners didn't pick up any of those chemicals down in Africa, but of course this is thanks to your Lontan instruments?"

"Quite," said Zhang. "In fact, the amounts were so small as to suggest that the contaminated objects or persons had been scrubbed to spectral cleanliness to just past the limits of Human-available technology."

"Covering their tracks ... " noted Townsend.

"Still," said Mallors, "there have been a few other arcology disasters that could have generated these residues, so why are we interested in Scandinavia specifically?"

This time Zhang, instead of answering, looked directly at Townsend. "Agent Townsend?" he prompted.

Since Townsend had interrupted him before, the mannequin was putting him on the spot now.

"What? Do we Humans have to think of everything?" he parried.

Zhang gave him a sly expression.

"It's because of Lindon Securities," Zhang turned to Mallors. "Specifically the corporate army it operates, which is based in Oslo. The ISSO has long suspected that Lindon has been smuggling down beyond-the-curve military technologies for his men. And, with his connection to Oslo and the Singularity, it's possible that the smugglers Lindon uses are connected to those who smuggled down the hypercomm."

"Or they might even be the same group," Mallors picked up. "Restricted military technology and a hypercomm are both ultra-hot items. Few smuggling rings would traffic in them."

"Correct. So we'll be setting up operations in the ISSO's Stockholm office. We'll manage surveillance on Lindon Securities and its subsidiaries. Especially the security branches, since Lindon may have delegated the smuggling out to one of them in order to keep himself insulated."

"Do we have any idea who these smugglers are?" asked Farrows.

"No, but there are only a dozen rings serious enough to be worth considering. We did recover evidence of one of them down in Africa, but at the moment they are too dimly correlated to be of note."

"Which group was that?"

He turned to Townsend and asked, "You remember the nanokatana marks on the table?"

"Yeah, from the ... the Yakuza mannequins?"

"Yes. These are them." Zhang forwarded them a set of dossiers.

One difference between skinjob dossiers and regular dossiers was that, instead of having a single mugshot at the top, these had dozens. Illegal aliens came down to the planet as only a deep copy of

171

some malevolent brain waves, and they had to be installed into mannequins in order to work their mischief. Since those shells could—and often did—change every day, a mannequin's dossier had to contain every one of their suspected likenesses.

"'The High Tide,'" Townsend read the group's name aloud.

"Serious criminals," said Zhang. "And the name also translates favorably into Japanese."

Townsend perused the group's members. While each had a native language name, also listed were their Human aliases: 'Crimson,' 'Snake,' 'Tides,' 'Chitin,' 'Surf,' 'Boil' ...

"Okay, I see how 'The High Tide' is vaguely Japanese," said Townsend, "but what's with the rest of these names?"

"Criminal skinjobs prefer aliases that are simple words so that they can translate easily into most languages. This would not be the case with purely phonetic names like 'Bryce' and so forth."

Townsend stared at him. "Yeah, I knew *that*. But what's with the water theme? 'Surf' and 'Chitin' and ... "

"Oh. The High Tide's members are originally Bentharrans, which is a species of advanced cephalopods. Names like 'Tides' and 'Surf' are typical slang aliases among their species—perhaps as common as 'Slick' and 'Blades' are in the Terran populace. Though I admit that these would sound somewhat odd to your land-based culture."

Townsend and the other Humans shot sarcastic glances between each other.

"What? Have I missed something?" asked Zhang.

"No, no," said Townsend. "But you just told us that sentient octopi are running around our planet in fake Human bodies and taking over organized crime. ... It's a little new to us."

Farrows and Mallors grunted.

"Really?" replied Zhang. "How quaint." He looked back down into the file.

Townsend was not sure, but he thought Zhang might have just told his first joke.

Chapter 18 - Indirection

General Roscher logged onto the *sub rosa* with the Home Guard. They had scheduled the call to start at 2100 hours, and so he had dialed in at 2106—not so late as to be inexcusable, but late enough to show that he didn't care about their schedule.

The Home Guard ASAPR was laid out as a medium-sized conference room. Brigadier Krohg and some staff were present, and Major Steffens was standing at the table's head, poised to make a presentation.

"Good evening, all," Roscher greeted them in one of his sculpted tones.

"General," Steffens replied—an unadulterated 'General.' Brigadier Krohg had instructed his staff to give the scare quotes a rest for this meeting.

"May I ask why we're meeting so late?" said Roscher. "And"—he glanced demonstratively around the room—"why is Colonel Hanssen absent? ... Firing him are you?" he half-joked.

"The Colonel's absence will be explained shortly," said Krohg. "This meeting is part of the due diligence in our agreement. We said we would consult you and get your approval before taking any action against the ANP—any action that made use of your intelligence. ... And we have such an action planned."

Roscher cocked his head. "Oh, indeed! Then you've kept it quite a secret. You'll be pleased to

174

know I've heard nothing about it from my spies." His tone was subtly sarcastic.

"As I said, we have an operation planned," said Krohg. "And ready to go. Tonight. In fact, everything's already in position."

Roscher squinted—and it was a genuine squint. Maybe he had not really known beforehand.

"Ah, and that would be where Colonel Hanssen is?" Roscher realized. "Ready to lead the troops?"

"Essentially. Now ... Major Steffens is going to outline our plan for you, and afterwards you'll be asked for your approval."

"Err, hold on here!" Roscher interjected. "This is hardly 'due diligence.' You're coming to me when you already have an operation in play, and when I have only seconds to consider it."

"Why should you need more time than that?" Krohg asked innocently.

Roscher ignored him and continued railing, "— And then these cloak and dagger proceedings!— only telling me about your operation in an ASAPR! Did you think I would broadcast the details of your plan to the corporate army?"

"Exactly that—Yes," Krohg pointed at him.

Roscher gave him a sour face. He liked to intimidate people by purposefully misinterpreting what they said and making them trip up correcting themselves. But Krohg's way of confronting him left him nowhere to run with his jokes.

"A fine trust you have in your allies," Roscher humphed.

"Look at it this way," said Krohg. "If something goes wrong with the operation, then we'll know the ANP couldn't possibly be to blame."

Roscher crossed his arms. He was not going to have any fun with Krohg in attendance. He might as well listen. "Very well. Shall the good Major proceed?" he motioned to Steffens.

**

Hanssen and Erlend were finishing their incognito approach to Östersund, Sweden. They had taken a civilian groundcar from Norway, traveling all the way over the lonely stretches of the H14 highway across the mountains. When the corporate army was combing back over the events of this night later, the Home Guard had to have left as little of a surveillance trail behind as possible.

After several hours driving in darkness, a gloam of light built ahead. The hills became dimly lit on their far sides as by a strong moon. Making a last, wide turn, they came into view of Östersund.

In the half century since First Contact, many cities had seen outrageous growth. Leknes was the most famous example of this. Back in the early aughts, the Lontans had made arcology constructors available in the form of 'shake and bake' kits: plant some nanites, dump in the required resources, and within weeks a pre-designed multi-hundred–story structure would arise. The Lontans had guaranteed that the technology was safe, but the handful of arcology projects that were proposed was tackled by astounding numbers of NIMBYer and environmental lawsuits.

The rest of the world was so gridlocked that Norway became the unlikely country to test the technology first. They used a sparsely populated island out in the Lofoten Archipelago as their proving ground, at a site outside of a town called Leknes. To everyone's surprise, the construction was completely successful, in a week erecting a mile-high arcology in a town of only 5,000. The only solution to this incongruity was to put enough people on the island to justify having a mile-high arcology there in the first place. Luckily tourists soon began flocking in, visiting the world's only alien-built arcology with the same alacrity that people had once lined up to see the electric light bulb. Thus was kick-started Leknes's horrendous growth spurt.

Östersund, Sweden, stood as a sound counterexample to this. A town from before First Contact, it had remained a town ever since. While the traces of augspace and the infostructure had propagated there in due time, the city was otherwise unchanged from a century previous.

Their car entered Östersund's meager downtown and parked. Exiting and walking down to the next block, they found a gauntlet of bars.

">*The Mayerling*—there it is," secure-texted Erlend, and he pinged the bar in their private augspace. ">The team's inside, ready to go."

">And the men at the airport?" asked Hanssen.

">The same."

While most of the bars were open, *The Mayerling* was supplying all of the ambient noise.

Its doors were propped open and bellowing out cigarette smoke and drunken cackling.

When they reached it, they saw the bar was packed with corporate army uniforms and a carefully maintained parity of prostitutes. Upon entering, their OHUDs became swamped with translations from all of the bar chatter, which looked to be spread across a dozen languages. Endless blurbs of Norwegian Bokmål appeared in their vision, each color-coded and aligned over its speaker, as if they were watching a foreign film where the subtitlers had attacked a crowd scene with particular zeal.

They proceeded to the bar. They attracted no attention from the soldiers because they were in plain clothes.

">Now to wait," texted Erlend.

***

"So the ANP's intelligence," Steffens started her presentation, "is giving us unprecedented coverage of the corporate army's bases. But from this we've only realized that they're far too fortified to attack directly. Even a surprise attack, for it to have adequate effect, would have to be so large and costly that we couldn't stage it. Which is why we've come up with another plan."

The first slide in her holo presentation appeared: a headshot from the personnel file of a corporate army officer.

"Meet Lieutenant Colonel Gregor Kurkland," she said. "He's the commander of several corporate army bases that are important logistics centers in their network. If we could attack those bases, it would be a crippling blow. And the most cost-effective way for us to attack those bases would be to steal some corporate army IFF codes—that's 'Interrogate Friend or Foe,' the system for distinguishing friendly from unfriendly units."

"I know what an IFF is," chided Roscher.

Steffens pursed her lips. "Well, with the proper IFFs we could fly past these bases' defenses. We could send in unmanned hovertanks to conduct suicide runs and take out most of their vehicles, munitions, and fuel.

"Of course it's difficult to steal IFFs. Corporate army vehicles have them, but not stored in a transponder or any part that we could simply break off and attach to our own vehicles. They're actually kept deep in encrypted memory on the main computers. For us to steal them, we'd have to rip out the computers and subject them to a full nanotech assault.

"Luckily Kurkland's men will present us with the chance to stage such a raid. Right now one of his units is rotating back from Africa, and they're spending two days R'n'R in Östersund, Sweden." A map of Östersund appeared on the next slide. It was a small 2,000-person town in the middle of nowhere. "As we speak, the corporate army soldiers are spread throughout town, and their vehicles are being kept at the airport under minimal guard.

"The plan is simple. We have strike teams spread throughout Östersund, one of which will incapacitate the men at the airport and give us the time we need to cannibalize their vehicles. Once we have the IFF codes, we transmit those to the hovertanks we have waiting to make their kamikaze runs. Then our teams evacuate Östersund and we call it a night. All we need is your okay."

"Problem," Roscher interjected, raising a finger. "I don't care what plan you have to 'incapacitate' their guards at the airport—it won't work. All corporate army soldiers are … 'booby-trapped.' Their body computers are always running a program that monitors their physical condition. If they're ever assaulted or knocked out—or killed—, this program broadcasts an alarm to the entire unit. And the unit commander can even forward it up to headquarters. As soon as you move against the guards, this alarm will go off, Kurkland's bases will be put on alert, and any suspect security codes will be invalidated automatically."

"We're aware of the security program their soldiers are running," said Steffens. "Our plan is to … 'overload' it. And we've already been working on this."

Roscher gave her a curious look.

"We have a dozen other plainclothes teams currently spread throughout Östersund. And, for the last hour, their job has been to find corporate army soldiers … preferably in bars … and … start fights with them."

Roscher's gaze narrowed.

"Every time a brawl has started, this automated system has alerted the unit commander, Major Lautner"—a new headshot appeared in her presentation. "And each time he's silenced it. This has happened half a dozen times in the last hour. He must be sick of it by now.

180

"Now, the next fight we stage will be in Lautner's location. And it will be timed exactly with our assault on the airport. The alerts will arrive simultaneously. And hopefully Lautner, in the confusion, will simply silence both of them. If it works, the corporates will only know something is wrong when the guards at the airport miss their next check-in an hour later. That should give us just enough time to retrieve the IFFs and stage our assault."

Roscher threw out a mildly impressed shrug. "I like it," he exclaimed. "It's such a shoestring plan that it actually has a chance. And, even if it doesn't, all you have to do is walk away and try again." He let out a long sigh. "So be it—you have my blessing. Now ... do you have a war room channel over which I might view the festivities?"

***

Erlend and Hanssen were keeping an eye on Major Lautner—though they were not doing anything so conspicuous as actually looking at him. Instead their body cameras were recording a fish-eye view of their surroundings, and they were using their OHUDs to watch Lautner from out of those feeds. He was sitting with several other officers— and an oversupply of prostitutes—at one of the well ensconced back tables.

As soon as they received the 'go' code from headquarters, Erlend began secure-texting to the five-man team they had inside the bar:

">Okay, everyone online." He opened a graphics pane in their private augspace and drew a quick floor plan of the bar. ">Okay, we're here, you guys are here, corporate army pigs are here, here, and here, and this is Lautner here," he narrated as he marked up his drawing. ">Hanssen and I will pick a fight at the bar. / Let it develop a bit, then you guys surge over here in the direction of Lautner." He was drawing arrows on the map as if diagramming a complex sports play. ">Once it reaches the good Major, we ping the guys at the airport to proceed. / Then just play out the rest like a normal bar fight."

The other men did not reply—per design. All of these secure texts might look suspicious when the corporate army was investigating the incident later. It was best if Erlend were the only source of the texts, and if none of his recipients made any telling replies.

">Just don't knock Lautner out," Erlend added. ">If he goes cold, then he can't silence the alarm, and it goes to his HQ by default. / We just want him roughed up and aggravated. / … All right," he finished.

A second later, Hanssen asked him, ">Who've you picked out to fight?"

Erlend sent a ping in this OHUD. It indicated a corporate army officer sitting down the bar. He was bent over a plate of noodles, eating slowly.

">Why him?" asked Hanssen.

Erlend actually looked at Hanssen in real life. ">What do you mean 'why him'—the guy's *perfect!* / His unit just got back from Africa, right? / Which means he's back in a first-tier country / surrounded by first-tier prostitutes / for the first time in *months* / and what the fuck is he doing? / … / He's *sitting* at a *bar*. / *Eating*. / *Bar food*."

182

Hanssen shrugged. ">So?"

">So? / It means he's a prig. / Probably the *company* prig. / When everyone sees him fighting / they'll *have* to jump in, too."

Hanssen gave an impressed wobble with his body language. ">You're really good at this."

">Fucking *shit yes*. / I could pick bar fights for a *living*. / I mean anybody can just throw a punch and get beaten up. / But I can find the *one punch* that will turn the entire place to bedlam. / —And I can make someone else throw it, too." He thumped the table with his fist.

Erlend stood and walked down to the corporate army officer. Once Erlend was standing next to him, the man stopped eating. But he stayed looking down at his plate of noodles.

"Lars. Reynard," Erlend introduced himself pseudonymously.

The man looked up. "Erik. Mohr."

Erlend gestured at the man's plate. "What are you having?"

The man examined Erlend carefully. "Spaetzle."

"Sounds German."

"It is."

He cocked his head. "Like you?" Erlend had noted the man's accent.

Mohr glanced back at him. "*Ja*." An answer to a challenge.

Erlend smirked innocently. "I didn't mean anything by it." He motioned back at the plate. "Any good?"

183

"*I* think so." Mohr stressed his 'I' as a disclaimer—'It's good for me.' This was a peace offering to the confrontational stranger.

Erlend nodded. As soon as the other party extended the olive branch, it was time to be truly affronting.

He took his hand, poised it like a claw, and dropped it into the middle of the man's plate. He dragged his fingers around sloppily, pushing half the noodles off onto the bar, until he had left nothing untouched.

Meanwhile the other corporate army soldiers had all been slowly noticing the brewing scene between Mohr and this stranger. With his attack on the plate they were now all fixated on them, and silence had taken the bar.

Erlend finally withdrew his hand clutching a single noodle, and surely the smallest one from the plate. He dangled this over his mouth, dropped it in, and chewed emphatically.

"Hm. … It *is* good," he heartily agreed.

Hanssen sensed how perfectly everything was primed. This Mohr knew all his fellow soldiers were watching him and demanding action. He had to respond with violence or else the entire unit would be shamed. And, once he threw the first punch, everyone would race to catch up.

Mohr picked up his plate and hurled it at Erlend—who dodged, so it went flying off behind him. He and Mohr then lunged at each other and opened up in a frenzy of blows. Hanssen quickly joined in—the corporate army soldiers behind Mohr joined in—other Home Guardsmen in disguise

184

joined in—the rest of the corporate army soldiers joined in—seemingly random civilians who just wanted to be part of the violence joined in—some of the more zealous prostitutes joined in—and it took only five seconds before the entire bar had devolved into a combat zone.

Sixty seconds later, Hanssen, Erlend, and their team members were being hurled out of the bar. "Get the fuck out!" "Go wreck someone else's shit!" "You're paying for my date!" were the most common things the soldiers yelled at them. They turned around irately and stalked back inside.

The Home Guardsmen spent the next minute sitting or lying on the street, nursing their wounds and checking for broken bones. They stood up gingerly and walked off.

Soon they received a secure text from the airport: ">Team Baker here, corporate army vehicles secured. / Any sign of an alert?"

Hanssen looked back over his shoulder at the bar. If there were an alert, then the soldiers would be streaming out in a panic. But … as they walked away … nothing happened.

">None here, Baker. / You're good."

Chapter 19 - Hangover

Erik Mohr and his fellow soldiers had just finished ejecting their brawling partners out onto the street. They yelled the customary "Fuck you!"s and "Get the fuck outta here!"s in various languages before turning back inside. Some of the men clapped Mohr on the shoulder, saying "Good one, man" and "Way to go." Inside they righted the tables and chairs, and the prostitutes gradually drifted back from the walls.

A quarter-hour later a new group of corporate army soldiers appeared at the bar's entrance. On seeing all the broken glass, chair legs, and spilled fluids spread around the room, they stopped in wonder. The lead man spread his arms wide—a beer in one hand and a cigarette in the other—and exclaimed, in iambic pentameter,

"So *what* the *fuck* is *with* this *town* to-*night?!*"

The rest of the soldiers looked up and grumbled back to him. The new party moved inside, and the lead man stepped up next to Mohr at the bar.

"Janus," Mohr greeted him.

"Hey, Mohr—so you guys got into a fight, too, huh?"

Mohr looked at him. "You, too?"

"Yeah. And they were some sturdy sons of bitches," Janus rubbed at the bruised knuckles on his punching hand.

"I thought you guys were across town."

"Yeah, we were." Janus shrugged.

Mohr first dismissed that. But then he stopped and looked down contemplatively.

"Really ... " he said. "'Cause I was just talking to another guy who'd gotten into a fight earlier tonight, too. Name was ... Kirkpatrick—was he with you?"

"No. Must've been a different fight." Janus swigged from his beer. "So much for Swedish hospitality, eh?"

Mohr's eyes narrowed. "That's ... a lot of fights."

Janus stopped. He bent down to stare into Mohr's face. "Whoa, whoa, whoa!—Snap out of it!" he waved his hand in front of him. "So there were a bunch of rowdy guys around tonight—so what? We're Lindon Securities—the corporate army—the scum of the Earth around here. That's our business as usual. Nothing to spoil our drinking over." He took another swig from his bottle. When it proved empty, he pounded a fist on the bar and shouted, "Beer!"

"Wait a second," said Mohr. "Yeah, we're unpopular, but that's still a *lot* of fights—especially for Sweden. I mean, if this were Norway, then sure, I'd already have expected a few people to have been killed. But out here ... " He rubbed at the stubble on his chin. "I was just thinking—"

"Yeah, *don't*," interrupted Janus.

Mohr hated himself, but he couldn't leave this be. He stood and walked over to the table where Major Lautner—their unit commander—was. The man was sitting with two other officers and four hookers, one of whom was on Lautner's lap.

"Sir?" Mohr interrupted.

The three senior officers had all been in the middle of a good laugh, and they did not recognize Mohr at first. Their attention only drifted over to him lazily.

"Captainnn," slurred Lautner, surprised to see him. "What the fuck?"

"Pardon me for interrupting, sir. But have you noticed anything strange tonight? ... Like about all the fights that have been going on?"

"Fuck—*yes!*" Lautner exclaimed. "It's like every fucking second I get paged for it in my viz! I don't need all this shit every time some idiot across town throws a punch ... "

"Hm." Mohr stalled, considering his options. He thought something was up, but, when everyone was off-duty and the commanding officer was drunk, it became a delicate matter how to proceed. "Maybe we should check into it, sir? All these fights ... maybe something is going on."

"Pffffff," Lautner dismissed him. His drinking buddies echoed this sentiment.

"Uh-huh ... How about ... you just call for a unit check in, sir?" suggested Mohr. "Have all the commanders report in. It would just take a minute. ... And HQ might like it if they knew you were keeping everyone on their toes. Especially during time off."

Lautner smirked amiably. "Huh. Officer thinking, Captain." He cleared his throat and sat up, poising himself to speak over his OHUD. "Major Lautner to all unit commanders, report in."

Another of the officers at the table jerked forward and did a spit-take. "Fuck—what are you doing in my viz!" he exclaimed. "Yes, Captain Kasparek here, *sir!* Checking in, *sir!*"

Mohr also received the same signal in his OHUD and replied.

Thirty seconds later, all the units had reported in, save for one.

"Captain Larcher?" Major Lautner said, tapping his temple. "Captain *Laaaaar-cherrrr* ... Report in. ... Report *innn* ... " he kept fishing for a request.

Mohr checked the duty roster and saw that Larcher's men were on guard at the airport.

Major Lautner tried a few more unsuccessful hails. And then ... he collapsed. He sank back in his chair with a crippled, despondent look.

"Ohhhh shiiiit," Lautner moaned, then he leaned forward and cradled his head in his hands. He knew something was wrong, but he was terribly drunk, incapable of dealing with it, and in a lot of trouble. "Mohr, um ... take some of these fuckers," he waved his hand at the room, "and get down to the airport. See what's up. Why Larcher won't report in. ... *Fuck*," he snapped at himself.

***

Ten minutes later Mohr was standing with a dozen other soldiers on the tarmac of Åre Östersund Airport. The guards they had left behind had all been knocked out, and the vehicles had been sabotaged—their engines crippled and their main computers removed. Mohr reported back to Lautner, who had begun the terrible duty of contacting headquarters.

Gregor Janus stood next to Mohr, kicking at some of the wreckage that had come off of the closest jet.

"Why'd you have to ruin my night, Captain?" Janus asked.

Mohr bobbed his head. "Oh, it's gonna get a lot worse than this, Lieutenant."

Janus looked at him, puzzled. "But ... this was just some vandalism," he said.

It's *bad*, sure. Someone's gonna get fired—most likely Lautner. But that's it. ... Right?"

Mohr turned to him. "This wasn't vandalism. You don't steal the computers out of military transports for that. You do that because you want to compromise our communications. Because you want to make a whole lot of impossibly bad shit become possible."

"... Oh," Janus realized.

"But it's even worse than that. Because these guys—whoever they were—knew an alert would get generated if they just attacked our men out here. So they started fights all over town to get Lautner buttered up. So that he would silence the *real* alert once they made their move. And they wouldn't have gone through all that trouble unless they needed to open up a window of opportunity to conduct a follow-up operation. And that shit's either happening *right now*, or it's already finished. *That's* what went down here tonight."

Janus blanched, then slumped down and rubbed at the back of his neck. "Now it's sounding like you wanna ruin my whole week."

190

Chapter 20 - Impression

Willoch was waiting in a conference room on Mars Haven Station, sipping lavishly at a cup of coffee. It was 0300 from her body's perspective, and so a persistent caffeine drip was necessary to stay awake. But she was meeting someone from another planet, which meant she was obliged to respect the local clock.

Looking out the windows into near-Mars space she spied the station that neighbored Haven, the partially completed Mars Gateway. It appeared as a speck to her naked eye, so she piped in magnified external feeds from Haven's cams. She appraised the station's construction progress—or at least where it had halted four years ago. Back then the Norwegian Navy had bought space on the new station, but its planned offices were located several decks below where construction had left off, and so they were yet nothing but vacuum. For Willoch, that painted amply the difficulty of her task: she was trying to sell something that did not exist yet, and that probably never would.

Her other party soon arrived, Hyram Goldam, Space Development Minister of Olympia—the largest nation on Mars. He wore the standard business fashion of his planet, which was a red-tinctured suit with battened-down lapels, and no tie but an oversized top shirt button to compensate. The planet had not developed this look naturally. Rather Mars had assumed that, being its own planet, it

191

might as well have its own fashions, and so it had just invented some.

"Minister Goldam," Willoch opened, extending her hand. "Thank you so much for meeting with me."

"Of course, Admiral Willoch," he replied. "Any way we can oblige ourselves to the Royal Norwegian Navy."

They took neighboring seats at the conference table.

"So I described my proposal in the message," Willoch opened, "but I thought face-to-face negotiations would be the most productive. And I know that Mars Gateway is a sensitive topic, so I wanted to be discrete."

The Minister nodded.

"Back at the initial offering for Mars Gateway, the RNN purchased space on the station. —As did all of the other Eyes navies. But by now the station is of course well overdue. And, even if it were completed, in our present state ... " she gestured.

"Of course," nodded Goldam.

"Because you must know of our budget problems, Minister. Every quarter funding from the Norwegian cities comes up short, and I'm forced to slash budgets and lay people off. And after five years of that, well ... by now the triage is pretty evident." Willoch had used to find it hard to talk about such things, but, after laying off several thousand people, the idea of being sheepish about it seemed phony and hypocritical.

"These are difficult times, of course," said Goldam.

"Thank you. ... I hear Olympia is facing some similar troubles?" Willoch was attempting to build empathy between them.

But Goldam only bobbed his head suggestively.

"... At any rate," Willoch continued, "the RNN is presently facing another budget shortfall. And for me to let anyone else go now would mean sacrificing not just individuals but whole departments.

"So I've been looking into liquidating the stake we hold on Mars Gateway. First I approached the other Eyes admirals about the possibility of acquiring our space. But, because of the production delay, they obviously weren't interested in acquiring a larger share of something that might never be finished. So I'm approaching you directly, Minister, to see about the possibility of securing a refund for the RNN's space."

Willoch hated having to perform this hat-in-hand gesture herself, but she had long ago fired the staff members she might have delegated it to. That aspect at least gave the trip the semblance of penance.

"Indeed," Goldam answered cryptically, as if he were only providing another ping back to her.

"... A refund *was* provided for in the contract we signed," Willoch added.

"Oh, of course. And, under the terms,"— Goldam at last spoke—"I believe you would be entitled to a fifty percent refund. Though you must understand the position of the Olympian government," he turned. "None of the tenants who bought space on Mars Gateway have seen their

193

contracts fulfilled. They could all ask for a refund—in fact, most of them have. Which is why the Olympian government has had to refuse. The money has simply been spent and is gone."

Willoch, "Hmm"ed—now it was her turn to provide pings.

"And please consider how it would do no good for us to provide those refunds," Goldam continued. "As it stands, no matter how bleak the economic situation looks, once a recovery starts we could see construction resume on the station immediately. All the contracts would be fulfilled. But, if we liquidated the project now, it would take years to gather new investors before construction could resume. For everyone who has a stake in the station, it's in their best interests simply to hold onto it."

"While I see your side, you must admit how risky such a stance is. I hear some governments and organizations are even suing you for the restitution of their funds." This was a veiled threat: that the RNN would initiate legal action of its own.

But Goldam grinned broadly. "And when they do they run into all the delicious complexities of inter-planetary legislation. It takes longer to get a Martian government to repay Terran money than it does for the ICC to convict a war criminal," he joked.

Willoch cocked her head. She had expected Goldam to parry her threat, but that was a curiously forward riposte.

Nevertheless, she had fully expected these negotiations to play out exactly as they had so far. The situation was simple: Mars Gateway was a money black hole; the Olympians were not paying anyone back; and so why should the Royal Norwegian Navy be made an exception? But there was a reason she could use, and it had to do with the 'Norwegian' part of their name:

"Though I was hoping," Willoch said demurely, "that you might make an exception in *Norway's* case."

That was all she had needed to say. She had just played the 'Singularity Sympathy' card. The only weapon she had come with, but a powerful one.

"Ah yes," Goldam replied, as if grinning through a sour taste. "And I am happy to inform you that my government has considered the plight of the RNN's valiant troops. And we are moved by your efforts to keep them compensated for their services. ... So I have been authorized to grant you a refund."

This seemed a favorable development, but Willoch sensed something fulsome in his reply ...

"Of course it would have to be kept secret," Goldam began adding caveats. "We are already involved in so many lawsuits that it could not even be hinted that we acceded in your case. The RNN would remain the titular holders of the space, with that only being changed at our convenience.

"And ... we shall only be able to offer you a refund ... "—a breathy pause—"in Olympian dollars."

Willoch stopped. "Excuse me?"

Goldam threw out a shrug. "For as much as depressions hurt developing countries, they hurt developing *planets* even more. There's no hard currency I can offer you."

Willoch's first impulse was to reply, 'And just what the hell am I supposed to do with Olympian dollars? Tell my men, "Hi, fellas, here's half your pay in 'money' and half of it in 'Martian scrip'"?' She struggled to bite that back ... —But this was almost an impertinence! Goldam had to know she would refuse such an offer, so why even bother making it.

"Please enlighten me ... " she began in a reasoned voice. "What is the scope in which my personnel could spend Olympian dollars?"

"Oh, many Martian businesses still accept them."

Willoch knew that this covered only a few cash-strapped casinos.

"Given your officers' easy access to interplanetary transit," Goldam added, "they should have no trouble in exercising that option."

"Hm," Willoch mumbled. This overlooked the fact that the safest place on Mars still had a crime rate roughly quadruple that of the most dangerous place on Earth.

"And what avenues," she asked, "might there be for converting Olympian dollars into credits?" This was a question that could only be answered in euphemism.

Goldam pursed his lips, "Oh, they're quite limited, I'm forced to say."

Translation: not a bank in the known universe.

"Ah," Willoch remarked.

But inside she was seething. She was still a chief Admiral, and her country—even now—had a population larger than that of Mars, and almost twice that of Olympia. Who was this Hyram

196

Goldam to patronize her? And his offer was all the more infuriating for how he kept his insults so thinly veiled. They were disguised just enough that Willoch had to keep up her etiquette while Goldam radiated effrontery.

Willoch replied, "If you had simply said 'no' to my request I would have accepted that. But to make such an offer sounds awfully impertinent."

Goldam smirked. "If you're interested in charity you might try that Lontan Ambassador you seem such good friends with. Of course then there's that Lontan doctrine of 'fairness' that you might run afoul of—how does it go? 'If we can't do something for everyone, we don't do it for anyone.' A nice way to rationalize doing nothing at all."

Willoch's gaze sharpened. Goldam had used the word 'fairness' and then made an offhand criticism of the Lontans. Both made her think of the Zaichi Ambassador, Laiidjokun, who had once done the same in strange synchronicity to Willoch's own thoughts. Some of Goldam's words even sounded like quotes from the Laiidjokun himself ... When no simple explanation for this presented itself, Willoch's impression hardened into an aversion. She wanted to leave.

She also knew this would be wise because, if she stayed any longer, she and Goldam would descend into personal attacks. She stood.

"Well, thank you for hearing me out, Minister," she said icily. "I bid you good morning."

"Oh, but it's afternoon in Olympia, Admiral," he returned with a condescending smile.

197

Willoch scowled—taunting her about her ignorance of the local time.

On her way back to her ship, her thoughts were still engaged by that troubling flash: 'the Lontan doctrine of fairness' ... 'that Ambassador you're such good friends with' ... Goldam seemed to have parroted Laiidjokun's words. And how could he even have known about Willoch's connection to the Lontan Ambassador? ...

Still, she was having trouble placing exactly what she suspected was wrong. That maybe Goldam was a mannequin who had been replaced by Laiidjokun, or someone else from the Zaichi legation? That was possible ... but highly unlikely. While mannequins admittedly did such things, it typically only happened in the criminal underworld. A mannequin had never dared replace a top-level Human official—even in such a third-tier nation as Olympia.

She took a lift back to Haven's docking levels and to the bay where her RNN shuttle was waiting. One of the benefits of being an admiral was she always had a personal shuttle at her disposal. Of course this was more expensive than taking mass transit—and perhaps a bit wasteful given all their budget problems. But Willoch figured it would be ridiculous for the commander of a black-water navy to fly coach to Mars.

The station had no artificial gravity in these levels, but, as a naval officer, Willoch was long-accustomed to weightlessness. She reached the shuttle, climbed aboard, and maneuvered into the pilot's seat. She urgently engaged the return course for Earth, and Mars Haven fell away out of the forward window. Soon the planet came into view behind it, filling the cabin with its rusty albedo. Within a minute she would be clear of the restricted flight zone, and then the shuttle would shift into hyperspace and finish the trip back to Earth at faster-than-light speeds.

Willoch continued trying to downplay her impression. 'Fairness' was no suspiciously rare word, she told herself. And it would be natural for Goldam to criticize the Lontans if he blamed them for the prolonged depression and Olympia's troubles. During rough times, people often blamed God, so why not blame the Lontans, who were the closest approximation thereto?

Still, she wondered.

Chapter 21 - Nocturne

It was a rain-mirrored, neon-slick night as Ingstad stood waiting by a Leknes overpass. He was flipping through his OHUD, looking for something diverting. And trying not to think of the surveillance nanites dusted over him, courtesy of the Leknes police. He was supposed to meet Roscher's second-in-command of the ANP's drug operations at midnight, but it was eight minutes past now, which meant 'Snake' was running late.

Ingstad went back to pacing up and down the street, kicking at puddles of water. Why was he doing this? he wondered again. How had Erlend talked him into it? His own glorious motivations about cleaning up the ANP aside, was this really something he was willing to get decapitated over? Because that was what would happen to him if they suspected him of spying.

Decapitation was something that had started back in the twenties. Back then, just after OHUDs had become widespread, the police had had their informants run recording programs on their comps to capture everything they saw and heard. But, when organized crime discovered this, the standard punishment became to saw through the informer's neck and yank out their body comps. Now, the Leknes police had not asked Ingstad to run such a recording program, since Snake would have him turn off his OHUD during the meeting. But dusting him with nanites was hardly more advanced, and decapitation remained the underworld's standard for punishing any subterfuge.

Ingstad checked the time: now 0016. Snake was definitely late.

A car turned down the street. Ingstad looked at it expectantly. It approached ... pulled up beside him ...

A cab.

Ingstad waved it on. The vehicle sped away irately, but it sent him an electronic brochure for its company.

He went back to pacing, and resolved to be patient and keep waiting.

... Until he thought that this might be a test from Snake. In fact, the man could be watching him right now. To see how long he waited ... Because Ingstad would only wait forever if he were an informer who *had* to wait around for Snake. If he really wanted to join the ANP's drug ring—as he had led them to believe when he had asked for this meeting—, by now he would be saying, 'Hell, I'm not hanging around all night to meet some fucker who can't keep time. I'm outta here!'

Ingstad spurred around and began stalking angrily back to the subway.

Shortly he heard a thunderous, mechanical gargling approach from down the street. A groundcar with tinted windows peeled out of a side street and pulled to a halt beside him. The rear door opened on Snake, who was grinning with the electrified yet half somnambulant eyes of someone who had been high on sledge for over a decade.

"Well, come on in, Ingy baby!" Snake said.

The car was a four-seater: Snake in the back, and two others up front.

Ingstad climbed inside, and the vehicle was soon back in motion. When he sat down, a glister of pixie dust billowed up from the fabric and danced around him. He was amazed at how brazen Snake was, driving around Leknes in a car that was actually wheezing drugs out of its upholstery.

Ingstad examined the two goons up front, but all he could see of them were their buzz coats and overcoats. —And the fact that each of them had more muscle mass than Ingstad's total body weight. Ingstad had heard rumors that Snake's bodyguards had had their 'muscular garbage collection' genes switched off. There was a simple retroviral therapy that made the Human body accumulate muscle mass monotonically, without the need for any exercise. Seeing the results in the flesh, Ingstad was convinced.

"Let's have some privacy," said Snake.

The windows became fully opaque. Ingstad knew this opaqueness would cover all usable portions of the EM spectrum: radio, IR ... He had no way to get a signal out now.

He imagined he should say something to appear nonchalant. He could laugh off his annoyance at being kept waiting. Or comment on the weather. Or tell one of the jokes he had heard about Colonel Hanssen. A thousand choices occurred to him, but he was too nervous and tongue-tied. He only sat still and examined this place where he would likely die.

"Uh, Ingy ... " Snake said, tapping at his temple.

Ingstad stared. "Oh, right!" he exclaimed, realizing what Snake meant. He went to the little-used 'Shut down' option in his OHUD and switched off his comps. All the additions to his vision sloughed away, leaving him with an oddly naked view.

That accomplished, Snake began again, "Soooo ... I heard from my man Vegas that you wanted to talk to me?"

Ingstad cleared his throat. "Yeah, Snake, I— ... Well— ... You see— ... " He had practiced this monologue beforehand, but now he found all of his preparation evaporated. "I— ... The thing is I was— "

"You have one minute—go!" Snake cut in.

Ingstad paused.

"Ah-heh-heh-heh, I'm just fuckin' wit' you, man," Snake chuckled. "No, seriously. Take your time. What you wanna talk about?"

Ingstad attempted a grin. "Well, you know ... you and I, Snake ... —Well, more like me and the guys you work with ... We've ... well, we've ... butted heads in the past. Over the drugs."

Snake gestured as if granting a point.

"I mean I joined the ANP thinking it was all concerned citizens standing up against the corporates. But then I go behind the scenes and see everybody doing pinch-hits of sledge, and wrapping up pallets, and making narco drops ... " He was not selling his point too well here ... "So I didn't want anything to do with the drug side back then. But now ... Well, yesterday we just had our first real fight against the corporates. And—"

203

"Oh, how was that shit, man?" Snake asked earnestly.

"It went okay. But ... it got close, you know? Closer than I expected."

Snake nodded, playing a therapist whose empathy was set on 'automatic.'

"And that got me thinking, this is what I wanted all the time, right? Some action against the corporates. A chance to do something. But now I realize that I'm risking my life, and for what? The same dirt pay I've been getting all along? Well, that was fine back when all I had to do was go joyriding all day, but not anymore.

"And meanwhile I've been watching you and your guys making all the money, getting all the perks. And, now that we're moving in with these Leknes guys, it seems like it might be your chance to go big time. At least that's what I figured. And so I was wondering ... if you still wanted my help. Me and some other guys I represent. See if we can't ... start pulling our weight." Kill me now, he added silently.

But, instead of killing him, Snake hooked him under his arm and beamed with paternal pride. "You see ... " he said, grinning ever wider. "You see this man? ... What did you always say, Mikhi?" he turned to one of the men up front. "What did you always say about Ingstad here?"

"I don't know, boss," Mikhi replied automatically.

"Oh, sure you do. How'd it go, something like ... 'Oh, Ingstad, that fucking cub scout—he doesn't even have the *ovaries* to do what we do.' Didn't you

204

say something like that, Mikhi? Come on, don't deny it."

"Well I guess I might have, boss." The answer was mechanical.

"Guess *shit*. You *did*. Seriously, Ingy, he wouldn't shut up about it. It was always 'He'll never step up to the plate' this, and 'He's plotting behind our backs' that. ... And I'll admit ... *maybe* I went along with him a few of those times. Truth be told, Ingy, I believed them. I didn't think you'd ever man your way over to our side. So thank you for proving me wrong, Ingy—*thank you*."

Ingstad wanted to smile and be at ease, but this overdone reception made him keep his guard up. He could only believe this was some stretching, facetious display on Snake's part.

"Well, if you're gonna be running with us, we gotta give you a new name, right?" Snake chirped. "Mikhi, Slim, you guys got any ideas?"

"Ehhhh ... none, boss," said one.

"Yeah can't think of any, boss," said the other.

"... You're useless," Snake retorted. He turned to Ingstad, stared for a second, and said, "How about ... 'Junk'?"

Ingstad eyed that.

"—Oh, yeah, kinda double entendre-y," Snake retracted it. "So how about ... 'Trip'?"

Ingstad shook his head.

"Or 'Sutch'?"

Again.

"'Treads'? ... 'Stilts'? ... 'Skies'? ... 'Bryan'?"

"—Uhh, what?"

205

"Oh no no no no no no, I got it, how about ... 'Dust-off?'"

"I ... suppose that works," Ingstad said. "'To dust-off' means 'to take-off.' ... I'm a pilot. ... Okay."

"Oh, I didn't mean it that way, Ingy. I mean it looks like you got a lot of nano shit covering you. Like we should break out the dustbin and broom and sweep you off—that kind of 'dusting off.'" Snake used his free hand to swat symbolically at Ingstad's jacket.

Ingstad's heart skipped a beat, but he forced himself to remain cool. Snake might only be bluffing.

"So what's it all from, man?" Snake asked, prolonging the agony of charade.

Ingstad chuckled weakly. "How should I know? Hitchhikers from the ... subway?"

"Ahhh, right," said Snake with a sly grin. "Sorry for prying, but you understand. Security and trust and shit. ... See, I got a lot of multi-spectral sensors up in my viz, and tons of security systems wired in there, too. One of these is always on the lookout for nanotech, and it shows me a viz pane of where anything suspicious is. 'Course the stuff *you're* wearing is a little too miniaturized and advanced to have been pumped out by the Ministry of Transportation or by some ad firm, but okay. I gotcha."

Ingstad at last realized that he had walked into a trap, but he smothered any telling reaction. Instead he became fiercely conscious of everything in the car: he noted Snake's arm around the back of his neck; where Snake's other hand was; what position

Mikhi and Slim were in. He noted where were all of the weapons that he could see; where all of the ones he could not see would likely be ...

"But, say!" Snake plucked up, continuing this odd foreplay. "Let me tell you about some of the other filters I got up here. Now this one is an electronics filter ... " he panned his head around the car. "Shows me everything that's hummin' with juice. So all the backs of your necks are burning from your comps—save yours, of course ... And the car is pumping the stuff like blood. 'Course this can't see outside because of the blackout curtain.

"Annnd ... here's a UV filter for picking out spectral signatures. I can see explosives residues, fingerprints, *semen stains* ... You might not want to know this, man, but the backseat of this car? It looks like a fuckin' *sperm whale* got it on in here. Annnd ... Oh! Here's one of my favorite filters— very useful—it's my *bullshit* filter; would you believe it?"

"Oh?" Ingstad managed to play along.

"Like, you see Mikhi up there?" Snake grabbed Ingstad's chin and manually rotated his head forward. "Under the bullshit filter, my man Mikhi burns a cool blue—hardly any bullshit about the man. And then Slim ... " he panned Ingstad's head to the next man, "well, shit, *he's* all the way down into that violet—indigo—fucking *ultra-indigo* range. No bullshit in him at all. ... Hell, there's hardly any *Human* shit in him, either—hey, Slim, your bm's must be as regular as an atomic clock, huh?"

"Fuck you," Slim called back perfunctorily.

"Heh heh, that's Slim ... " Snake turned his gaze portentously onto Ingstad. "But *you*, Ingy! —I mean *you*, 'Dust-off.' You know what color you are?"

"Um ... Burnt umber?" Ingstad ventured.

Snake sat deadpan for several seconds. Then, "A-HAHAHAHAHAAA—well aren't you just hi-goddamn-fucking-larious. ... Heh. —But no, man," he became deathly stern. "Sorry to say it, but you burn solid *white*. You're so full of bullshit it's just oozin' out your eyeballs. Dripping down your face like Goddamn tears. You're *crying* bullshit, man.

"And you been that way ever since you got in this car. Hell, since you were standing out on that curb. —Shit, ever since the first fucking second I saw you. And you only been gettin' brighter and brighter ever since."

Ingstad belatedly realized that he had not walked into a trap at all, because how could this be a 'trap' if he had never had even the pretense of being believed? When he had called up Snake's men to arrange this meeting, he had not been engaging in intrigue but plainly making an assisted suicide appointment. Now Snake and his men were only fulfilling their end of the deal.

Snaked sighed, settled back, and began speaking honestly for the first time that night: "See, I figured the Leknes flatfoots would try some Serpico shit to break into my racket. Like you said, this is the ANP's big chance, right? They gotta know that, so they gotta try something to stop it. And so when I hear that *you're* interested in joining my crew—*you* of all fucking people—I was like, 'Hell, couldn't they have sent someone *more*

208

obvious? Dig up Saint Therese of Lisieux perhaps?'
... " He shook his head. "Soooo, what now? ... I
guess I could just pitch you out of the car—those
nanites on ya haven't seen anything useful. And
maybe you and your newfound friends will give up
after this.

"*But*,"—Ingstad felt this word like the kiss of a
lash—"if someone tries to play you for a chump,
then there have to be *consequences*. I gotta send
them back a message, clear as day. Something that
spells out the words 'Better luck next time,
douchebags' in skywriting letters ten klicks up." He
brought their heads together and waved out a hand
as if painting that spectacle. "Tell me, Ingy," he
slipped back into his coy, pretending voice, "do *you*
have an idea how I could do that?"

Ingstad moved rapidly—he snapped a fist into
Snake's face while he used his other hand to try the
door handle—just to make sure it was locked—
before using both hands to grapple for Snake's
weapons. Snake was strangely not putting up a
fight. There was blood trickling from his nose
where Ingstad had hit him, but it was not an
incapacitating blow. Ingstad could only think that
Snake was sledged out of his mind—fortunately for
him.

He pulled out Snake's pistol and buried the
muzzle into the man's forehead, cocking the
hammer. Mikhi and Slim turned around too late to
intervene.

"Open the doors!" Ingstad yelled. "Open them
or I'll blow his head off!"

Snake, despite having his head riveted under the barrel of a Colt .45, was grinning.

He reached up, grabbed the pistol, and depressed Ingstad's trigger finger himself. It clicked empty.

"You dumb fuck," said Snake, smiling with bloodied teeth.

Ingstad felt blows from Mikhi and Slim land on his back, and Snake attacked with all the promised ferocity of a supermeth addict. Ingstad was thrown into frenetic confusion by the impossible sequence of wrestling that followed. In alternating half seconds he was on his back, slammed up against the side, crashing into the ceiling, throwing Snake backwards, kicking at the window, being thrown down to the floor mats, pinned against the front seats—

Until he felt lightning lance into his back as surely as if Zeus himself had stepped down to author a blow in their duel. Ingstad's conscious thoughts flew apart in a burst of agony and he crumpled to the floor. He saw Snake hovering over him wearing a pair of electric-fanged brass knuckles that had just discharged. That would explain the pain, Ingstad thought dimly.

Too soon the knuckles crackled with a fresh charge. Snake notched his arm back and looked intent on stamping the knuckles into Ingstad's face. Ingstad was actually glad for this, as he reasoned that it would either cause him to die immediately, or go into an instant coma. Either way he would not feel the blow itself.

But this was prevented when the car was jounced violently into the air as if they had hit a wall. The car's Impact Foam deployed and billows of pink exploded from every seam, filling the cabin. The foam wrapped around their bodies and cushioned them from the impact.

All motion stopped, all sound surceased, and time itself held briefly static. With four of Ingstad's senses blacked out, the only thing left to concentrate on was the foam's all-surrounding, amniotic warmth—toasty with the heat of its rapid deployment.

When Ingstad felt a chill at his ankles, he knew the foam was melting. His legs came free up to his pelvis, and he wondered how he would continue fighting with Snake once the foam was gone—but he was preemptively yanked out of the car instead.

On the street outside he was surprised to see a mass of police and firemen. The two officers who had pulled him from the car were now manhandling him into custody, but one of them said, "It's him," and they let him go.

Instead they dove on Mikhi. He had just been pulled from the same side of the car as Ingstad, but he was ragdolling the two officers assigned to restrain him. The addition of Ingstad's two officers—and then two more—still did little to subdue this brick of muscle. Finally a seventh officer appeared and peppered Mikhi with tranquilizer darts, clustering them in his stomach like rabies hypodermics. A normal person would have dropped like concrete under such a narcotic assault, but Mikhi only sank to the ground like a deflating balloon.

Ingstad saw that the car's front had been crushed to no higher than a foot off the ground. The cabin was intact, though, and all the occupants had been retrieved bodily from the wreck. Snake and Slim were being wrangled into custody on the other side.

Erlend jogged up.

"I didn't get it," Ingstad said immediately.

"Oh well," said Erlend.

"But, uh ... " Ingstad gestured at the crushed car, "what did that?"

"Hovertank. Had it on standby in case we didn't like what was going on."

"How could you tell it had gone bad?"

"The car started rocking, so either you guys were fighting, or you were having sex. Either way, we figured something wasn't going according to plan."

"Ah. Good thinking." Glancing back at the wreck, Ingstad added, "And *exceptional* aim."

Chapter 22 - Riposte

"I said 'immunity,' sir!" cried Roscher, almost rising to his feet before the Brigadier. He voiced the word 'sir' not as to a superior officer but as one affronted gentleman to another.

"Yes, you did," replied Brigadier Krohg calmly. Roscher was meeting over telepresentation in the Brigadier's office, which gave Krohg the home court advantage. "But, as I recall, we only agreed on 'retroactive' immunity. We certainly never said anything about it being 'perpetual.' And in return you agreed to clean up the ANP's operations. Yet now we discover that one of your most senior officers, Major Carl Linge—a.k.a. 'Snake'—" the Brigadier added the alias with disdain, "has had the gall to smuggle drugs into Leknes itself."

Roscher huffed. "If you're talking about that stunt your men pulled with Ingstad last night, then I don't know what you could mean. There wasn't a gram of sledge in that car."

"You're right. There wasn't."

Roscher drew back. "Then I don't understand—"

"But one does not have to be carrying sledge '*on* their person' to qualify as smuggling it. '*In* their person' also suffices."

Roscher squinted at the legal camel-through-the-eye-of-a-needle that the Brigadier was proposing. "That's ludicrous."

"Actually, it's precedent. According to 'Bergen v. Storheil' in '33,'"—Krohg forwarded Roscher the document—"given modern extraction techniques, it is possible to dope oneself up with supermeth in a deactivated form only to have it extracted later, yielding usable product. This clearly constitutes smuggling."

The Brigadier was surprised that Roscher was ignorant of this. Maybe the man did not bother with such details that were better left to his traffickers. —Or, as was more likely, maybe Roscher did know this, but he was playing innocent for appearance's sake.

"And, from samples of Major Linge's blood," the Brigadier continued, "we found him to be carrying approximately four grams worth of supermeth—many times the normal lethal dosage."

Roscher considered. "But what if that was merely the residual from recreational practices, and not meant for extraction?"

Krohg eyed Roscher. "Are you telling me that one of the ANP's highest officers ... has been doing so much sledge ... and for so long ... that he can carry around enough of it in his blood to kill a *whale* ... and that's just his morning buzz?"

Roscher shrugged. "Still, as long as the concentration was not achieved for the express purpose of later extraction, then—"

"Sorry, 'General,' but we can't take the doper's word on whether they were acting as a mule or not. Otherwise we'd be offering them a get-out-of-jail-free card. A legal limit was set to tell the difference between plain users and mules, and that is half a gram. Your Major Linge is obviously in violation of this."

Roscher sank back in his chair. He glanced at the vidwindow, which was depicting the sunrise conditions outside. "What's the fallout?" he asked with resignation.

"Linge will be sentenced before Leknes courts and likely receive several years. His two ... bodyguards, however,"—he had almost said 'henchmen'—"were not in violation of the same law, and so they will be released.

"... Though of course Leknes does not have the resources to keep a skyrocketing number of narcotic offenders in jail for their assigned terms. So, in Major Linge's case, if, during the rest of the ANP's collaboration with the Home Guard, your forces perform exceptionally, and there are no other such infractions, —and if the Major himself serves his time with good behavior—, then we may see fit to parole him in only a few months. Likely before next year."

Roscher rocked in his seat. "You have my gratitude," he said with seeming magnanimity. "And might I extend to you my sincere apologies for Major Linge's behavior. You have my assurances that such a thing will never happen again."

Krohg recognized the coded response: Roscher was not referring to the misbehavior of his men as the 'thing' that would never happen again, just the incident of them having gotten caught doing it. It was the difference between promising immaculate behavior versus invisible nefariousness. But that would do for now.

***

After Roscher's telepresentation signed out of the Brigadier's office, it next appeared in the same hall that Colonel Hanssen was in. Hanssen knew the meeting the man had just been in, and, seeing Roscher, he stopped.

Roscher's image approached within a step of him, and the two squared off. Hanssen used the opportunity to survey the man in detail: the grey, bristling beard, the face cracked with lines, and the edgy eyes of incipient withdrawal.

And Roscher grinned out of the slightest corner of his mouth.

Hanssen knew there could be a thousand meanings behind that grin. But he caught one distinctly: it was as if Roscher had said a crisp and condescending, 'Touche, sir.' Which meant that the man was already concocting his own elaborate riposte to Hanssen's strike.

Hanssen nodded near-imperceptibly back, accepting the challenge.

Chapter 23 - Blame

Mohr and his men were back at their base in Norway, digging air raid ditches. Rarely was his unit given so primitive a task as 'digging ditches,' and in added insult they had been given nothing more advanced than shovels and entrenching tools to do it. The only modern aspect to the job was how the earthworks they were to dig had been diagrammed for them in augspace. But otherwise this work could have been outsourced to Roman construction slaves.

Straightening up from his work, Mohr groaned at the unfamiliar strain in his back. He looked up and down the half dug, zigzagging trench line. All around his men were gyring through their rutting dance, pitching earth over their shoulders, making progress only in a gruesome trickle. It was humbling to know that such manual labor still existed in the year 2045, and that it could be just as laborious as ever.

A meeting reminder popped up Mohr's OHUD: he and half a dozen other captains were due to meet with Major Karpinski. He stuck his shovel into the ground and handed command off to Lieutenant Janus. He headed back towards the administrative building cluster at the center of camp.

Nearing his destination, Mohr saw the rest of the captains who had been summoned to the meeting, all approaching from different directions. Solemn nods passed between them. They suspected that Karpinski had called them together to discuss the Home Guard attack back in Östersund, which meant that the agenda would likely involve them being yelled at and criticized a great deal. Hence why they had all headed over at the last minute, not wanting to be in Karpinski's presence a second longer than necessary.

Mohr and the other captains entered the building, located and swept into the small conference room, and took their seats at the stroke of the hour. Karpinski was at the table's head, sitting facing the side, and drumming his fingers back and forth. He frowned at the saucy promptness with which his men appeared.

Without introduction, Karpinski started, "Well, I must tell you I'm sorely disappointed. The kind of rumors I've been hearing around this base, it makes me think I'm the XO of a sewing circle instead of a military unit. A little shit happens a few days ago, a few things blow up, and suddenly everyone's all *Apocalypse Now*. I mean, shit!" He spun to face them and rested his arms on the table. "I've heard it all. Men saying the Home Guard destroyed every base north of Trondheim. That they abducted Lindon in a commando raid. Even that they nuked the Bunker in Oslo.

"So I've called you captains together to put a cap on this gossip. Now, Marshal Atkins doesn't want to let the general ranks in on the details of this Home Guard offensive yet, but I'm gonna share the big picture with you. That way you can take some assurances back to your men and put your houses in order."

218

Mohr was relieved that they would be hearing something. In the days since the Home Guard attack, the corporate army's in-house news had gone silent. Neither Atkins, nor Lindon, nor the colonels had said anything. With so glaring an information gap, it was only natural that the men would invent outlandish rumors to fill it.

"—But first," turned Karpinski, "let me share with you a few facts in my possession. They're about 'winning.'"

Mohr winced. This foreboded a rant, since Karpinski liked to trowel down general rules before he went into vehement specifics.

"Specifically, it's about how there are two ways to win. The first way is for *you* to 'achieve victory.' This comes from things like hard work ... strategy ... out-thinking and out-flanking your enemy, et cetera. It happens, and it works. I've even seen this very unit do it on occasion.

"But *more often than that*," he stabbed a finger into the table, "you win by the second method. Which is you don't do too much, but rather the other side 'achieves *defeat*.' By screwing up. By incompetence. By any number of things. Because it's damned hard to find a damned good commander who'll 'achieve victory,' but damned fools are everywhere every day 'achieving defeat.'

"So here's the truth," he leaned back—to make room for a series of holos that appeared over the table. "Last Saturday we were attacked by units of the Norwegian Home Guard from the city of Leknes. They threw together a nice raid on this and

219

other nearby bases—doing their share to 'achieve victory' ... "

Karpinski gave them a full outline elaborated with spreadsheets and unflinching damage reports. Mohr was relieved to see that the attacks had had limited extent. Only six bases had been hit, and, despite the mountains of infrastructure and vehicular damage, there were only two fatalities. Granted there were over fifty in the infirmary, but the attacks had clearly been conducted with non-lethal restraint.

However, even though only six bases had been attacked, they were six crucial ones in the army's infrastructure—an infrastructure that was now obviously overextended. And, as Norwegian military activity was continuing, this looked to be only the first blow of a sustained offensive. The Home Guard's opening strike had been designed not just for shock and awe but to put the corporate army on the back foot, and to give them a prolonged advantage to press.

"And *now* ... " said Karpinski after completing his summary. "*Now* it's time for a little audience participation. Because we've had time to sift through the details of the clusterfuck in Östersund. And with details, of course, comes blame."

The captains were instantly on their guard.

"So let's turn ... to Captain ... *Mohr*."

All heads whiplashed in Mohr's direction.

Oh shit, he thought—but "Sir?" he was cognizant enough to answer.

220

"Do you recognize this man?" Karpinski asked him. A graphic appeared on the holo over the table, evidently a still from an OHUD capture.

After some recollection, Mohr recognized it as likely coming from his own OHUD. He had been afraid of this. After their return from Östersund, all of the men had been required to submit their OHUD logs of the evening, for the investigation into the attack. Many were also running the same program as Mohr that saved the last minute of everything they saw. While this program threw away the video data that was over a minute old, it also archived snapshots at 15-second intervals. The image Karpinski was showing him must have come from one of those saves.

And, worse yet, he did recognize the man in this picture. "Yes, sir," he admitted to Karpinski.

"Can you explain how you met him?"

"Yes, sir. It was ... at a bar. The man and some others entered, and ... they started a fight with my men. We kicked them out."

"Oh, good for you," said Karpinski patronizingly. "And do you also suppose you recognize this man?"

Another graphic appeared. Mohr answered, "Yes, sir, he was the one who started the fight."

"And, say ... this man?"

Another image: "He ... was also one of the brawlers, sir."

Karpinski glowered. ... And sighed. ... And shook his head. Each action was timed to best show his mounting disgust.

221

"Well, Captain Mohr, it appears that you and your men all have three strikes against you. Because here's who the last man really is."

On the holo appeared a personnel photo of the man, who was now wearing a Home Guard uniform.

"A lieutenant in the Leknes HG," said Karpinski. "Strike *one*. ... And here's who the second man is."

Another personnel shot, and another set of lieutenant's bars.

"Strike two," said Karpinski. "And finally ... "—the last graphic—"*Colonel* Hanssen, currently the field commander of Leknes's Home Guard, and so doubtless one of the men running this campaign against us. Strike ... three."

Fuck ... me, thought Mohr in synchronicity.

"These three were all in Östersund conducting a covert operation that kicked off the attacks there and back here. Yet in the course of that they picked a fight with Captain Mohr's men. What luck! In fact, we provide you all with facebook applications covering the Home Guard brass just in case we run into situations this fortunate.

"... Yet not *one* of you dumb-asses—nor all your dumb-ass men—recognized these three. Nor passed the slightest alert up the chain of command. ... And, if this is the state of Captain Mohr's men,"—he raked the others with his contemptful gaze—"then I have to assume that all the other dumb-asses on this base are in just as piss-poor shape.

"*This* ... is 'achieving defeat,'" he said in grave full circle. "Because of your carelessness, you allowed an attack against the entire army. And two of our guys are dead because of it."

Even when Mohr was the target of a reaming, he could always appreciate the sardonic humor of it. And this one, he was admitting, would have been hilarious to recall perhaps a year later.

But Karpinski's last had spoiled that.

Two or three years it would take now.

"So, of all the units that have to dig themselves out of a hole in this coming fight, ours is the deepest. By *far*. ...

"But luckily," Karpinski unexpectedly brightened, "we've been given an opportunity to redeem ourselves. We're being deployed to the front."

Mohr was ambivalent about this. The corporate army did have a technological advantage over the Home Guard, but, numerically, if the whole Norwegian state took up arms, Mohr was afraid they would fare like Napoleon in Russia.

A new holomap appeared showing Norway overlaid with the logistics web that connected the corporate army bases. "In detail," said Karpinski, "now that all of this has become hostile territory, we're having a hard time supplying our outlying bases. Home Guard forces are continuing to harass those, and our guys up there are running out of ammo and supplies. Our main forces are working to reestablish our internal lines, but that will take time. And, before they can finish, there are a few dozen

223

bases that are in danger of simply running out of food.

"So *we* will be re-supplying those bases individually. We'll be going out into hostile territory, leading armored convoys with heavy escorts. And, in fact,"—the holo flipped to show a tactical map diagramming a single convoy route— "our first mission is tomorrow."

Chapter 24 - Quartet

Cheryl spied the bar: a quaint twentieth-century affair, heralded by a neon sign whose letters were half burnt out, making alphabet soup of the proper name '*The Queen Rania*.' The place's augfront was similarly dilapidated, sporting many broken image tags and links, as if decorating with tiles of '? GraphixError: Unreadable data format' were a valid fashion statement.

Cheryl had the place sized up in an instant: a low-end salaryman bar whose patronage would consist of men and prostitutes in around a 3:1 ratio. It was only the lack of a second floor and some beds that kept the place from becoming an outright brothel. In fact ... on a hunch Cheryl looked around and saw that *The Queen Rania* was situated across the street from an hourly 'bed-and-fuckfest'—as expected.

On entering the bar she spotted her mark right away. The man was sitting on a stool, clutching a beer bottle in one hand and cradling his head in the other. Despite the dim lights Cheryl could make out his slovenly appearance and bristly face. There were many hookers present, but this saturnine figure was one of those left unmolested. But that would only make Cheryl's job easier.

Whenever the Mafia handed Cheryl a job, they gave her pictures of her targets but never their names. Any additional information was dangerous because Cheryl was often put up against high-class corporate targets whose OHUDs never stopped recording across a dozen intrusive wavelengths. If Cheryl knew any details about her target beforehand, then she would not be surprised—in the biometric, physiological sense—when the mark told her them in conversation. Then later, when security was fine-toothed–combing through the OHUD vidage, the deception might show and Cheryl would become useless to her employers. Best-case scenario she would end up like one of the many hookers busying *The Queen Rania.*

Cheryl knew it would be too obvious to dive on her mark right away, so instead she took a turn about the room. She responded warmly to the smiles that came her way (from the regular patrons, excited at seeing a new girl) and ignored the vicious stares (from the regular hookers, affronted at the same). Finally she circled back to her target and hopped onto the stool next to him.

As he was still wearing his work clothes, she chirped, "Hey, honey, I think business hours are over."

The guy looked up, surprised. "Heh," he offered in her general direction, then looked back at his beer.

Tough customer ... "Cheryl," she introduced herself.

"... Vlad."

"*Ooooo*, like the vampire?!" she said in an eldritch leer.

Vlad shrugged. "I guess."

"Girls like you to suck their blood, huh?" she added with a vocal kink.

Vlad grinned. And said nothing.

226

Cheryl nearly rolled her eyes—she was serving up tee-balls, here ... Okay, start again, slower. "So where you work?"

"Lindon Securities," he said more easily.

"*Really?*" Cheryl's surprise hopefully masked her genuine concern. If this Mafia job had something to do with Lindon Securities, then it meant her margin of error was nil.

"Yup!" said Vlad, grinning smugly. At least the honesty of Cheryl's reaction was helping him open up.

"Whadaya do there?"

In reply he performed a twitch to activate his badge, and a card-sized holo appeared over his chest. Cheryl craned her head into position to read the words—and made sure to slather ample touch onto Vlad in the process. In a schoolgirl starcher she read, "'Stockholm Human-Mediated Computational Services.' ... You're a mentat?"

"Yup!"

"Wowwww," Cheryl said. Granted, mentats technically did the least amount of 'work' of any class of 'work*ers*' anywhere, but it was still white collar. And this was helping her cover: instead of appearing like a dumb hooker beating on a dead horse, Cheryl would now look to be going after genuine candy.

Cheryl warmed Vlad up for a few more minutes before dropping the line, "Hey, Vlad-y, why don't we get out of here?"

Vlad grinned and levered himself up from the bar. But he almost toppled over when his alcohol-clouded nerves had trouble finding his legs. Cheryl

227

ducked under his arm to prop him up, then walked them both to the door.

On her way out, the other prostitutes shot Cheryl murderous glances. Even though Vlad was clearly not trophy pickings around here, Cheryl's attempt to stake a claim—as paltry as it was—was a direct challenge to *The Queen Rania's* regular supply-side sex workers. Those glances told Cheryl that they would let her get away with this one for now, but if she came back there would be war. But that was fine, as this was a one-off job.

Once outside, the rest of her mission was blessedly simple. She guided Vlad across the street to the bed-and-fuckfest. She procured a fuckpad and was given a fuckkey. She made sure the room was on the first floor so that there would be no doomed ascent of the stairs.

As soon as they were in their room, Vlad began pawing her with the reechy alacrity of a caveman. He was pushing her towards the bed, and Cheryl let him walk them over. Just before he was about to push her back onto it, however, she stuck his neck with a nanoinjector that deployed from one of her fingernails. Vlad was immediately stricken unconscious, and Cheryl stepped out of his grasp and out of his way as he collapsed sack-like onto the bed.

She pulled a satchel from her back. From inside she produced a nanotechnology patch, wafer-thin, the size of a postage stamp. She attached this to the back of Vlad's neck, over where his body computers were located.

She had not been told what the patch would do, but it would likely fight a battle with Vlad's defenses, after which it would be free to reprogram his comps at will. Then, along with whatever its primary objective was, it would also erase all the records that Vlad's comps had recorded this evening—including all evidence of 'Cheryl.'

Attempting such a hack on Vlad would have been risky before the depression. At work mentats were plugged directly into guarded corporate networks, so they were supposed to have top-rate body security. If this were the equal of Cheryl's invading nanites, then they might get caught in a war of attrition for control of his body, and the waste heat from that might cook Vlad's brain. But Cheryl's job was covert infiltration, so it was unseemly to leave a trail of corpses behind.

But the depression and its mass corporate cutbacks meant that mentats were no longer such walking safes. Within three seconds the patch sent Cheryl a message saying that it had compromised Vlad's systems. Then two seconds later it announced, 'Mission accomplished.' Cheryl removed the patch and tucked it back into its case.

She straightened up and demonstratively wiped her hands. To complete the deception, she undid Vlad's pants, and she plucked out his wallet and retrieved his cash card. She tried to draw down twenty credits—a measure above the going rate—but it only had 13.481 on it total. Cheapskate.

Only once Cheryl was out of the hotel, around the corner, and several blocks away did she relax, congratulating herself on another job well done. She sent an encrypted data burst back to her organization—announcing 'mission accomplished'—, then thought ahead to the long, cleansing bubble bath that awaited her at home.

***

Vlad was being dredged back up to consciousness by the shriek of an alarm clock. He was about to hit 'snooze' and slide back down the depths—until he saw that it was his OHUD's 'deadman's alarm.' So named because, if he slept through that, then he would be late for work, which meant being fired, not finding another job, running his savings dry, and eventually ending up on the street, buying it like all the other vizhuffers.

He bolted off the bed—Where was he?—What had happened last night? The fact that his pants were undone provided some clues—but no time for that now. He jumped into the shower—clothes and all—and gave himself a vigorous once-over. He leapt out, quickly blasted his hair with the dryer, and was out the door, 60 seconds elapsed—he would let his nanofabrics dry along the way.

Stepping out of the hotel fired an electronic tripwire that compiled his room bill, charged his card, and chucked the receipt into his OHUD.

"Fucking extortion!" he cried back at the desk.

—And that was just the cost for the room, he realized—he couldn't even remember what the sex had cost him. In fact, he couldn't even remember the sex itself—what a rip last night had been!

Out in the street he saw *The Queen Rania*. It was almost lugubriously unrecognizable in the daylight, but that at least told him the way to the

230

nearest subway station. He broke out running—and his sprint lasted precisely three steps until the sledgehammer knocks from his hangover forced him to slow down. He jogged the rest of the way, striking a balance between speed and neural trauma.

He arrived just in time to grab the next train. Only once he was underway did he check the time ... and sighed with relief—he would just make it. Granted he would be going in to work wearing the same clothes he had left in yesterday, but he would be changing out of those anyway once he got back.

At the facility, he blazed through security so frantically that the guards must have thought he was late for a workplace killing spree. He charged down to the locker room, where the other mentats were already finished suiting up. As he hurried by, he bore their expected jibes of, "Fuck, man, you look like *shit*."

He reached his locker, stripped off his clothes, and took one of his fresh coolsuits off the rack. The suits were skin-tight, rubber-hard, and jutting with plumbing protuberances. Vlad attacked putting his on just as the chime sounded in the locker room, marking one minute to first immersion.

Somehow, besting all his previous records, Vlad had the coolsuit on and was staggering out onto the floor just as the countdown expired. *Victory*, he cawed. ... Technically he was already supposed to be in immersion once the countdown was over, but at least he had achieved another day where they could not fire him.

"We're *waiting* ... " came his supervisor's—Sarah's—voice over the comms. She was glowering at him through the plaz windows on the far side of the farm. Vlad saluted sarcastically and jogged to his open immersion creche.

"No running in the pit!" Sarah shouted.

Once Vlad was at his station, his job was almost over. The creche was a small pool sculpted in the outline of the Human body. It was deep enough to hold a decimeter of water, but it was dry at the cycle's start. Vlad climbed in and positioned himself meticulously over the pads and grips.

The pool flooded with something more viscous than water up to his ears, and the cap came down on his head. A myriad of sensors and feeds wormed out from the creche's sides and latched onto Vlad's body, staking their claims as in an American land rush. Soon the creche would induce unconsciousness, and then, once Vlad's brain was cleared of cluttering thought, it would become a razor-edged tool for intuitive computation.

***

Sarah Spikes used to love her job. Five years ago, mentating was like running a ballet academy: all of their subjects were educated women with brains wired like grand pianos. Once in immersion, one wrote the data into their brains, simulated the routines, and got speedy, muliebrity-powered intuition back. And it was a pleasure to work with those women, too, to chat with them at break. For them, mentating was just part-time. Because they all heeded that certain shame that mentating was, after all, selling their bodies. Granted they were specifically only selling their brains, and then for intellectual rather than sexual use, but it was selling

232

nonetheless. So they had goals and ambitions for which mentating was just a stepping stone.

But then, the depression. One might have thought that it would have improved mentating's conditions, what with more better-educated and -qualified people looking for work. And this had happened, but only simultaneous with the demand for mentating dropping by a much greater margin. After all, who could afford to farm their computational routines out to Humantime anymore when late-model hypercomps were just as good— and had no rights? So cuts were made, drastic and deep, and the mentating firms were forced to turn to the lowest common denominator for their subjects. It had come down to the burnouts, the slackers, and the people who would only 'work' if it meant going to sleep for eight hours. That now for three years Sarah's job had just been nannying after filthy men.

Ah, Vlad had finally shown up, Sarah noted. "We're *waiting* ... " she said over the comms. "—No running in the pit!"

If Sarah could cut anybody in the program— perform the slightest bit of amputational triage—, Vlad would be it. They typically had to run detox on him for the first half hour of his immersion just to clean up his brain enough to do any work. Otherwise they got the results one would expect from an inebriated computer. And twice this month already he had had wet dreams while in immersion. For as much as the computer being drunk screwed up the results, the computer having sex during calculation left no byte intact. The only things they could run him on were the embarrassingly parallel jobs where his high loss rate fell just in the range of 'acceptable.' Looking at Vlad's profile, Sarah saw three crucial gauges where he was hovering just above the cut rates. One dip below and they would fire him—but he had not made it yet. Lucky, he was. Lucky and filthy.

Once Vlad was in his creche, Sarah engaged his immersion, and at last all of their mentats were away.

Five minutes into the sequence, a warning chirped. Sarah checked it ... anomalous beta jitter in grid five. That was a little odd, but nothing to—

And now in grid three. Grid two. Five, one, eight—

A klaxon flared and all the lights went red. Sarah's screen flashed with messages crying of a deep infiltration, and the entire facility advanced to some dire alert state. All the mentating sequences were halted and the facility's web links were hard-severed. They were in quarantine—Sarah had never seen this before.

The other supervisors were soon on the channel: "The hell was that?!"

"I got jitter alarms in all sectors—"

"What did that mean? What do we—"

Shortly they were all lassoed into a conference call coming from their hotline into Lindon Central Security. They were brought before the dark avatar of a security chief.

"All right, what the fuck is going on over there," the chief said, not inflecting a question. Meanwhile his eyes looked extraordinarily busy with OHUD work, suggesting that this call was occupying perhaps only 3% of his attention.

Sarah, being chief supervisor, had to answer: "Uhhh ... we don't know, sir. We got some beta jitter across grids, then everything shut down—"

"You were used for a backchannel attack," interrupted the man—supplying an explanation that had apparently come from the other 97% of his attention.

"We were hacked?" said Sarah, shocked.

"No, not you—who'd want to hack a fucking mentat plant?"

Sarah flustered. But she reminded herself that security chiefs spent their days upbraiding peons for causing major breaches, so they ought to be excused their brusqueness.

The chief continued, "They used your facility's line into the Spire to trigger the doors for a much larger piece of work. They're already in and out."

"... It's over?"

"Of course, it's been a quadrillion clock cycles."

"I ... can't tell you how they got in," Sarah started making excuses. "We run very strict standalones. —And—And there wasn't a single blip on our security boards ... "

Down in the pit, the mentats were all sitting up in their creches, looking around, surprised that the clock read only minutes later.

"Send me everything," said the security chief.

Sarah dumped him their complete morning records. The transfer would take five seconds, but, even before it was done, the man answered,

235

"Yup, a noosteganographic implantation in one of your mentats. Once he went under, a noetic trick launched a mindvirus to the others. It incubated, then sprang open the attack on the Spire. Nice job. Brain surgery."

"Iiii ... " Sarah stalled. "Have you found the source of the virus, sir?"

"Impossible—it spread untraceably, then launched its copies randomly ... " He sat with irked attention on his face, rubbing his chin. "But we need to get to the bottom of this—we're sending a team to ziplock your facility. Sit on everyone till it arrives."

Sarah went wide-eyed. She had heard dread tales from other supervisors about being 'ziplocked.' Her immediate fear was of their entire department being scrapped—of them all being out on the street — unemployment — destitution ...

"I ... Uh ... yes, sir, we—" she stammered. "Right away—we'll just—You don't have to be concerned about—"

"Oh, don't worry, honey," the chief interrupted her patronizingly. "So much other stuff just got fucked up right now that you're way too low on the food chain to worry about sacking."

Sarah frowned. But returned to work.

***

Lindon was having after-dinner tea in Tokyo, wrapping up a business negotiation, when a peon crept servilely into his vision from the back of the room.

He could always tell the severity of a disaster by what manner the company chose to inform him of it. Significant inconveniences would perhaps

236

reach him as a memo or a CC; major setbacks would prompt a director to email him directly; a catastrophe meant a flesh-and-blood VP would present himself in his presence. But, for the summit cataclysms, they would send an underling with a bound report, since no one of rank would be brave enough to weather his wrath.

Lindon had seen preliminary reports on the web attack an hour ago, and now that he finally saw this young employee appear with a binder in his hands and a mortified look on his face, he knew how dire it was. —And they had already used the binder method to inform him of the Home Guard attack two weeks ago. This would be the first time two such disasters had occurred so close together.

"Please excuse me, gentlemen," Lindon said to his associates. They bowed as he departed.

He approached the young man, who dared not look him in the eye. He merely said "Sir" and held out the report. Lindon could have gathered all the information online himself, but this report would at least show him the perspective his organization had. He leafed through the opening pages.

He appreciated the scale and sophistication of the attack. The assault had been conducted with the precision of a commando raid, yet with the global sweep and smothering breadth of forces more familiar to blitzkrieg. The attackers had compromised the mainframe and raided a host of sacrosanct systems, in and out in 10.72 seconds. The damage was the worst in their history—perhaps in most companies' histories.

Scanning the details, Lindon saw that the attack had used the 'death by a thousand cuts' strategy. Every company had vulnerabilities, but most of them were too minor to be worth exploiting, and so neither were they worth the trouble of patching. Yet this attack had pooled hundreds of just such negligible flaws from across all sectors of Lindon's company, and played them off against each other in multiplicative synergy until they became a single weakness that was crippling in its scope. The number and diversity of exploits employed was stupefying: a flimsy hard line running to a deep sea oil rig; lax subject screening at a mentat plant; known bugs in logistics software running across the corporate army bases ... Ultimately Lindon saw that there were no more than a dozen Humans total who were capable of such complex orchestration.

And the list of organizations that would undertake such an endeavor was equally small. The ISSO and the national security agencies were always suspect, but law enforcement would never have over-exposed themselves in this manner. That left the illicit organizations, which were far more likely to be involved. Lindon and the other companies that engaged in extraterrestrial smuggling were always trying to steal from each other, as pilfering something that was illegal to begin with entailed little risk of being called out and prosecuted. Many organizations had already tried to steal the 'secrets' of Lindon's success.

Yet this attack had not been such a desultory raid but rather a surgical strike. And Lindon knew of only one organization that had such a specific interest in him at the moment: the Russian Mafia. And he also knew why that was. Which meant that his next thought was a simple and long-coming, Goddammit, Peder ...

Chapter 25 - Perspective

Approaching the Lontan Museum in their hoverlimousine, Peder found little remarkable about it. Granted it was twenty times the size of the Taj Mahal, levitated on a platform larger than Stockholm itself, and constructed at a cost that dwarfed the Earth's current GDP, but, in a world already planted thick with hyperbole—arcos, space elevators, and Mach-5 maglevs—, it took hyperbole's hyperbole to leave him impressed.

The Lontans had built their Museum on a floating platform not just to show off but so that it could change venues every two weeks. That way it could honor all of the scattered Human cities with equal visitation. The alpha world cities had all had their turns, and now it was gracing Stockholm while the Museum made a tour of the Baltic Sea. And Zuzanna had found opening night to be the perfect cover for another business outing with Peder.

"So, the Lontan Museum ... " Peder mused. The structure had long dominated the forward view of their limousine, but their only creaking parallax towards it said how far away they yet were.

"I'm excited—aren't you?" said Zuzanna, bright-eyed.

Peder gave a euphemistic squirm. "I must admit ... my expectations are low."

"... Low expectations?" she balked. "Of the Lontans? ... This is the *Lontans*, you understand."

"I'm aware of that."

"And this is their official museum of galactic art and heritage on Earth."

"Yes."

"They sunk a *hundred trillion credits* into this thing."

"I understand all that."

"Okay, then *I* don't understand *you*," she sat back, yielding the floor.

Peder gathered his thoughts, making ready to venture out into hostile territory. "I don't doubt the time and energy they put into this place. But ... it's just a bunch of art made by long-dead aliens, isn't it? I can't imagine it being anything other than hopelessly esoteric. I mean, for as little regard as I have for the works of *Humanity's* own avant-garde, what chance is there that I'll enjoy the Lontans' 'Third Quaternion Movement'—or whatever the hell they're gonna have in there ... "

He expected some fast rebuke from Zuzanna, but instead she looked off in thought. "Oh. You're thinking the Lontans are only going to show us a bunch of junk, then give us the old, 'You just don't understand it' ploy? Try to psych us into fawning over it?"

"Exactly! Isn't that the story behind so much art?"

"Is it?"

"Well, yeah ... I think it started back when some respected critic wanted to seem hip and cutting-edge. So he picked some hack artist out of nowhere and called him a genius. But then no one wanted to lose points by gainsaying this windbag, so they forced themselves to say the same. But then, soon enough, other critics wanted to see if they commanded the same cachet. So they started picking out their own hacks to champion. And soon enough there was so much faux–avant-garde crap being legitimized this way that it spontaneously aligned into a 'movement.' And so other artists figured they'd better stop making what they thought was good and make what everyone else said was 'good' instead. Which made it easier to find hacks to champion—and right there you have a positive feedback loop. And it went on and on like that, like some arms race of The Emperor's New Clothes, until we got to the point where a monocolor canvas gets exhibited in the Prado, with everyone yelling, '*C'est magnifique!*'"

Zuzanna had been grinning throughout his polemic, and was continually trying to jump in by waving her hand. "—While I follow you," she finally managed to interrupt, "I can't imagine that the Lontans would be so petty and pretentious as that. They already know they're our superiors, so wouldn't they honestly try to impress us with their good art rather than to bluff us with their bad?"

"I suppose ... " Peder shrugged. "But any species that makes a floating museum that big must be a *little* fond of pretentiousness, wouldn't you say?"

Zuzanna chuckled admittingly.

They turned forward and watched more of the Museum's infinitesimal slide closer. They were both searching for a topic of conversation.

"Oh!" said Peder. "Here's a bit of a sensitive question ... " He refreshed her wine glass to try and maintain his nonchalance. "Is your organization still in its high-security mode?"

Zuzanna looked at him. "You want to know because ... "

"—I was only wondering if that was why we were still meeting in person."

"Oh! Yes," Zuzanna realized. "We're on the tail end of the alert, though. Don't worry, you won't be bothered with this anymore," she said in a hurry.

Afterwards they both looked off awkwardly.

Peder had been stung by that 'Don't worry.' He had only asked about the alert out of curiosity, but it seemed Zuzanna had taken it to mean that he was getting annoyed, so she had apologized: 'You won't be bothered with me anymore.' On the contrary, he enjoyed spending time with her. ... —Though that was certainly all there was to it. They were good friends, yes, but he was not so foolish as to want to get involved with his Mafia handler.

And Zuzanna had lamented that 'Don't worry' herself. Peder's question had caught her off guard and she had overreacted. Because the Mafia's alert actually was over, and so Zuzanna should have scheduled this meeting as a regular *sub rosa*. But she did have the prerogative to meet with her clients however she chose, and she actually did enjoy spending time with Peder. Amidst all the bastards of her bosses and clients, he was the one mostly decent person she did not have to be on constant guard against. And she had taken a defensive posture to his question lest he suspect something.

—Or get any ideas. While she did enjoy spending time with him, that was certainly the limit

243

of it. And, even if she wanted a lover, she was not so foolish as to consider getting involved with one of her clients. Not that the Mafia frowned on such things—it was actually encouraged insofar as it drove customer satisfaction and repeat business. But Zuzanna did not want her love life to be doing anyone any favors.

The rest of the trip to the Museum passed with them both engaged in their disparate broodings.

When they finally arrived, their limousine deposited them at the VIP reception platform. The Museum loomed ahead as a majestic palisade. An autowalk conveyed them the long distance to the reception hall, where inside they found a 'hall' more on the scale of a basilica, with walls of lavish decoration and a roof as brightly lit as a daytime sky. Artistic holoworks flashed and melded across the great ceiling space.

They moved about casually, exchanging pleasantries with the other glitterati. Part of attending the social event of the year was leaving behind evidence of one's attendance, and in all of these people's OHUDs would be proof that Peder Kjaerstad and Zuzanna Mukhina had been there, and vice versa.

When the time came for the ribbon-cutting, a glut of dignitaries appeared at the far end of the hall, standing before the titanic doors that led to the exhibit space. In attendance were the Governor of Stockholm, his entourage, the Museum staff, and a copy of the Lontan Governor himself wearing a Human mannequin. The requisite speeches commenced. From where Peder and Zuzanna stood far back in the crowd, they watched the stage through vidstream close-ups offered on the common channels.

Peder remarked to Zuzanna how the Lontan Governor was wearing a mannequin. "You know, Zuska, I've never seen an alien in the flesh ... "

"Me neither," she replied, but lightly. "Though I suppose that's their standard policy. Must be to keep from frightening the natives."

Peder frowned. "That might have made sense right after First Contact, but that was fifty years ago. Isn't it time they dropped the facade?"

"Perhaps not," Zuzanna shrugged. "Fifty years isn't so very long from the Lontan perspective, you know."

"Granted, but ... it still seems condescending. It's as if they think we're too childish to accept the reality of aliens among us."

"They do wear their real bodies to some official functions," she granted.

"Yes, but never when among us 'commoners.'"

The speeches up front were coming to a close. The Lontan Governor ended his remarks with his customary declaration: "I bring you the universe ... " Then he cut the ribbon and its fluttering halves genuflected before the opening doors. Applause followed and the assembly herded forward.

***

The experience ended up far surpassing Peder's expectations. True to Zuzanna's prediction, the art had been simply exceptional. Exotic, to be sure, but undeniably good. This became obvious to him in hindsight when he considered how there was

245

roughly a quadrillion times more Lontan art than Human art. Within such a colossal oeuvre, there was bound to be enough Human-like art to out-mass Human history itself, so all the Lontans had to do was sort out whatever was suitable.

It turned out that every Terran aesthetic period was mirrored by hundreds of alien cognates: the Lontans had their own Renaissance and Baroque and Impressionist periods, and each with their own titans to set against Michelangelo and Rembrandt and Van Gogh. While the portraits Peder and Zuzanna saw were all of grey-skinned, four-limbed Lontans, and the landscapes only rarely donned Earth-like color schemes, their underlying value was always striking.

And the Museum was more than just an alien Louvre, as it also hosted full-sim walk-throughs of famous galactic landmarks. Peder and Zuzanna spent hours strolling through everforests, world canyons, and Möbius oceans, with their senses offered a million xenoteric delights.

Over the course of the evening they ended up perusing only a small fraction of the exhibit space, and Peder was sad to be going. But he was also elated and xenophilic. He would have given anything to be out in the real galaxy just then, not just viewing it through these simulacra. Only a few hundred Humans had ever visited that great beyond, and they had all been world leaders, dignitaries, and Nobel laureates taken on a free tour by the Lontans. But Peder, too, wanted to know the true face of the future.

That was the great question that always loomed over the modern age: 'What will tomorrow be like?' And it was a new question, because, in the past, there had been nothing like the modern concept of the future. For most of Human history, progress had taken centuries to accumulate, and life had stayed fundamentally unchanged from generation to generation.

But now the only constant was change, and the only law was that the change was accelerating. — And this had only been the first two centuries after the industrial revolution. Now Humans lived on different planets, space elevators planted the horizon, Jupiter had been ignited into a star called Jove, and the only safe assumption going forward was that all bets were off. They were spiraling out into undreamed fantasy, and yet the future *would* have a face. Even if it were a whirlwind that changed from second to second. And Peder wanted his glimpse.

He wondered why the Museum did not have the same effect on more people. Why it did not shake them out of their malaise, rekindle their excitement, and get them to put their shoulders back to the mill, at last ending the depression. There was so much out there and they only had to reach for it.

They exited the Museum and strolled to the valet parking lot at the edge of the platform. The view offered a stunning vision of nighttime Stockholm, with the Museum's elevation giving them an aerial perspective on it. The city floor was a thick carpet of light, broken only by the waters of Lake Mälaren that carved the city into an

247

archipelago. Pyre-bright arcologies and high-rises stood lording over the expanse, circled by the firefly sparks of the city's air traffic. Peder found himself attaching a museum-style placard to the sight: 'Human city, Earth, c. 21st century.' The Museum had contained many such panoramas of various civilizations throughout their development, and with pride Peder thought that this vista would not be out of place in the 'Human Wing' of another Lontan museum on another first contact planet.

Though the view did hold one eyesore. There was one arcology that was not lit up at all, visible only as a black silhouette stolen out of the city's nightscape—a kilometer-high tombstone. Peder knew its story: finished at an inauspicious time just after the Singularity, the arcology had lost all of its tenants in a few months and quickly found itself taken over by squatters, gangs, and homeless. It was the grim first in a phenomenon that was being observed the world over. Poverty arcos.

And on that note, Peder realized why the Museum had no stimulant effect as he had imagined. It was because the depression was too lived-in. If they were already putting out the lights in the arcologies, then the Human race must feel it had been left behind.

With First Contact, the Lontans had come promising endless space and limitless technology, and Humanity had accepted the bargain. And, for the first forty years, it looked as if the aliens had kept their word. The exponential growth had been relentless and resplendent. Occasionally perforated by the minor bubble, of course, but those curtailed shocks assured them that that would be all the sting that tragedy would have in the modern age: a return of 6% instead 10, and the slack more than made up for by next year. The stars—and the paradise they represented—had seemed so close. They were living beyond their means and gliding in a dream.

But it was that very complacency that had so magnified the shock of the Singularity, because it was every deferred bubble piling up at once. And the worst part was that the disaster had been caused by the progress they had so blindly followed. A city was destroyed and the only explanation they had in hand was that there had been 'too much technology' in 'too unstable a configuration.' Which meant that every other city hovered under the same unpredictable threat, and it would inevitably happen again. So not only had the stars proved distant and hazardous, but now what they promised to bring— far from paradise—was but more of the same outrageous catastrophe.

To pull through this they needed to rely on their inner strength, but that was precisely what all the decades of excess had shorn them of. They were here not just because of one, brief catastrophe but because of all the soft years beforehand that had gradually unfitted them for these struggles. That was why, when the future had suddenly no longer glittered gold, their reaction had been the death instinct. The depression.

And Peder admitted that this was a natural response. For there was a fatal allure in how easy it was to surrender to the tide. To love the idea that it was better to die by one's own hand now, than slowly by the million, trillion unnatural shocks their future had become heir to.

Before, Peder had seen the Museum as a wondrous showcase of all that was within reach. But it took only a small change of perspective to see it instead as dangling over them glimpses of their once promised but now unreachable future. No longer a lavish invitation but a gaudy display of exemption.

When their limousine pulled up, Peder was at least consoled to think of spending the rest of the evening with Zuzanna. He opened the door for her, but then—

"Oh, I'm sorry, Peder, but I'll have to be heading home," she interjected. "I have a big meeting tomorrow that I need to prepare for. But you have a good night!" She squeezed his hand quickly and was off, heading towards the cabstand.

Peder stood behind, bewildered. Under normal circumstances, he would have read this clearly as his being cut. But, in the context of their Mafia job, he knew that Zuzanna had squeezed his hand so as to deposit a nanocapsule there that would contain a canned report, which would tell him everything he needed to know. Since nothing had to be discussed face-to-face, it meant that the Mafia considered his Atkins/Lindon contract finished.

Zuzanna had already turned around and was walking away, that he had not had a chance to take a last look at her should they never meet again.

Chapter 26 - Arrears

Once back in his ASAPR, Peder extracted the capsule and decoded the report. It included a holo recording, and, activating it, he saw Zuzanna materialize before him.

"Sorry for the surprise, Peder. I wasn't expecting this to be our final report any more than you were, but ... " she shrugged. "That's how it worked out. Af—"

Peder paused the recording to check its length. Only ten minutes. He was incredulous that everything would be explained to him so quickly.

"After our last meeting," continued the unpaused Zuzanna, "we put together a raid that would answer the questions we had about Lindon's prototype augspace system. We carried out this raid successfully, but ... " she made an open-handed gesture, "it turned out to be worth very little.

"For one, we discovered where the remote hypercomp center is. We got a snapshot of the company's data traffic and saw a huge channel going back and forth to Stockholm with about the right info density that this system would need. Only problem was the source of it was Oslo. Which means this augspace system is located inside the corporate army's superbase there, the Bunker.

"This location was obvious to us in retrospect. We've never been able to get full blueprints of the Bunker, but we do know that it's massive enough to house such a hypercomp facility. Perhaps even without the base's soldiers knowing it's there. And

Oslo's also perfect from the security standpoint. The city's controlled by Lindon's personal military, so there's no way for anyone to secret their way in. Not even us."

Peder could not fault the Mafia for saying that Oslo was impenetrable. Even he, who supposedly 'commanded' several hundred men stationed in the Bunker, had no way of getting one unauthorized electron in or out.

"And as for the ghosts?" said Zuzanna. "Well, it turns out that they're all personality fronts." A ream of financial information appeared beside her, and she walked Peder through an example with an employee named Joakim Ivarson.

"The man's salary is 78,000, and at the end of the year Lindon takes out his withholding, covers his corporate housing and livelihood, and pays his share of employer taxes. Mister Ivarson pays his own taxes, and so the Skatteverket is satisfied. But Ivarson himself receives nothing else. Lindon's payroll system holds no disbursements to him for his net salary."

This was a sure sign of a personality front: Lindon was paying all the taxes to satisfy the government of this 'Ivarson's existence, but the identity was really an invention being used by someone else as a cover. Typically someone whom it would be illegal or unethical to hire outright, such as an industrial spy or a hacker with a criminal record.

"And, with all the data going back and forth from Oslo," Zuzanna continued, "it stands to reason that the people running Ivarson and all the other personality fronts are located there. Which means we can't get to them. And we don't even know any of their real names. So there's no way of turning any of them into sources on this system.

"That's why the job's over. We've found out what we could about this prototype system, but we've also found out there's nothing else to do.

"And one last thing ... " she said with a troubling turn. "You can tell that our raid recovered a lot of financial information. And from this we were able to piece together a significant discovery. Everyone was wondering how Lindon could finance such gargantuan projects during the depression. First the salvage operations in Oslo, then his corporate army, then the Bunker ... The company was showing explosive profits in some areas, but it was still a stretch. How could it sustain all of this?

"Well, we've found the answer is it *can't*." Another glut of charts and spreadsheets appeared beside her. "The Spire isn't just 'in debt'—it is debt incarnate. The amounts are preposterous, but Lindon's kept it hidden by juggling his loans between hundreds of creditors and thousands of aliases. He was actually doing a superb job of this ... " she turned and looked wistfully at the spreadsheets. "But it looks like the charade will finally fall apart next month. A couple big loans come up in August and Lindon simply won't have the cash to cover them—nor even to keep the creditors quiet. Once that leaks out, it won't take long for everyone to realize that the company's insolvent."

253

So far Peder had accepted everything Zuzanna had said, but he balked at this—Lindon Securities going bankrupt? Impossible. He paused Zuzanna's holo and began sifting through the numbers himself. He checked the investment histories and portfolios, he flipped through every promissory note, scanning the dates, signatures, and amounts ... In awe he found himself retracing Lindon's astounding juggling of the debt. The man had been keeping an army of creditors in double-blind confusion, using every financial institution from the First Bank of Switzerland to the Martian Credit Union like the stacked bricks in a fantastic pyramid scheme. Whenever one of them became frustrated and started handing down ultimatums, Lindon would throw some last-second cash together, or just procure a different loan through a front company, so his debts looked good and no one was the wiser. But it was a plate-spinning act that spanned the entire solar economy, and everything was synchronized to fail in cataclysmic unison.

In the end Peder slumped back in his chair, dumbstruck. What Zuzanna had said was true, and that meant that a sizable chunk of the European economy was about to disappear—and cause a shock that might even measure up against the Singularity Crash itself.

He un-paused Zuzanna's holo:

"At least," she continued, "this explains why Lindon hasn't gone public with the augspace system. At this point it wouldn't matter. Sure, it would kick up a few hundred million in investment instantly, but they're in debt billions—*hundreds* of billions—by now. No way to dig themselves out.

"So there looks to be no way for us to turn any great profit out of this augspace system. The only thing left for us is to place the mother of all put options on Lindon's stock and clean up after the crash in August. That's what my bosses are doing—some windfall calibrated for the millions. And out of that, you—as a senior investor—will get your share.

"Now ... where does this leave the original investigation you contracted into Atkins? Well, both you and he are going to be out of your jobs in a month, so do you really need blackmail material on him anymore? Your original objective is moot. And there's also nothing more we can find out about the augspace prototype. All that's left is the put option.

"We also believe that it's time to back off," she added delicately. "This investigation has been high-profile for us, and at times it's even brought us close to the *ISSO*." Like anyone connected with organized crime, Zuzanna would only whisper those four letters. "Of course it's now obvious why they'd be looking into Lindon's company. But the potential Lontan scrutiny attached to that we find ... off-putting."

After a few more apologetic sentences, Zuzanna's image shimmered away. The report was finished.

Peder stayed sitting a long time, aghast. He flipped back through the numbers, looking for any way to disbelieve, but the deductions were irrefutable. Lindon had killed the company—and for

255

what? A private army, a fortified base, and some sleeper projects that had driven them to bankruptcy. Peder had often worried about what designs Lindon had for his army, but now it did not matter. No James Bond would need to storm the company's secret base and thwart its evil plans, because an army of irate creditors was about to dismantle it all far more thoroughly than any secret agent's slapdash destruction could accomplish.

Back at the Museum, Peder had been struck by the disquieting thought that Humanity no longer had a future. Now he had to add to that the far more destitute knowledge that, with his company about to collapse spectacularly, he had even less of one.

Chapter 27 - Poisoned Pawn

Erlend and Märtha were in one of the base's hovertank garages. The tank they stood before was damaged along its port wing, whose leading edge was marked by a dozen fist-sized dimples. Their shapes were swept backwards in teardrop forms, as if the tank had been hit by dollops of hyper-puissant acid rain. Erlend had given Märtha a jar of grey goo and a spatula and instructed her to spackle over the holes. Whenever she scraped a helping of the nanite goo off into the dimples, the material would slythe over the bowl and grow the surface back outwards. Once it had re-formed the original shape, it hardened and blended in perfectly with the existing body.

"Good ... " said Erlend, watching her progress. Though this was the most elaborate praise he could offer—spackling was perhaps no more difficult than eating cereal.

"What exactly are these dimples I'm filling?" Märtha asked.

"This tank took some fire on our last mission. All these tanks are repair cases," he motioned around the garage.

"You mean bullets did *that?*" Märtha balked, pointed at the wing.

"Nanorounds, yes. Didn't they teach this stuff in school?"

"Well, sort of ... We started covering nano in my science classes back in Oslo, but then ... the *Singularity*," she dropped her voice duly. "When my grandfather took me to Steigen, it was like the teacher there hadn't even heard of evolution."

Erlend grunted. "Well, the way it works is the tank has a macromolecular body—which just means it's stupidly, unimaginably strong. So, if it gets hit by plain bullets, they just glance off. The tank takes a global change in momentum—thanks to Newton's Third Law—, but it's far too strong to take any local damage. So anti-armor bullets nowadays are really just wads of catalytic nanomachines. They splash onto the skin and start eating through the body atom by atom, hence the dimples."

"But then ... why didn't they eat through the whole wing?" she asked.

"The tank skin has its own defensive nanites sewn into it. Most of the time they fight off the invaders and keep the damage to just lost mass—like with these hits. But then we have to go and patch them afterwards. Hence your job."

Märtha finally nodded with total understanding.

"So take care of the rest of the tanks in here, then call it a day. We actually have all the patch jobs highlighted in an augspace pane somewhere—I'll ask Liljedal to send it to you."

"That's fine. Though ... when you said you were going to teach me some tank maintenance, I thought it would be a little more ... *involved* than this."

Erlend shrugged. "Hell, I thought repairing battle damage would be a lot sexier than doing plain grease monkey work."

"True. But still ... "

Erlend wavered, but ended up saying, "Fine. Next time I get a chance, we'll crack open one of these things and do some real surgery. But it'll have to be next week, though. I'm going out on a long mission soon."

Märtha smiled thanks, and Erlend turned away.

She interjected, "—Or maybe you could ask Hanssen to show me how? ... "

Before turning back, Erlend flashed a wry grin off into space, as if he were soliciting the sympathy of an unseen audience. Märtha probably thought she had been amazingly subtle with her 'ask after Hanssen' bit.

"Well, *Colonel* Hanssen is a busy man," Erlend replied, turning back. "Even more so than me."

Märtha wondered at his emphasis on 'Colonel.' "Still ... I haven't gotten to see him at all lately."

Erlend stifled a sigh. He had been trying to wean Märtha off of her Hanssen infatuation, but by now he had long ago exhausted the slow approach and was thinking it was time to employ some honest demolition. Yet here he restrained himself and said only,

"Yeah, but the Colonel is second-in-command, you realize. And we're still in the middle of fighting a war? ... These tank hits I'm having you patch weren't just picked up from target practice, dear."

"I know that ... " Märtha squirmed.

Erlend could have left it at that, but instead he asked, "Why are you so interested in the Colonel anyway?" Of course he knew the answer; he just wanted the pleasure of watching this spoony teenager attempt to dissemble.

259

"—Oh. Well ... —Hanssen saved me and my grandfather, you know. Of course I'd like to spend some more time with him."

While this was a plausible answer, Märtha's stuttering delivery showed that she had probably first thought to say, "My undying love for him!"

"Hell, *Colonel* Hanssen's saved my life a dozen times," said Erlend, "but you don't see me taking him out to dinner or anything."

Märtha blushed. But then, hoping to seize the offensive, she asked, "Why do keep calling him '*Colonel* Hanssen,' anyway?"

Erlend cast another glance off into space. "Because I'm trying to insinuate that that's what *you* should be calling him."

"... Really?"

"He's been your superior officer for two months now. You may just be an intern, but he still gives you orders. ... And, if all that weren't enough, the fact that he's twice your age shoulda tipped you off to the asymmetrical power dynamic."

Märtha ratcheted back into a defiant posture. "Fine. '*Colonel*' Hanssen. Thank you for informing me, *Lieutenant* Erlend," she said haughtily.

Erlend gestured as if tipping his hat, and finally turned away. Though he was mentally scheduling when he would perform his intervention on Märtha. He sympathized with Hanssen, who was nearly uncomfortable walking around his own base now. Hanssen had even had to become almost inquisitive in keeping up with Erlend and Kitano on what they had Märtha doing on any given day, just so that he could be safely elsewhere.

260

Chapter 28 - Suspicion

For the first time Willoch charged into the Ambassador's office without pausing to adjust her appearance outside. She was mad as hell—here to kill—the phrase 'pounds of flesh' was stubbornly on her mind.

"Good evening, Admiral," the Ambassador received her hurriedly. "—And may I say at once how distressed I am by the necessity of this meeting."

"Ambassador," she gave an icy reply.

"I did not consider it a serious possibility that the Hezokeen would seize *all* of the ships you sent in the tithing attempt. As I said, we might have expected one or two to be taken. At most three, but—"

"Ten out of ten," Willoch said, a little glibly. The report had just come through from the Lontan Governate that all the tithing ships had been seized. Willoch had asked for an immediate meeting with the Ambassador and had been accepted. But even if it had been turned down she still would have stormed his office.

"Let me assure you that the Lontan Governate will absorb the cost of the lost freighters," said the Ambassador. "It was my advice that led you down this unfortunate path, and we insist that we simply waive the losses."

"That is ... gracious," Willoch tried.

But in her mind she was reciting what Laiidjokun had warned: that the Lontan

Ambassador had sold out the Earth's location to the Hezokeen himself. That theory had found her incredulous at first, but now she was giving it more than an agnostic's entertainment. The Hezokeen seizing their entire tithing attempt meant that it had only been a foolhardy idea to begin with. Perhaps the Ambassador had talked them into it solely because he was set to receive his own 'tithe' on whatever the Hezokeen stole. Willoch's poisoned trust of the Lontans was fast becoming active suspicion.

It was almost odd for her to look at him now ... She had once believed the Lontans to be all-powerful but benevolent. Despite the utter unknowability of an alien mind, she had willed herself to believe that they served honestly as the guardians of Humanity. Yet now here sat one of those guardians who had betrayed her entire species for personal monetary gain. No matter how 'unknowable' aliens might be, they were apparently not exempt from sharing Humanity's basest vices.

"As I said," the Ambassador continued uneasily, "pirates are business-like, professional—... e-evolved even ... " He was almost stammering.

This was the first time Willoch had seen the Ambassador out of sorts, and she realized she might have been over-severe so far. She reminded herself that she was here with a purpose, not just to dynamite bridges.

"Excuse me if I have seemed ... abrupt so far, Ambassador," she said calmly. "You may have recommended this tithing to us, but I helped sell it to our leaders. I take this as a personal

262

embarrassment. ... But I apologize if that has soured my mood."

The Ambassador nodded, and he quickly recomposed himself.

—Though so quickly that it made Willoch suspect that she had just watched a performance.

She knew that the Lontans did not really need to wear bodies. Their brains were all hosted on some noetic hardware on the Embassy, and they merely dialed down into whatever mannequins they wished to animate. But that meant their host bodies should never display an emotion unless their conscious thoughts willed it so. A Human's facial expression might be inextricably tied to the neuro-chemical feedback loops bubbling over in their cerebellum, but the Ambassador's avatar should not have appeared flustered unless he let it be 'rendered' on the mannequin. But Willoch was dubious that this millennia-old alien consciousness could be reduced to stammering.

Of course, even if he were acting, it might have simply been another attempt to appear more Human and to keep an authentic feeling of interaction between them. But it might also have been meant to deceive.

"So, Ambassador ... " Willoch began afresh, trying to mask her thoughts. "Obviously we're concerned about what this means. These pirates are certainly not the breed you expected, so who are we really up against?"

"Indeed," said the Ambassador, now back to his usual ease. "And I must stress what little sense their actions make. If they had tithed you, they would have received much more in the long run—and far more easily. But now they have left you no choice but military retaliation."

"Then they must think they can get more out of us with an all-out attack?"

"Unlikely, as your system is still not advanced enough. The most they could come away with are raw materials, but most systems possess those in similar abundance. And yours is protected by Lontan warships and defenses. Even though the pirates outnumber you, they would abhor the cost of overpowering you in an engagement."

Willoch nodded favorably. Even though the Ambassador may have contrived this entire situation, at least he was offering sound advice. ... Of course that tithing idea had seemed 'sound' itself at the time.

"Perhaps they took your actions," he continued, "—the *immediate* seeking of a tithe—as a sign of weakness. So they stole your entire first cargo shipment as a lesson. To suggest that you are unworthy of such accommodation. But, now that they have made their point, they might be amenable to—"

"You're not suggesting that we try tithing again," Willoch interrupted. It was not a question.

And was that the first time she had ever interrupted him? she wondered.

"No, no, of course not," the Ambassador conceded. "I can see why that would be impossible for you. I was only trying to analyze the Hezokeen's actions. And, even if you tried a second round of tithe ships, I admit that they would likely all be seized again."

"Do you have any other explanations for how the Hezokeen have acted?"

The Ambassador 'sighed.' "None."

Willoch suppressed a frown. Even if she had no reason to distrust the Lontans, it was just as Laiidjokun and Goldam had said: what good were they anyway? They had helped her species advance for a while, but now they were sitting back while Humanity languished in depression. Even now that they had this real, physical threat hanging over them, their Governor was washing his hands while their Ambassador was padding his bank account.

"Then might I pass by you the response plan the Admirals and I have prepared?" Willoch asked.

"Of course."

She cleared her throat. "We now know something of the Hezokeen's size and strength, but no longer of their location, which seems essential to pin down. Otherwise, we're giving a hostile force free reign with our system. The ability to attack anywhen, anywhere.

"So our plan is to send a detachment of a dozen ships out to the Hezokeen's last-known location. Our ships will reacquire them in stealth, and start weaving a giant sensor grid around them—like an island extension of the Monitoring Lines that surround the solar system. If the Hezokeen make any move out of that pocket, we'll have a heads-up. We won't have much ability to counter them *after* that, of course, but this will be our way of telling them that we're still here, that we have a military, and that we're not afraid to use it. If they don't like the prospect of having to punch through our fleet—as you said—, then the least we can do is show them that, whatever they try, we *will* be in their way."

The Ambassador was nodding—not Lontan-nodding, but bobbing his head in imitation of the Human fashion. "Yes, that is the right response," he said.

"No recommendations?"

"None. Except to send your ships as soon as possible."

***

Back in her office Willoch was assembling orders, but she was still in a foul mood. On top of the failed tithing attempt, she had also recently come to a conclusion on her supposed connection between Ambassador Laiidjokun and Hyram Goldam. The truth had turned out to be mundane. She had checked the Zaichi Ambassador's itinerary and found that he had visited Mars and dozens of other places while campaigning for Zaichi interests. Goldam's anti-Lontan sentiments would have made him a natural ally for him to approach, and they had actually met half a dozen times, most recently only a month ago. So there was nothing sinister in Goldam having used Laiidjokun's words. It only meant that an alien ambassador was doing some effective canvassing.

But, while this had quelled Willoch's worst suspicions, it had also had a disquieting side effect. Back when Laiidjokun had come to her in confidence at the concert, Willoch had felt he was making a bold move. Here was an alien—one of the gods themselves—who was defying Lontan hegemony to come to Humanity's aid. One who spoke out against their crooked doctrines and dared to shine a light on their shady dealings. And, most importantly, Willoch had assumed that he had approached no one but her, and that had given him the air of an informant.

Yet now it seemed that Laiidjokun had only been bruiting those same sentiments all over the system, in places as insignificant as Olympia, and to people as irrelevant as Hyram Goldam. The words she had imagined as a prize for her alone were but junk mail, and she was merely one of the more credulous recipients.

Willoch had felt this as a betrayal. Back when Laiidjokun had infected her with her first doubts of the Lontans, she had naturally been compelled to trust him instead. For a time she had even imagined that the Zaichi and the other species were Humanity's secret allies, knitted into a cabal resistant to Lontan dominion.

But now it seemed that Laiidjokun had only been manipulating her, feeding her his customary talking points, and trying to lure her into their camp. So he was obviously not someone she could trust. And yet neither could she run back to her old faith in the Lontans. So there was really no aid for them to reach out to. No true friends among the other species but only enemies of enemies.

Willoch's thoughts turned back to her meeting with the Lontan Ambassador some weeks ago, where he had first told them to deal with the pirates themselves. At the time she had been thrilled to accept the challenge, but that reaction now struck her as foolishly naive. Back then she had been gazing on the world through a dozen rosy preconceptions—Lontan benevolence; the goodwill of the other species; there being plenty of time for Humanity to grow and learn ... Now, with those preconceptions shattered, everything was framed by their jagged edges, and for the first time she was looking on a vicious and conniving universe.

Every species was prodding Humanity in some direction, but all for their own gain, and without the slightest concern for the newfound species. Willoch could not guess at what high-stakes game they were playing, but it was clear that Humanity's life or death was already part of the wager—and maybe even had just been the ante.

Chapter 29 - Philosophy

Leaving the kitchenette, Townsend was met by Agents Laake and Mosely—two of the local Sweden ISSO agents they were working with.

"'Morning," said Townsend.

"'Morning," Laake replied. "So what do you think about those Hezokeen guys turning out to be dipshits?" he proceeded immediately.

"Sorry?" Townsend asked.

"You know, this 'tithing' bullshit the leaders tried? That backfired? ... The Hez bastards grabbed all our ships and are picking their teeth on the cargo?"

"Oh," he recalled. Laake often started his conversations a sentence or so too far in for Townsend to follow him immediately. He seemed absorbed in a perpetual internal monologue that only prevailed on the outside world as an occasional sounding board. "Well, I always figured the Hezokeen were dipshits to begin with," answered Townsend, "so they're just hitting par for the course as far as I'm concerned."

"Ah. Well, I'm glad," said Laake. "Because, otherwise, this Operation Mal Voisin wasn't going anywhere. I was afraid they were gonna start scaling it back. And the *last* thing I want is to go back to the shit I was doing last month."

"Hear! Hear!" added Mosely.

Townsend grumbled affirmatively.

They started walking back to their office.

"So you see that new film that came out?" Laake asked on the way. "*From Lontus with Love*?"

"No," said Townsend. "Any good?"

"Well, yeah, it's hilarious. But you shouldn't see it—it'll just make you depressed about our job. Made *me* depressed about it."

"How so?"

Laake shot him a blank look. "You *do* know what it's about, right?"

"Um ... some sort of spy thing?" Townsend said dumbly.

Laake sighed. "It's a comedy. About a Lontan secret agent who comes down here in a skinjob to fight alien intelligence wars. ... You get it? That's *Zhang*. We're *working* with that. And yet it's so much more boring in real life ... "

"Most things are."

"Yeah ... " added Mosely.

"—Oh, speak of the devil," said Laake, as Zhang rounded the corner and joined their group.

"Good morning, agents," Zhang said trimly. The mannequin slept who knew where, but he was always on time for work, starched and pressed.

"Hey, Zhang," Mosely greeted him. "*You* seen *From Lontus with Love*? —Errr, wait, look who I'm talking to ... " he caught himself. Whatever the mannequin did in his spare time, it was certainly not going to movies.

But Zhang paused for a beat, then replied, "Now I have. Did you have any specific questions about it?"

The three agents glanced at each other.

"Hey, what was that shit you pulled just there?" Mosely asked. "—I mean, obviously you just zipped through the film in fast-time, but I hope you didn't download a bootleg copy to do it. That shit's illegal, you know."

Mosely did not really care about copyright infringement—which to him was as arcane a legal entitlement as *prima noctis*. He was only trying to rattle the Lontan.

"Of course not," Zhang replied. "The Lontan Governate purchased and downloaded a legal copy of the film for my perusal once you brought it up."

"Oh," Mosely shrugged, defeated.

But, "Waaaiiit ... " said Laake. "The Lontan Governate just bought a copy of the film? ... You guys pitched ten credits into the Terran economy, just like that?"

"Yes."

He balked. "Then I got a question, Zhang. Your Governor is always making speeches about helping us out of this depression, right? Hell, that's where 'credits' came from, isn't it? It's some Lontan-stabilized reserve currency we use now that all the old ones were killed by inflation. But, if you really wanted to revive our economy—and like that—" he snapped his fingers, "why not pitch in like you just did but on a bigger scale? You Lontans probably have the spare change to start buying up shit from all over the place."

"That is true," said Zhang.

"Then why don't you?"

"The answer is quite involved."

"Oh, I'm a big boy."

271

"Very well." Zhang drew a deep breath. "The first, most obvious reason is that we Lontans simply have no use for current Human exports, and so our purchases would constitute nothing more than charity masquerading as economic stimulus. And this would not be encouraging true economic growth but rather only propping up certain sectors. This would eventually require either withdrawing our support—causing a crash of the inflated markets—, or leaving the Human economy sempiternally dependent on us insofar as we indulge you in buying goods we have no use for.

"The greater reason, however, is that such a program would also start a dangerous chain reaction. Any program that involves substantial Lontan assistance would incur accusations of favoritism—no matter how well-managed and egalitarian was our approach. People would denounce us for showing preference to one country over another, or one economic sector over another. And this resentment would actually drive us deeper into interventionism. We may begin by acquiring only export items—which is perhaps an innocuous form of stimulus—, but an export-poor country may argue that this policy leaves it as a disadvantage. In compensation it may demand direct Lontan investment in amounts equal to what other countries are being assisted with in exports. This would open the door to alien ownership of Human companies and property. Then, if our management were shown to be beneficial, other Human corporations would be pressured to follow suit, lobbying for Lontan ownership, if only to keep from being left behind.

"This would begin an inexorable march towards an increasing Lontan stake in the Human economy, eventually culminating in perhaps outright monopolization thereof. Such an outcome is anathema from a first contact perspective, as our mission is to modernize Humanity while keeping it an independent culture. And even you, Agent Laake, must admit that that would be disagreeable simply from the standpoint of Human pride."

In the course of this speech, the agents had arrived at their office, but they had stayed hovering outside.

"Uhhhh ... " said Laake, who looked to be still digesting words somewhere back around 'sempiternally.'

"Listen to this guy," Mosely interjected. "Like we got the Lontan Governor himself among us."

"The argument I just related is actually one of the Governate's standards," Zhang replied.

The three Humans looked between each other. 'Governate-standard arguments' ...

"Well, let's get to work," said Townsend, at last turning them into their office. "You guys saw that flash from the Chief this morning?"

"Uh ... " Laake slurred.

Townsend sighed. "What he said is the situation's heating up. With the Hezokeen seizing our convoy, the fleets will be sending out another wave of warships soon. And, the next time we run into each other, we may just start shooting. Finding the Hezokeen agents planet-side is getting more important by the minute. So let's actually start earning our pay."

Chapter 30 - Presumptuous Ewokistry

Mohr's six-tank unit pitched and banked between the hillsides. The surrounding slopes formed a great 'v,' at the trough of which ran the highway—in the place of where a river would have flowed had nature had its say. Mohr's flight was the vanguard for one of the corporate army's supply convoys, this one consisting of five megatrailers. Its full escort included two tank platoons, a flotilla of anti-air vehicles, and enough firepower to throw a decent war.

And Mohr knew it was all doomed. This convoy was passing through three hundred kilometers of woodland, which left it open to about a thousand opportunities for attack. Their only real defense was secrecy: the fact that the Home Guard should have no idea when their convoy was leaving or where it was going. But in reality the Norwegians seemed to know the corporate army's schedule as thoroughly as if they were being CC'd on all troop movements. So that was it; mission over; convoy lost. Just like the dozens of others that had met fiery ends all over Norway in the last month. Mohr figured they could have saved a lot of money in fuel and escort costs if they had simply sent these convoys out naked and unarmed like Viking sacrifices.

"Contact on the cliff," said one of Mohr's men on the comms. "IR; Human bodies." He highlighted the contacts with red crosshairs in their shared tacspace. Mohr saw two men lying on their bellies atop the cliff. One of them was surveying their tanks through binoculars.

"Spotters. Probably for some highway robbers," Janus observed.

"Out during the day?" asked Bakhtin.

"They're out all the time now."

The other spotter had something pressed to his ear. In an EM visualizing pane, Mohr saw it iris with purple and fuchsia, meaning old-band radio waves.

"He's active on his wireless," said Bakhtin. "He's called us in."

"That was just SOP," said Mohr. "No robbers would be dumb enough to actually attack us."

He said this to reassure the men, but to himself he wondered whether these spotters could be part of the inevitable Home Guard attack. It was rumored that the HG had already teamed up with the ANP, so for them to further ally themselves with highway robbers would actually be a step back towards legitimacy. —And yet this, Mohr knew, was exactly why the convoy was doomed. Even if he was right and had seen this threat coming, he could still do nothing about it. This juggernaut could not be steered clear, and he could only continue escorting the prey into whatever ambush fate had laid.

A minute later they were rounding a bend in the road—when a chorus of master alarms shrieked into their ears. The tactical computers told them to break high and wide, and the autopilots even seized control of the tanks themselves if their Human pilots proved too sluggish.

Mohr saw the source of the alarms: their sensors had detected a bomb buried under the highway. It was large enough to incinerate the lead megatrailer of their convoy and leave a crater that would consume the rest.

Mohr thought this was a silly move. In order to hide a bomb from the corporate army's sensors, it would have to be buried so far down that, when it exploded, it would hardly make the road burp. Mohr had expected more from the Home Guard ...

"Captain Mohr, status!" yelled Major Klein from back with the convoy. He had received echoes of their master alarms.

"Sir, we've detected a bomb in the road, sized to kill the convoy," Mohr replied in adrenaline-accelerated speech.

"Take care of it," Klein barked back, as unconcerned as if Mohr had only announced an abandoned ox cart. "We're slowing the megas to seventy percent. You have two minutes."

The convoy's megatrailers could not stop in the middle of these woodlands, as doing so would make them easy prey for even a lone Ewok with an RPG. Mohr's vanguard had to clear all obstacles so that the convoy could barrel through undeterred.

"Clear out and ready your nanopave," Mohr said to his group. "Bakhtin, touch off the bomb with a grep."

Lieutenant Janus—Mohr's pilot—gunned their thrust and took them up to the top of the hill. Bakhtin's tank swooped low over the highway and dropped off a Ground Penetration Round. The grep began chewing through the asphalt down to the

276

explosives cache. Mohr counted three ... two ... one ...

—And the 'zero' was provided by the nuclear-loud combustion of the bomb load. Flames leapt out exuberant and debris hailed over the hillside. With smoke blanketing the area, Mohr used his tank's sensors to survey the ground. In place of the explosives cache was now a fifteen-meter crater where the road had been erased from the earth.

"Tanks one and two, cover," Mohr ordered. "All the rest, rebuild the road."

Four tanks lined up before the crater. The first surged forward, opened its ventral doors, and dropped a dozen grapefruit-sized pellets before the rim. These burst with hyperactive quicksilver that seeped up to the crater's edge. The sludge interfaced with the tanks' 3-D scans of the area and diagnosed the repairs that had to be made. It dug a molecular foothold into the ground and began extending itself into a shelf that reached out three meters over the gap.

The second tank charged forward and dropped a reinforcing group of pellets. Their quicksilver merged with the old and sped the construction's advance. With this second dose the makeshift bridge now spanned over half the crater's length.

Mohr found it odd to see a bridge building itself supportlessly from end to end like this. He had to remind himself that the shelf—being nanoconstructed—would weigh only grams and be far stronger than plazsteel, and so could easily support the megatrailers. Despite having 'grown up' with nanotechnology, Mohr still found its

277

superlatives strengths counterintuitive. But maybe his hypothetical children—or grandchildren—would at last find it commonplace.

Once the last two tanks had dropped their pellets, the bridge was complete. Its hasty construction left it boiling with steam, which added to the general smoke and haze still belching from the bomb crater. Mohr flashed a 'road clear' back to Major Klein.

From around the bend came the six tanks of the mid guard group. Their leader, Captain Davies, signaled Mohr: "We'll take the fore position. You guys fill in mid guard."

Davies's tanks had to race ahead to make up the lead that had been lost by Mohr in ironing out the bomb. Mohr signaled to his men and their tanks formed back up, heading out along their old course.

They were only ten seconds down the road when their master alarms erupted again.

"Fuck!—Contacts! We got contacts!" yelled Scheele.

Fifty Home Guard tanks—an overwhelming force—had popped up from behind the hills on both sides of the road, three hundred meters distant. The convoy was surrounded, in a dictionary sense, but ...

That was all. The Home Guard units were sitting still.

"All tanks, fall back to the convoy!" yelled Major Klein. "We're maintaining speed! Cover us as we cut through!"

Mohr's group executed wing-tip turns and charged back.

They had just returned to the crater site when they saw an unexpected addition to the scene.

"Uhhh ... " Mohr said on the comms. "—*Logs*. We got logs, sir."

"The fuck you mean '*logs*'?" asked Klein.

"Logs rolling down the mountain," he explained, and he piped him one of their tank's cam feeds. On the bend past the crater there was an avalanche of lumber tumbling down the hill.

"Well—fuck—*shoot* something!" Klein yelled.

Mohr's men obliged. They fired cluster shots of shrapnel and high-fragmentation loads, isotropic explosives and waves of sonic pounders. Their every volley turned great chunks of the logs into matchwood, but it was all too little. The first logs had already reached the road and were spilling across, creating an impassable barrier.

"It's no good!" Mohr called back. "The road won't—"

"Just clear it!"

Mohr's tanks doubled their onslaught even as the squeal of the megatrailers' brakes sounded from around the bend. A final blaze of minigun fire kicked up a blizzard of mulch from the jam, but the logs remained locked tight in the road.

The first mega pierced the crater's haze of smoke, still shrieking on its brakes. Mohr's tank lay precisely in its way, so Janus hit max thrust and lifted them out. Their engine exhaust sent wood chips flying as from a titanic leaf blower gust.

The megatrailer hit the logjam and jounced up as if it meant to fly over the tangle. But it came down only halfway across, jackknifing helplessly.

The other megatrailers managed to stop in time, however, and formed a line behind it.

With their burst of vertical speed, Mohr's tank was carried over the hilltops. They crested just in time to see the Home Guard units launching a stupendous missile salvo—every one of their tanks must have emptied its batteries simultaneously.

"Holy fu—Pack it in around the convoy!" said Klein. "Defenses and interceptors to full!"

Their tanks scrambled into a hasty defensive formation covering the trailers, but they were far too disorganized and outgunned to present a solid defense. The Home Guard missiles came mecca'ing in, dodged the paltry screen of interceptors, and struck home on the megatrailers dozens of times over.

While Mohr's tank was being buffeted by the mushroom clouds and heat blooms, he deciphered what had happened. The bomb they had spotted had been a lure—the Home Guard had hoped they would see it. Because having to deal with a modern bomb would keep them from noticing the other, primitive trap hidden in plain sight, viz. the pile of logs stacked around the bend, primed to roll down the hill and pulverize the convoy. And their advanced alien sensors were tuned to look for only metals and explosives and EM fields, so they were colorblind to a lethal configuration of lumber within lumber. Mohr had derided the possibility of such presumptuous Ewokistry before, but now it had just paid embarrassing dividends.

When his tank stabilized, Mohr saw that the area below had become a sea of flames, with no sign of the trailers. At least there had been no fatalities, as the trailers had only been driven by computer, and none of their own tanks had been downed in the onslaught.

Though perhaps that was even more embarrassing, he thought. The Home Guard had demonstrated that, not only could they blow the corporates' asses out from underneath them, but that they could do so so surgically as to leave the rest of their bodies shamefully intact.

Mohr looked out at the armada of Home Guard tanks, which was now turning around to retire. They had done their damage, so there was no need to belabor the point with a dogfight. They were heading home.

And Mohr said to them, in wry apostrophe, "Good one, Hanssen."

Chapter 31 - Jackpot

Lieutenant Commander Frisch sat in the waiting room of Admiral Willoch's office, passing the minutes by OHUD-reading. Every few pages he looked up and wondered at the delay: Willoch was running late. Of course with any other admiral such a delay might have been expected—and maybe even prerequisite. But Willoch was excessively punctual, so any setback in her schedule was subtly disturbing.

Frisch was finally summoned a few minutes later. He entered her office and stood at attention ... then waited a while longer as Willoch's eyes made the rummaging dance of someone clearing their OHUD desktop. At last she stood and greeted him:

"Good afternoon, Lieutenant—I must apologize for the wait, I've been behind all day. It's very frustrating."

"That's quite all right, ma'am."

"No, it's not. I'm in charge—if I can't stay on top of things, how can anyone else?" she sighed to herself. "But, please ... " she motioned to two armchairs in the center of her office. They took their seats, and Willoch paused to collect her thoughts.

For as long as Frisch had known Willoch, she had always looked fatigued. This was understandable, since her job of maintaining the Royal Norwegian Navy after the Singularity could at best be described as a prolonged act of going down with the ship. The strain of this had shown on her increasingly over the years, and Frisch had had a first-hand view. Even though he was just a lieutenant commander, he was one of the only seven ship captains in the RNN, so he was used to meeting the Admiral face to face.

"So, Commander," Willoch began, "I know you—like all the other skippers—have been busy running combat sims against the Hezokeen."

"You might have started off with 'So, rain was wet today,' ma'am," Frisch joked.

Willoch grinned slightly. Admiral Stennis's reconnaissance mission had been the first extraterrestrial military action in Human history, and every officer was now doing double or triple simulator time to prepare for the next encounter. Even the restricted line officers, who, like distant heirs to a throne, were not qualified to take command of a ship until thousands of more-qualified people above them had all perished.

"By now you must have heard that we're organizing another mission," Willoch continued. "This one will be under the Confederation's Admiral Hadamard. They're going out to establish a sensor picket around the Hezokeen fleet. We're sending a smaller number of ships this time—only a dozen. But I elbowed my way in with the admirals and secured one of those slots for Norway. It calls for a destroyer, and I've selected you and the *Jotunheim* to go for us."

Jackpot! Frisch cawed. This was exactly why he had expected Willoch had called him in. His dream assignment had landed.

"Is your crew up to it?"

283

"Certainly, ma'am," Frisch said confidently. ... But when he saw that Willoch expected more, he embellished with, "You won't find a better destroyer crew in any of the fleets. We trained harder than anyone before this incident, and even since then we've still been outdoing them. You've seen our numbers, that's why you brought me up here. And, above all, we're eager to go."

Willoch nodded. "Of course on paper you're one of the best crews we have. You've performed exceptionally in all of the sims and field exercises. Now, normally calling a crew 'simulator good' carries with it a caveat, but our Lontan simulators provide exactly the same experience as being on one of their ships. There's absolutely no physical difference between the two.

"Except, of course, for what we can never simulate. And that's the reality of it. In every sim we've ever run, all our officers have known that they were just squaring off against a fancy random number generator. And that psychological difference is key. Especially for a crew in the black-water fleet."

She leaned back in her chair and clasped her hands. "You know, I often think that, if we'd known what we do now about Lontan ships back when we were first buying the things, we might have put the entire program under the Air Force instead of the Navy. But back then all we saw were these large, impressive ships, and the fighters and corvettes were all unmanned, so naturally we gave it to the battleship pushers.

"But, when we started training skippers for the black-water navy, it turned out that naval aviators made the best captains by far. And it was because those large Lontan ships—once they were in hyperspace—turned out to be just as fast and as agile as fightercraft. In our early trials we routinely saw one good aviator with a destroyer being able to defeat an entire flotilla commanded by typical fleet skippers. And afterwards those captains just said, 'But things aren't supposed to happen that *fast*.'"

Frisch kept nodding in timed reinforcement to Willoch's speech.

"And that's why piloting a spaceship is so much more stressful. As with fighter combat, it's life or death with every split-second decision. And so there's that much more pressure once everything at last moves outside of the simulator.

"... A lot of officers think Stennis's recon was the fleets' first 'real' mission. But it was nothing. The Hezokeen never came within mid-range missile shot of our ships. All we've gained is a few captains who've *seen* an enemy, but that's it.

"But this mission under Admiral Hadamard *will be* real. We're sending a small group out to find the Hezokeen's main body and stick with them. And it's almost certain that they'll be hostile from the start. This task force will have to deal with constant harassment; react swiftly to strategies designed to destroy them; and they'll have to keep this up for weeks, all while the closest reinforcements are half a day away.

"So you can see why I have to be absolutely sure about whom I send." Willoch finally yielded him the floor.

Frisch paused to organize his response. Willoch may have selected his ship, but this interview meant that the job was not yet his. He had to make a case.

"I know I can't ... sugarcoat it for you, Admiral," he began in earnest. "I can't say not to worry. That, 'I know my men backwards and forwards, they'll hold up, you can count on us.' Because you're right. We've never been through the pressure we'd face out there.

"But ... there's more that sets the *Jotunheim* apart than just our simulator scores and our performance. It's the reason we achieved all of those in the first place. It's because we are a *crew*. A lot of the ships out there are staffed by ... by a bunch of coworkers. They see this as just another job, with the same opportunities for slacking off as anywhere else. I've served in commands with little more discipline than a fraternity house.

"But on my ship, on the *Jotunheim*, we know we're soldiers. We're fighter pilots—as you said, ma'am. We're the type of people who fought the Battle of Britain, and Midway. We're the ones they send on the impossible missions, like landing on the Moon, or flying spy planes over enemy territory.

"So we know that we're here to fight, and to do it for something worthwhile. And we know that our survival depends on each other. And that's why we want to excel—not just to rack up points. But because the only alternative is one day you're in a life-or-death situation, with time to make just one lightning decision, —and you're unprepared."

Frisch was sprinkling his speech with well-timed pauses, gestures, and inhales. Here he stalled and looked down somberly before continuing:

"I can't honestly say whether we'll be able to handle everything that comes at us out there, ma'am. But ... I *can* tell you that, whatever it is ... we'll handle it as a team."

Willoch leaned back and steepled her fingers. Frisch was her best destroyer skipper, and he had just hit a home run with his interview, but it would still be unseemly for her to confirm his appointment without a little show of hesitation.

She rose and extended a hand. "Thank you, Commander. The mission is yours."

"Thank you, Admiral."

"Bring them all back in one piece."

"That I will."

Before dropping their handshake she added, "Make damned sure of it."

Chapter 32 - The Ecstasy of Agitprop

Mohr was sitting at a table in the base's mess, having his lunch. Janus walked over with his own tray.

"'Afternoon," Janus greeted him, sitting down.

"'Afternoon," Mohr replied. He was just taking another bite of steak when he cried, "Aw, fuck!"

"The hell—you bite yourself?" Janus asked.

"No, I just got another EC-2 in my mail ... " Mohr's OHUD desktop had just alerted him to another form to fill out.

"Ah, another one marked 'Please fill out ASAP'?"

Mohr grunted.

"Good, so I'm not the only one. It's been raining forms on me for the last couple of days."

Mohr mumbled distantly—he was already busy whipping through the form's fields and checkboxes.

"You know ... " Janus continued, stirring his mashed potatoes pensively, "I'm thinking maybe this has something to do with that last convoy we lost."

"—Don't remind me," Mohr groaned. "I'm surprised they didn't sack me after that one. Major Klein got reassigned ... "

"Yeah, that was tragic," Janus sarcasmed—he hated Klein. "But, see, the paperwork volume was pretty standard over the last month. Then suddenly after that convoy—BAM! Nothing but forms."

Mohr looked over. "So? You think that means something?"

Janus shrugged. "Well, something like this happened at a company I worked for once. Back before I joined the army."

"Oh?"

"Yeah, we suddenly got all these forms coming in. They were standard ones, but all for old shit. Like someone was trying to fill up the databases— get all the 'null's filled in. Kind of like what we're seeing now. And the reason they needed everything tidied up ... " he paused for suspense, "was because the CEO was preparing for this fucking *blitzkrieg* bankruptcy filing."

Mohr frowned. "You think Lindon's going bankrupt?" His voice dripped incredulity.

"Well ... this *did* start just after we flushed another big wad of money, huh?"

Mohr held to his dubious look.

"Just an idea ... " Janus shrugged innocently, and went back to his food.

Mohr looked off. He had never considered the possibility of Lindon Securities going broke. It violated this core impression he had formed three years ago in Oslo. He had been eating dinner at base, and he had suddenly realized that Lindon Securities could afford to feed him dinner, and two other square meals a day, and put a roof over his head, and give him a hovertank to fly around in, and do the same for five thousand other guys, and all atop the ruins of Oslo, and in the middle of the worst depression in world history. And if all that

289

were true, then the corporation had to have bottomless pockets.

This was the first time Mohr found himself reconsidering. The war with the Home Guard had been running for two months, and all he had ever heard about was convoys being blown up. There were never even any battles; the Home Guard was simply slipping in, exacting tens of millions in damage, and slipping out. The corporate army must already have been expensive enough beforehand, and now they had to be hemorrhaging money ...

He was distracted when someone ran in and shouted, "Hey! Check out local news!"

The men sitting in front of the main holo had been watching a rugby game, but they changed the feed to a local Norwegian plug. Mohr was drawn to look up at the screen when he caught flashes of raging fires and debris. His first impression was of a terrorist attack somewhere, or of massive civil unrest, but then he noticed the situational splash text at the bottom of the screen:

Corporate Army Attack

After a double take, Mohr shunted his paperwork aside and piped the plug directly into his OHUD.

"The hell's this?" said Janus, now watching the feed himself.

The newscasters were saying,

"—buildings were hit. One of the transit department's, a fire station, and several fuel ports. Again, what you're seeing is live. The corporate army tanks first entered Røros only fifteen minutes

290

ago. They've been gone for about ten minutes now, but of course the fires are ... "

"What, Røros?" said Janus. "That's, like ... *here*. It's just thirty klicks away."

"Yeah, but ... our tanks?" said Mohr. "No fucking way."

A new caster interrupted: "—Excuse me, Lars, but we've just received an urgent user submission over our site. This is from a vetted user, A. Hovland, and they've managed to extract freeze frame enhancements from the Rørosers' OHUD vidage. This should give us a better idea of the attackers' identities. Let's put that up on the stream ... "

The feed showed a vid of two tanks flying overhead. Choice frames were highlighted and sharpened, so that the tanks' decal art and names became good enough to read. Seeing them, the entire room groaned.

"Oh my God ... " said one of the casters. "That's terrible! I hope our viewers can see this—we've identified two corporate army tanks. The first one is named the 'Widowmaker' and the next one is the 'Orphanizer'—absolutely terrible!"

"Despicable!" and "Wretched!" chimed in the other casters.

"Oh fuck us," said Janus. "Those tank names— is that *Shabanov's* unit? *His* patrol?"

"Wha—they just left here an hour ago," said another soldier.

"Right. So did *they* do that?"

The screen swelled with new vidage of a building fire. The flames lapped high at the sky, and delayed explosions were sending up more mushroom clouds.

"Fuck!"

"Shit, why couldn't we have sent out the 'Friendly Skies' or the 'Food Drop' this morning ... "

Every few minutes the plug debuted more OHUD vidage, submitted by Rørosers, that showed their first-hand views of the attack. These sequences were filled with stampedes of pedestrians, the roars of tank engines, and explosions erupting in gauntlets forward and behind. The plug cycled through the most popular ones like greatest hits, and it repeated vociferous quotes from city officials, police chiefs, and average citizens, all building up a rhapsody of opprobrium.

While watching, Mohr was maintaining two perspectives. One was the earnest and reverent one that solemnly thought only of the Human tragedy and made all the proper *de rigueur* statements of, 'Our thoughts and prayers are with those in [place] who have lost their loved ones,' etc. The second perspective was a cynical and amoral one that thought only of how screwed the corporate army was by this. Whenever the plug showed more shots of the burning fire station, Mohr paid service to his dual perspective by first thinking, 'Oh, those poor people—and now Røros will be out one badly needed fire station,' before quickly segueing to a, 'Oh, come on, they're *firemen!* Of all the people who'd get a bomb dropped on them, you'd think *they'd* at least be able to handle it. —They probably *let* their station burn down, just for the cameras.'

The main caster returned with a serious look as he started a new topic:

"Since the start of this tragedy we've been looking for what caused it. And online now we have Adeleide Castberg, a security expert from Bergen, who's been following the events. And he thinks he has an explanation for us ... "

The security expert showed up in a sub-picture. He was wearing casual clothes and sitting on a couch. Mohr figured the man was unemployed and spent his days doing freelance news contributions. His moral side was grateful for such a resourceful citizen journalist; his amoral side scoffed at this hippie.

It took a few halting sentences for the caster and Adeleide to establish their rapport. Once the interview began, the man was saying,

"—Yeah, what struck me was how the first building to be hit was one owned by the transit department. Turns out that that's the building that housed the city's air guidance radars. I did some digging and found out that the radars were replaced a couple of years ago. Because of the depression, the city hired a contractor who retrofitted some salvaged Russian CB-12s. The only problem is the CB-12 is an anti-aircraft missile platform. It *can* be used for air guidance because of its high-quality tracking radar, but maybe the corporate army tanks mistook its scans for an attempted weapons lock. And that could explain why ... "

"Wait a minute," said Janus to the room. "Shabanov should never have been in Røros. The guidelines say that Norwegian cities and towns are off limits."

"Right," said one of the men watching the main holo. "But ... I don't know, maybe he got fed up. Wanted to ride in and show the flag."

"And then they were acquired by the CB-12 ... " said another man as they all pieced the incident together.

"And, since no other patrol's ever gone into Røros before ... "

"They thought it was an ambush."

"—And so they shoulda bugged out."

"Right. But instead they do *this*," one man threw out a disgusted hand at the feed.

"Yeah, they commit a fucking war crime ... "

"Total fucking idiots ... "

"Goddamn fucking morons ... " concluded Janus.

It was amazing, Mohr thought, how quickly news of atrocities could spread these days. It no longer took months or years for rumors to leak out, condense into stories, and precipitate investigations. Case in point, Shabanov and his men had not even returned to base yet—they were still out on patrol—and already the details of their handiwork were being cast across the country.

And the story was spreading faster than a net virus. Flipping through the other Norwegian casts, Mohr saw that each had become but a unique veneer of icons and newscasters framing the same shots of billowing smoke, building carnage, and OHUD replays. Each channel had worked up its own biographies of the five Røros dead—*only five?*,

Mohr's amoral perspective caviled—three of whom were firemen. There were collages of the deceased's family photos and vids, graduation shots from the academy, even vids of them responding to past fires and rescuing actual children and puppies in the line of duty. And all overset with tearful words from family and friends. Tallying up those points, Mohr saw they became a direful sum. Few classes of citizens were granted such knee-jerk hagiography as firemen, and here Shabanov had cut down three of them in their prime—and in the lull before the evening news cycle.

With dread Mohr realized that there was nothing standing in the way of the story spreading to Europe as a whole. All of the Continent's latest newsworms were in remission: the Lord Offendene trial was out to jury, the Turkish youths had stopped rioting, the French President was not pregnant, and the Pope was still dead, so what was left? He even checked VizPlay—the world's top sharing site for OHUD captures—and saw that several Røros clips had already cracked the top ten. Mohr knew the only way to drown out the screams from Røros would be for a massive natural disaster to strike somewhere around the world at that moment. But barring that it was far too late—the perfect storm of propaganda had arisen.

The base loudspeaker broadcast an announcement into all of the men's OHUDs:

"Patrol one-five arriving pad C; service personnel to standby."

It was Shabanov's team. They were returning.

The men in the rec room looked at each other with smoldering intent. They flashed with a psychic communion like the crack of a whip, and then bolted out the door, streaming in the direction of the tarmac—Janus included. They would jump Shabanov's men as they deplaned. Only Mohr had stayed behind.

Considering everyone's frustration, Mohr expected it would be a brutal brawl. He pulled several cam feeds from the landing field into his OHUD to give himself a prime spectator's view. Then he set these off to the side in his vision while he resumed his paperwork.

Chapter 33 - Bergen

Through the cockpit, Hanssen saw a line of arcologies resolve in the distance. There were a dozen of them, in a matched design, with their successive heights drawing a parabolic curve. These were the gleaming sentinels that ran along Bergen's central valley, which meant that Norway's *de facto* capital had slipped into view.

As their jet drew nearer, however, the city's grittier details came into resolution. Their approach took them in over the old industrial core of Fana Borough, which every month was looking increasingly like one of the more infamous siege grounds of the Soviet front. Most of the buildings were stripped down, fires blossomed from many barricades and roadblocks, and even from flight they could see the graffiti that delineated the gang territories.

"Humph," said Erlend, examining the view himself. "How are these Bergensers supposed to help us fight the corporates if they can't even clean up their own city?"

Kitano shrugged. "They've done pretty well, considering."

"Oh please, the Singularity was five years ago," Erlend said loudly. "I mean, Leknes may have some slums and some homeless people, sure, but nothing like *this* … "

Kitano gave him another shrug. "So you're saying we should reject their offer? Turn around right now?"

"Not a bad idea. We're kicking the corporates' asses because we're lean and mean, while they're slow and top-heavy. But Bergen's Home Guard is slow, top-heavy, bureaucratic, self-important, *and* already has its hands full. Some allies are more dangerous than any enemy."

Hanssen sighed, listening to Erlend's and Kitano's conversation. On some points he agreed with Erlend, and yet they could not reject Bergen's offer to join the campaign. Leknes's efforts had been successful, but the problem was that they had become too successful. The city government had originally authorized only a short operation—just enough to get public opinion off their back. But after those dazzling initial successes, the public had demanded an unending stream of sensational headlines. The city had had to keep expanding the campaign's budget, but by now Leknes's Home Guard had exhausted its supplies and the city coffers were spent. They needed Bergen's help, even if it was only to open up a money spigot.

Their jet landed, and Hanssen and his staff were met by a retinue of Bergen Home Guardsmen, led by a Major Schulerud. They were driven back to the Ministry of Defence.

Bergen's military infrastructure had been built with some mind towards making it the backup command center in the event that Oslo were ever knocked out or unreachable. Of course they had been living that exact disaster scenario for the last five years, which gave the place much more intrinsic urgency about everything. Compared to Leknes's MinDef, Hanssen thought the people rushing through the corridors here were rushing more, those speaking in hushed tones were hushing more dramatically, and every activity was engaged in to some more-exigent extreme.

They descended to a wing of the Ministry that was safe within ASAPR-level security. There Schulerud presented them to some of Bergen's brass. After the Singularity, generals had piled into Bergen like shipwreck survivors, and so Hanssen was introduced to eighteen of them. Their combined rank totaled an astounding forty-one stars.

Soon arrived Bergen's field commander, Hanssen's opposite number. Schulerud presented him:

"Colonel Hanssen, allow me to introduce Colonel Brechts."

He and Hanssen exchanged salutes, although Brechts purposefully put a lag on his motions so that it looked like Hanssen was saluting him. Everyone in the room took notice of the slight. The Leknes officers balked, and even some of the Bergen officers behind Brechts winced.

">Wait, what just happened?" Kitano secure-texted Erlend.

">Brechts thinks he out-ranks Hanssen," Erlend replied.

Kitano double-checked their insignia. ">But … he does. / Colonel versus Lieutenant Colonel?"

">Yeah, *before* the Singularity he outranked him. / But afterwards each city is like its own country. / All that matters is their job, so they're really equals."

">Oh. / … *Asshole*."

">*Yeah* ... "

"Colonel," Hanssen had said, finishing his salute and extending a hand.

"Lieutenant Colonel," Brechts replied. "We've been following your campaign closely. I'm glad that Bergen has finally decided to join up. I think there's a lot we can bring to it; a lot of improvements we can make."

Hanssen waited a beat. "Oh?"

"Yes, new tactics, a lot of fresh ideas—we'll get the whole thing straightened out. Am I correct in assuming that you've held overall command until now?"

Hanssen read a great deal into that 'until now.' He was about to puncture some lofty hopes:

"Not really, Colonel. In the field I command Leknes's units, Colonel Feiring commands Trondheim's. We have other units that have volunteered from other cities, and they serve with us as convenience dictates. ... The only person that's close to an overall commander is Brigadier Krohg."

Brechts glared back with alarm. "Well ... that may just be the first thing we have to change— having no unified direction and oversight. Plus these very troubling collaborations you've made, most notably with the ANP. You're just asking for travesty to befall the entire operation going on recklessly like that, Lieutenant Colonel."

Hanssen sensed that Brechts was insistently calling him 'Lieutenant Colonel' to try and get him to call him 'sir' in return. So he shrugged and replied,

"I'm sorry that you feel that way, Brechts."

300

Brechts opened his mouth again, but Major Schulerud intervened, saying defusingly, "Wellllll, should we move to the conference room? ... "

Brechts nodded and they moved to the new setting.

***

Waiting in the conference room was Bergen's mayor, Jakob Laurantzson. He was accompanied by a valence of politicos, but even without them the man's identity would have been obvious. With his advanced age and mane of wild, white hair, he looked like a 19th-century naturalist poet who was only stopping through civilization while on the way back to his shed. A fitting look for a man who had taken a city with one foot in anarchy and dragged it back to civilization. Hanssen and the other Leknesers were introduced briefly before all took their seats.

Brechts's aide stood and sent out an officious OHUD document. It was a Bergen operations plan, code-named 'Solstice.' He began a presentation:

"The purpose of Operation Solstice is to bring new organization to the anti–corporate army campaign. So far only two cities have participated: Leknes and Trondheim. Operations up till now have been successful—but sporadic and unfocused. And, despite the amount of damage Lindon has sustained, he still refuses to negotiate.

"But perhaps his intransigence stems specifically from the partisan character of the attacks against him. —An aspect which can only be exacerbated by the Home Guard's cooperation with the ANP. Thus, by centralizing the campaign, and

301

giving it a distinct and visible leader, we'll finally be legitimizing our efforts. Bergen's participation will also give a national stamp to what has so far been only a regional insurrection. This will pave the way not only for more rapid progress on the ground, but also at the negotiating table."

Hanssen's eyebrows arched. This introduction had a lot of effrontery for being given by only an aide. Though at times the man sounded embarrassed by his own words, as if he were reading unwillingly from an OHUD script.

As the details on Operation Solstice unfurled, Hanssen understood them as follows: the current, successful operations would halt, everything would be reorganized under Bergen's aegis, and then Colonel Brechts would personally direct the new, suicidal war effort. Hanssen wanted to object, but, even though this plan was excrement, it was excrement that was vigorously backed by a great number of star-studded shoulders. He resolved to wait at least until the presentation was finished.

But, as he listened, the plan only descended deeper into madness. Almost unbidden he heard himself interject an,

"Excuse me—"

The room's many heads whiplashed towards him and time itself jumped into sharper focus. Hanssen's first impulse was to backpedal, but he knew that he personally had to put on a strong show if Leknes hoped to engage this friendly power.

"I ... think there's been a ... miscommunication," he proceeded carefully. "Leknes and Trondheim have been ... fighting a

302

successful guerilla campaign against the corporate army for nearly two months now. It's working. And, pardon me for saying so, but we don't even need Bergen's help. Lindon is bleeding money and he'll soon come to terms." The part about not needing Bergen's help was a lie, but there was nothing that said Hanssen could not bluff.

"All this"—he waved a hand at their meeting—"is only because the Bergen public was so outraged by the attack on Røros that you had no choice but to sign up with us. And this meeting was supposed to be for us to tell you how Bergen could participate in our campaign, not for you to arrogate the whole operation. And I had to tear myself away from my men for an entire day to come down here. So, if you're just going to go on about how you plan to get us all killed without even asking for my input, I might as well leave now."

Hanssen had felt a swell of pride when he started down this reproach, but by the end he was fearful he had overdone it. Yet Brechts had remained strangely composed throughout.

"Well, Colonel," Brechts said coldly, "if you think there is something lacking in our plans, then, by all means, please point it out." He gestured to the front of the room, and his aide stepped back to his seat.

Hanssen was delighted. Apparently Brechts thought he was bluffing about Bergen's plan being moronic. Perhaps Brechts had drawn up Solstice himself and so believed it to be imbued with an *ex cathedra* infallibility.

Hanssen stood, paged back to the beginning of the aide's presentation, and began his deconstruction.

"First off, you plan to bring all Home Guard forces up to these new forward bases around the corporate army's territory. But that will take at least two weeks, probably three, during which time we won't be able to launch many attacks. But our campaign relies on keeping constant pressure on the corporates to prevent them from being able to fully re-supply. That's the difference between making their resource situation just desperate or actually unmaintainable. Just doing this reorg will give them such a breather that it'll erase all the gains we've made so far.

"Second, you may want to build these impressive forward operating bases, but we specifically didn't do that because, by stationing ourselves at small, shifting locations, the corporates never have any idea where we're concentrated. That way they have to defend every point of attack equally. But building these bases will be announcing to them where they can count on us to be all the time. So after this it'll just be our few, large bases against their few, large bases. Stalemate.

"Third, you propose to do this so that we can launch pitched battles against the corporate army, but that's ludicrous. Our campaign has lasted this long precisely because we've avoided all direct engagements. If we tried to take out their tanks and jets in straight combat, we'd have to pay at least one of ours for every one of theirs we destroy, and probably more because of their technological edge.

If we'd been running these kinds of attacks since the start of the campaign, we'd have lost half our operating power by now.

"And, really, what reason is there to go after their tanks and airpower? Those are useless in Norway. They can't attack our cities because of the public backlash—Røros proved that. And they can't attack the Home Guard so long as we don't present ourselves as targets. You only want to go after them because you think it'll hurt them the most, but these guys are a *corporate* army—they answer always to their bottom line. So all we have to do is go after anything that costs money. —Which tanks and jets do, but there are a lot of things that are easier to blow up for all the red ink they spill. Like the convoys and outlying bases we've been going for.

"If we go head-to-head with the corporates, at best we'll start trading punches and giving them victories, and that will give them an incentive to keep fighting. But, if we keep blowing up their money with asymmetric warfare, it'll be pointless for them not to meet our terms.

"So you want to know how Bergen can help in the campaign? ... Simple. Just move your forces forward in small units up to the fringe of the corporate army's territory. You don't even have to attack by yourselves, because, with just the threat of Bergen's strength, the corporates will have to shift away from our fronts, which will make our attacks more successful. No huge reorg or change of command needed. Just move a few men forward and stay out of our way. We'll carry home the job that we started."

After he finished, the room hung with the taut quiet of an expected execution. Brechts sat with a pursed look on his face, looking disdainfully in Hanssen's direction but not precisely at him. Despite everything Hanssen had said, he knew Brechts was not actually wondering who was 'right' between them. More likely he was just railing internally about Hanssen's 'insubordination' and 'impertinence.'

Brechts stood. "Well, Colonel,"—his voice was murderously icy—"if that is your opinion, then I see there is no chance for constructive cooperation between our two cities. And I would hate to keep you from continuing *your* brand of campaign."

He spurred about and began to leave. The brass stood a moment later to precede Brechts on his way, and the junior officers followed after.

A walkout by the entire Bergen contingent was now in progress, and Hanssen had precipitated it. He looked at his own people, most of whom returned shrugs and sardonic looks. Erlend, however, was plaintively eyeing the buffet table, wondering if the food might now be considered off limits under the changed circumstances.

But there soon proved to be one person remaining along Bergen's side of the table: Mayor Laurantzson. Indeed, he was feigning obliviousness to any walkout taking place at all.

When the Bergen officers saw this, they froze mid-step. They looked between each other, attempting to decipher this awkward situation. ... If Laurantzson were only a mayor, then they might not be obliged to stay, and so maintaining a unified walkout should be their objective. But, with Bergen more of a 'city–state,' that made Laurantzson rather a 'head of state,' and so they were obliged to treat him as their commander in chief. Then they could obviously not disobey his wishes and leave him naked of any staff ...

So, hesitantly, the Bergen officers drifted back to the table. In the end, only Colonel Brechts held to walking out.

Once everyone was reseated, Laurantzson looked to Hanssen and said brightly, "Colonel, if you'd please continue ..."

***

A half hour later the meeting was concluded, and Bergen's officers were scrambling to scrap their old orders and draw up new ones. Out in the reception hall, Laurantzson moved to intercept Hanssen. For as frail as the man looked, he could still walk under his own power—not briskly, but not decrepitly, either.

"Colonel Hanssen, I'm so glad to finally meet you ... " he said heartily, taking his hand again. "And I'm thrilled that we have you at the helm of this operation."

"Thank you, sir," Hanssen replied, drably modest. "Though I'm ... sorry to have caused a row with Colonel Brechts."

"Oh, bah. Brechts will get over it. And luckily his aide stayed at the meeting, so it will only be as if the Colonel were delayed and missed it." After a pause he asked, "Spirits high in Leknes?"

"Yes, sir. ... As Brigadier Krohg said, our campaign's all about reasserting some Norwegian sovereignty on Norwegian soil."

"Ha! Glad to hear it! I'd love there to be more talk of Norwegian sovereignty around *here* ... " He shot a glance at his military contingent. "Mostly it's just rants about Lindon's presence, and Leknes's recklessness, —and all oblivious to the idea that perhaps Bergen could do something itself.

"I tried terribly hard to get us involved in the campaign before this, you know. I even called your Mayor and Brigadier Krohg, hoping to arrange something with them. But the Bergen legislature blocked me at every turn.

"Finally, after Røros—God rest those poor souls—they had to yield to public pressure and let us join in. But even then I was afraid that they would foot-drag our participation out into nothing of consequence. ... So you were just the person I needed to come down here and shake things up."

Hanssen grinned deflectingly. In his opinion, Bergen had an understandable obligation to be cautious. With Norway's capital city gone, its 'successor capital' must necessarily feel more vulnerable, and be more sensitive to the greater incremental harm that would befall the country if it, too, perished.

Laurantzson put a hand on his shoulder and turned him from the crowd, walking them off together confidentially. "And so now ... " he said in a lower voice, "I'd like to know a little of where you see us ending up after this campaign is finished."

Hanssen looked at him. "Sir?"

"Where do you see Norway as a whole."

Hanssen wondered briefly. "Not much changed, sir."

The Mayor gave a self-amused sigh. He had expected a certain answer so thoroughly that he had forgotten that Hanssen was not on his train of thought.

"You may know that I'm an outspoken supporter of reconstituting the nation. —Of course I would be. I'm nearing a century old, and Norway has been a whole country for nearly all of that time. Now that I'm on my way out, I don't want to leave seeing one of my only constants dashed. So I'm hopeful for anything that I think may effect that.

"And this campaign has already seen two large cities cooperating ... Now the news in Røros capturing the entire nation's attention ... And here's Bergen finally joining in ... I would like to think that this could grow into something more after it was finished."

"Perhaps, sir," answered Hanssen. "But ... re-forming the country? Has the campaign been that momentous?"

"Well, I backed two referenda a few years ago on putting us back together. Both failed—not just in terms of their outcome but also in terms of how few ballots were cast, how little interest was shown. But now we've seen a military campaign against a common foe that has drawn the entire country back together. That seems far more motivating material than just a referendum, don't you think?"

"True, sir ... "

Laurantzson was obviously prodding him for an in-depth opinion. These were typically something outside of Hanssen's purview. He either gave orders or he took them, and having an opinion either way was just court-martial fodder. Yet this was the Mayor of Bergen who was soliciting him now, and courtesy demanded he not shirk him off. But, more than that, Hanssen did feel the tingling of a point he wanted to relate. It was something that had been touched off by Laurantzson's words. But it was vague and half-formed, not within easy reach ...

"Well ... I think— ... the problem is— ... that nothing's *happened*, sir," he blurted out.

Laurantzson eyed that, waiting for clarification.

"The country is ... the way it is now ... because of the Singularity. I don't just mean how we lost Oslo, I mean everyone's attitudes and opinions— how everything changed. I've ... heard the breakup of the country called the 'dissolution.' It makes it sound like some event where all the mayors got together, signed some accord, and that was the formal end of it. But that never happened. In reality everyone simply stopped trying to put it all back together. That's all the 'dissolution' was. That's how drastically the Singularity changed us. The country came apart from just the ... the climate that was left."

Laurantzson struck a considering pose.

"It's like—the line of succession," Hanssen continued, trying to paint a simile. "Our prime minister after the Singularity was the twenty-third in line for the office. When she resigned, we started pulling up people in the forties and fifties—and even further down. But, past the top slots, succession is just an academic exercise. You can only lose so many people before you lose the whole idea of what you're succeeding to. And that's what it was like for us. We'd lost Oslo, which was our capital, in every way. And, once you lose your head, your body can't simply take it in stride.

"So it feels like ... we're hiding now. Because, the more you have, the more there is to lose. And the more you reach for, the more you come up short. That's why people don't want to put the country back together. It would just be tempting fate. Inviting the same disasters—or worse—to happen all over again."

Laurantzson nodded in dawning understanding.

"So you want the country to come back together? But the Singularity was too great a shock—it redefined who we are. We can't simply hold enough referenda and public support will re-materialize. Because of the drastic way everything changed, there has to be something just as big to take us back. —If 'taking us back' is even possible. But that's what hasn't happened."

"I see ... " Laurantzson nodded. "And you're *certain* this campaign couldn't be the catalyst that you speak of?" he coaxed.

"No," Hanssen shook his head. "It would have to be ... something bigger."

Chapter 34 - Bitter Peace

Peder drummed his fingers on the conference room table. He was the only person present, and sitting in the only chair present. It was an odd setup, but this room was for telepresentation meetings. The other participants were all in different locations, each sitting around an identical table but at unique positions. Once the meeting started, projections of them would be sewn into everyone else's augspace, and their images would come along with the chairs they were sitting in. Thus any extra chairs already in the rooms would have to be airbrushed out by the rendering software, and that extra work would mean wasted energy and money. With the large number of telepresentation conferences a company like Lindon Securities did, keeping extraneous chairs out of these rooms probably saved them a few Megacredits in electricity and hardware every year.

But Peder huffed at this, thinking that meanwhile Lindon had a secret hypercomp cluster in Oslo that was burning through money like a blast furnace. The old saying 'penny wise, pound foolish' was here an understatement by several orders of magnitude. Really they were tightfisting some sou in their right pocket while letting gold bars slip out their left.

At the nanostroke of the hour—14:00:00.000 000 000—Lindon, Atkins, and seven other corporate army CEOs appeared around the table, with Lindon and Atkins at its heads. Lindon had grown increasingly gloomy over the course of these weekly meetings, and for this one he appeared in his dourest mood of all. The other CEOs quickly adopted a meek and deferential posture.

The meeting began with a staff member reporting on recent Home Guard activity. Since this was both a corporate and a military headquarters, the briefing was conducted in a hybrid of the tactical and financial viewpoints. First came the summary of losses tallied in terms of vehicles, equipment, and casualties; then these were converted into their more-liquid equivalent, credits. Maps of Norway appeared showing red 'x's for the locations of all attacks, which were then tagged with red figures showing the monetary losses there incurred. Eight-figure sums appeared like tombstones over where each hovertrack, battletank, and superjet had met its demise.

To Peder, this twice-as-dire dual view highlighted the inherent dissonances in maintaining a 'corporate military.' Traditionally, national militaries needed only to think about protecting the motherland—let the money cost of it be damned. And corporations needed only to think about staying in the black—let the Human cost of it be damned. But conflate those two and one was suddenly torn in service between starkly opposed masters.

"The greatest change since last week, of course," the presenter was saying, "has been the entrance of Bergen into the campaign. Their units, however, have had little direct impact as they participate in far fewer actions than their Leknes or Trondheim counterparts. Still, in order to

313

counterbalance this new threat, we have had to shift substantial forces towards the western front. This has reopened many of our vulnerabilities in the north, breathing new life into the other cities' attacks.

"But Bergen's primary importance is undoubtedly as a fresh supply center. Before this, we had confirmed intelligence that the other cities' logistics situation had become critical. They would have had to cease all major offensive operations within two weeks. But, now that Bergen has opened its stockpiles, the Home Guard will be able to sustain its campaign apace for at least several more months. Within that time, however, our *own* logistics situation—"

"Right—off!" blared Lindon.

The underling's holo rippled and disappeared in a violent whiff. This was so different from the standard disappearing effect that holograms performed that Peder wondered whether Lindon had not actually vaporized the man.

The room focused on Lindon. He was drumming his fingers on the table and staring shiftlessly downwards. After a frightful pause he perked up and said,

"The military situation is only half bad. Munitions are low, Home Guard actions come almost daily, half our colonels are arguing for withdrawal from our frontier bases—but this we can manage. What concerns *us* is the far greater damage to the army's image. Every minor victory for the Norwegians is being bruited and magnified by their media, and the rest of the world is *seeing* it. We are

314

trying to build the army's image as a go-to force for national security needs the world over, and instead everyone is seeing us being given the runaround by a bunch of backwoods partisans! ... I need solutions. *Now*."

Lindon never asked questions—he only demanded answers. And he only dropped the Corporate 'we' in moments of heightened passion.

The CEOs remained frozen, each silently daring the others to speak first. Nikolai Rokotov offered his head on the chopping block:

"Do you mean a ... a military solution, sir?" the man ventured.

Lindon looked at him cuttingly. "You mean besides the obvious solution of taking the gloves off, going on an all-out campaign, and wiping the Norwegians out inside of a month? ... Because that *would* work, but then our resources would be spent, the troops run a little ragged, and world opinion a trifle sour on us, wouldn't you say? So you wish to suggest a military solution other than that?"

Since Lindon did not ask questions, the only times he actually inflected them was when he was being sarcastic, rhetorical, or he was firing someone, e.g., "You do remember where the door is, yes?"

Peder knew no one else would speak. What was there to say? From doctrine they knew that at least a ten-to-one superiority in forces was required to win a guerilla war; and, failing that, one had to start carpet-bombing cities. —Not that that actually accomplished anything, it just gave one something to do while otherwise slowly losing. But here they had nowhere near the numerical superiority required, and their 'accidental' killing of only five civilians had caused a media sensation. Even the UN Secretary-General had branded them with one of his busybody condemnations.

"Pardon me, sir," said Atkins, entering the meeting with calm force. "No one wants to say it, but this battle is lost."

These words shocked Peder and the other CEOs. Peder had long ago learned the trick of speaking to bosses—and especially to Lindon—as if they were hostage-takers: one never used negative words like 'no,' 'can't,' or 'won't.' And here Lindon was in one of his most sardonic moods yet, but Atkins had just used the word 'lost.'

"We lost"—Atkins brazenly repeated—"because the Norwegians knew what they were doing. They executed a perfect guerilla campaign and hammered our weak points—which were plenty, seeing as we built our infrastructure here with little mind to having to defend it against domestic terrorism. We were overextended in every measure.

"And, as you said, sir, this battle was fought on more than just a military dimension. It was also a war of publicity and image. And here we always had both hands tied behind our back. There was no reprisal we could have made that the public would have turned a favorable eye on. —And that's not even factoring in their Singularity Sympathy."

Peder had to credit how Atkins kept saying '*we* lost,' '*our* infrastructure,' '*we* built,' etc. The man was accepting total responsibility for the war even

316

though he had only come to the army's helm a few weeks before it had started.

"But just because we've lost this battle doesn't mean we need to lose the *next* one," Atkins asserted. "In my opinion, we have to accept the Home Guard's demands, but we can do so in such a way that will give us an imperturbable stake in this country."

Lindon was looking off askance. If he were ever going to fire Atkins, Peder thought, then that magic moment was nigh ... Of course Peder knew it was pointless to covet the man's post now—they were all going to be unemployed soon enough. But he still held it as a matter of principle to see this ringer ousted.

But Lindon said only, "Proceed."

... This was a reaction far outside all of Peder's predictive models for the man.

Atkins continued, "The only reason the Home Guard's campaign was successful was because we staked out too much territory in this country. So let's forget about how much we have and ask how much we truly need. Of the nearly two hundred bases out there, which are the indispensable ones?

"The answer to that is only one: the superbase in Oslo. It's a hardened installation with enough space to house all of our men and vehicles. With the Bunker secure, every other Norwegian base becomes vestigial. And the Bunker is so fortified that the Norwegians never even attempted to attack it. The entire Oslodistrikt infrastructure has been left untouched by this offensive.

317

"So, to stop this conflict, we accede to the Norwegians' territorial demands. They wanted us to withdraw from at least three quarters of our bases, but we can be even more generous than that. We'll offer to withdraw from *all* of them—all except for Oslo. We agree to pack up every base more than fifty kilometers away from the city.

"From the Norwegians' perspective, our footprint will shrink to nothing more than a sliver of poisoned land, so they should be pleased. And, from our perspective, we'll be cutting a great deal of dead weight in exchange for turning that fifty-klick plot of land into a stronghold. Once invested there, we could cut down a combined attack from even the entire Home Guard with impunity. Without that threat of force, the Norwegians could never again dictate terms."

Lindon bobbed his head. "A fifty-klick radius would give us an adequate footprint, yes … But suppose the Home Guard deciphers our intentions and they launch a preemptive strike while we're in the middle of relocating."

"That's possible, sir, but we'll be able to finish this relocation inside of a week. Securing the Oslo perimeter will take longer, of course, but we can have all the men and essential equipment back to the city within six days. That would leave the Home Guard only a small window to attack, and every day we'd be concentrating our firepower."

Lindon leaned forward. "While we like the idea of making the army impervious to all *future* attacks, this move will still look like total capitulation. It seems there's no way to save face."

318

"Actually, sir, we will benefit from any treaty we make with the Norwegians. Before this, our international status was that we were squatters on Norwegian land, and that was exactly what dissuaded many governments from soliciting our services. But now we're going to make a settlement with the Norwegians, and, no matter what form that takes, it gives us recognition. After this the corporate army will be a completely legitimate enterprise."

Lindon had been nodding in ever increasing amplitude as Atkins spoke. At the end he thumped the table soundly and said, "Now all we have to do is get this down in electrons. —Kjaerstad," he snapped.

"—Yes, sir," Peder replied.

"Get over to Norway. Get a meeting with the Home Guard, the mayors—whoever's in charge of this travesty—, and lay out our proposal. Just the preliminary agreement for now, with a framing committee to script out the full version later. But we'll need a ceasefire while we effect this relocation to the Bunker. So lie, cheat, steal, do whatever, but *get us that ceasefire* within twenty-four hours."

"Yes, sir. ... Um, would you like me to leave—"

"*Now*. Right now."

"Yes, sir." Peder stood and walked out. When he breached the conference room door, his connection was severed and the men in augspace blinked away.

Peder hovered some seconds, stupefied by the spectacle he had just witnessed. Lindon had always been a terror of a CEO, and yet Atkins had just played the man like a recital piece. If Peder had said the things Atkins had, Lindon would have obliterated him. Yet, coming from Atkins, Lindon had taken them as calmly as if they had both been acting out a script. Peder could not imagine what would usurp Lindon so totally …

It was also surreal to watch the efforts Lindon was making to secure peace with the Norwegians all while ignoring the catastrophic debts his company faced. He was obsessed with perfecting a sandcastle while a mile-high tsunami approached the shore.

And now Peder had to go to Norway, where he was one of the most hated people alive.

He allowed himself one seething, *"Fuck,"* before he went on with his day.

Chapter 35 - Eyes

Townsend was watching a real-time vidstream from a security cam at Stockholm–Arlanda Airport. On it Peder Kjaerstad was walking across the wind-racked tarmac to a jet that stood impatient for his arrival.

"So what's so special about this guy?" asked Townsend, tapping his stylus over the image of Kjaerstad.

"Very strange," said Zhang. "Three months ago he contracted an underground investigation of Lindon's company."

"Who'd he use?"

"Mid-level Swedish group first, then graduated to Mafia."

"Heavy hitters," Townsend grunted. "What's he looking for?"

"Unclear. The Swedish group didn't seem to accomplish much, but the Mafia conducted several operations, each one increasing in elaborateness. You know the Leipzig–Stockholm hack six weeks ago?"

"Yeah. … Wait, that was for *him*?"

"Yes. The Mafia arranged it, and apparently for something related to Kjaerstad's job."

Townsend drew back, impressed. "Shit."

"We know that they obtained some of Lindon's internal security data and financial information, but we don't have a copy of it. Since then the Mafia have made a few more infiltrations, but all of them minor."

"Who's Kjaerstad's contact?"

"Zuzanna Mukhina."

Zhang forwarded him a dossier. It sketched in Mukhina's criminal connections with typically turbid resolution—the Mafia's security was a model of thoroughness. But, for as murky as the last decade of Mukhina's life was, there was surprising detail on her from the ages of 13 to 26. This was thanks to the fact that people of Mukhina's age had put their entire adolescence through early adulthood up on the nets.

"Okay," said Townsend, "I grant you it's odd that Kjaerstad would be investigating his own parent company. But beyond that why do we care?"

"We're interested in the financial data the hack may have recovered. We suspect it shows disbursements that have never been seen outside of Lindon. It may help reveal the channels he uses to pay off his smuggling contacts, which could lead us to those who smuggled down the hypercomm."

"Ah, okay. Promising."

"And there is another anomaly. We believe Lindon is aware of Kjaerstad's and Mukhina's actions, but he hasn't done anything about them."

Townsend blanched. "Lindon *knows* that these two pulled the Leipzig hack on him … and he hasn't even given Kjaerstad a reprimand or … some concrete shoes?"

"No. Lindon has kept them under surveillance, but he has left them otherwise unmolested."

"Any idea why Lindon's letting them alone?"

"Haven't the foggiest."

Townsend knew that was a polite lie. Not that Zhang was concealing something, but, if all the resources of the Lontan Governate 'had not the foggiest,' it really just meant they were working on a thousand equiprobable explanations, none of which was frontrunning enough to bring up.

"So what this all means ... " said Townsend, stalling while he thought it through, "is that we can use these two."

"Yes," Zhang affirmed. "The ISSO operations so far have been high-profile, and our raid in the Sahara was not a subtle opening move. Every unregistered mannequin planet-side knows that the ISSO is moving hard, and they even suspect that we Lontans are behind it. They're laying low, so we have little chance of following up on the soft leads that we have."

"—But," Townsend interrupted to show that he was following, "these two are civilians with legitimate underground connections. So they might be able to follow up on some leads for us. Without it looking suspicious, and without alerting anyone that we're on to them."

"Exactly," said Zhang brightly, as if complimenting a pupil. "We would like to obtain the Lindon internal data that Mukhina has, and then maneuver her investigation down the avenues we're interested in. That could put us onto Lindon's contacts, and perhaps even the Hezokeen agents."

Townsend nodded. "Great. So now the question is how are we going to, one, get the hack data from Mukhina, and then, two, 'maneuver' her to follow up on the leads we care about?"

"As to that, for the moment we are at a loss."

Townsend scoffed. "But you're the Lontans. Can't you just ... implant the desire to help us in Kjaerstad's and Mukhina's heads? Then they'd give us the info and—"

"That would be violating a great body of law, both Lontan and Human," Zhang interrupted.

Townsend shrugged. He realized he had probably just asked Zhang to commit what the Lontans would term 'mindrape.'

"So for now we sit back and wait?" Townsend conceded. "Maybe Mukhina moves after whom we want, maybe not? Maybe we think of something better later?"

"Yes."

"Not much of a plan."

"No."

"Well, as long as we're in agreement."

Chapter 36 - Departure

The departure orders still glistened in Frisch's OHUD: 'instructed to depart with your ship'—'no later than 1900 hours'—'rendezvous with Admiral Hadamard's task force'—'Godspeed' were the snippets that his eyes were retrafficking. He kept the orders open in his OHUD even as he rushed for the ship, afraid that they might dematerialize otherwise.

He rode a lift down to the military docks of Gateway Station, and the gravity eventually decayed to imperceptibility. The civilian portions of the station were serviced by a Lontan artificial gravity generator, but down here zero-g prevailed. Frisch grabbed hold of one of the small transhandles protruding from the lift's sides. When the car stopped, the handle drove out along the wall and into the corridor, pulling Frisch along.

The corridor was a wide cylinder whose inner walls were flocking with transhandles pulling people and equipment along, all guided by a hypercomp traffic system. Frisch gave his destination as the *Jotunheim's* berth and the handle started taxiing him off. He was pulled down progressively smaller corridors and accelerated in the emptiness. Shortly he arrived at a cul-de-sac bulb that was the last docking port connecting to the *Jotunheim*. All the ship's other umbilicals had been severed, and this was the only connection left, waiting to ferry him over.

The handle pulled him over to the far side of the bulb. A patch of the wall shuddered like a drumhead losing its tension, and it irised open into a man-sized tunnel. Frisch fed himself in headfirst. Inside he felt an invisible tug infuse his body, and the Lontan ship was now propelling him.

Ahead the tunnel curved away, occluding forward sight. Glancing down Frisch saw the iris closing behind him, sealing the momentary gap in the ship's hull. This capillary, too, was collapsing as soon as he passed through it, shriveling like a used umbilical cord. It had been created only to transfer Frisch to the bridge, but it would not be needed again until they were back in port. So for now the ship was reclaiming the space, and even reclaiming the mass—the carbon used for the umbilical's walls, the nitrogen and oxygen for its air, the heating elements for its environment. All were melted back down and returned to the ship's element stores.

This capillary was not a gangway transferring him onto the ship—he was already in the ship. Opening a schematic in his OHUD, he saw the *Jotunheim* as a great wedge shape, with this tube threaded through her as a minute blood vessel—and with Frisch the sole corpuscle busying it. Outside of that, 99.9% of the ship's volume was a vast sludge of biotech trunks, nanossemblers, and reactor cores, all of it Lontan-made and inaccessible. Frisch's destination was the only Human-habitable portion of the ship, the crew capsule. This was the ship-within-a-ship that housed their compact living quarters and bridge. The Lontan ship was a giant organism, and the Humans interfaced with it through just the stem of its nervous system.

After a minute, Frisch arrived at the capillary's stubbish end. He felt a tug in the reverse direction, and his body came to a stop with his head a foot from the 'ceiling.' Beneath him the capillary pinched off and sealed him inside of a body-shaped pocket. He felt like a torpedo that had been locked into place, ready for firing. Gravity reinvigorated his bones, bringing with it that pseudo-falling sensation as his body reaccepted an orientation. His weight came to purchase on the floor and the wall melded open before him.

After all of this replicanty Lontan technology, Frisch was relieved when the portal opened onto a concretely Human view. He stepped off of the cushy, organic feel of the capillary floor and onto the stolid steel of the crew capsule. Inside the fourteen officers of his crew stood at attention and saluted. His XO, Lieutenant Alexandra Khlebnikova, was at their head.

Frisch stepped forward and began shaking hands. He did not need to engage in any banter with the crew—he had last seen all of them a few hours ago, and he had been practically living with them for weeks. But the handshakes did acknowledge the special occasion.

Once finished, Khlebnikova asked, "Care to conduct your inspection, sir?" She was always one for procedure.

Frisch grinned wryly. Normally he would not have bothered, but, as the crew capsule had only the square footage of an apartment, it would not be much trouble to oblige her.

327

He glanced around the first floor: a cylindrical room, twenty meters in diameter, and ringed with vidwindows simulating a cityscape. This was their recreation deck, complete with sofas and game tables. Khlebnikova made sure to keep it spotless, though it did not strictly need to be. The crew capsule was not a fighting vessel with battle stations and munitions stores, but really only a 'vacation home' for when the crew was not on the bridge. Frisch had seen ships where the crew capsule was in a constant state of dorm room dishevel.

"Looks okay down here," Frisch said.

He went up the narrow spiral stairway in the center of the room, and the crew followed. The second floor was of smaller diameter and held the mess and infirmary. Again his inspection was cursory. As long as there was no butchered deer carcass on the table, the room would pass muster.

"Good here," he commented.

The final floor was sleeping quarters. Individual capsules, piled three high, stood in five bookshelf stacks covering one half of the room. The other half—the bathing area—stood with its doors open, peering onto atomically clean showers, sinks, and stalls.

"Fine here, too," he delivered his verdict.

Here the main stairwell ended and only a ladder rose up to the bridge.

"Let's get underway," said Frisch. "Current shift, we're up. Everyone else, dismissed." Frisch climbed up the ladder, and Khlebnikova, Bruusgaard, Evensen, and Riiser followed him.

328

The bridge was not a full deck by itself but rather a small cupola crowning the three-level crew capsule. It was just large enough for the five reclining chairs that were placed at equal angles around the ladderway's opening. There were no displays, blinking panels, or any electronics in evidence. Only the dome-shaped ceiling had a vidprint surface, which was simulating a blue sky— a guard against claustrophobia.

One by one, Frisch and his officers climbed the stairwell and crawled into the chairs. Settling in, Frisch took a last glance around with his real eyes, then he gave his mind over to the ship. This was more than just having his vision or senses overridden like augspace. The ship was tapping directly into his brain, opening his mind's eye in a way that was unknowable to plain Humans.

Once the interface was complete, Frisch was now in tacspace—and so truly able to inspect the ship. His view started off floating outside of the *Jotunheim*, where she was still moored to Gateway Station. Frisch switched to an omniscient perspective and was now viewing the ship from every angle simultaneously. From here he could manually verify—indeed, he already knew—that all physical connections between the ship and station were cleared. The only things left were the EM moorings, whose radiation he could see in a new color channel, orthogonal to those provided by Human visual receptors.

Switching back to a real perspective, Frisch peeled away the ship's skin to look at her reactors and her pulsing, electric skeleton. With another gesture he scrutinized her brimming element stores and traced the feed arteries that tributaried her nanofabs. Here was more nanoconstruction horsepower than was currently harnessed by Human civilization.

In tactical view, Frisch saw that the ship was currently unarmed. But this was no oversight, as the ship's nanofabs could construct all of its munitions on demand. With that ability, what reason was there to have tons of explosives piled up inside the ship while she was only sitting around in port. None at all—or so the USS Arizona might have argued.

Giving the ship a test, Frisch ordered her to prepare a standard alert package of weaponry. In response, power fired the nanofabs and they drank from the element stores, punching out missiles, intercept platforms, and countermeasures. Dozens of vacuoles formed on the inside of the hull, and interstitial nanofabs used the ship's broth to construct the needed gun nests. Munitions were blazed along conveyors and locked into place. In all, it took only 1.7 seconds for the ship to go from being an innocuous pleasure craft to packing the firepower of a doomsday machine.

Having finished his inspection, Frisch turned to the other officers in tacspace. None of them had a physical presence in tacspace, but he could feel their focus on their respective stations: Evensen invested in the propulsion systems, Bruusgaard finessing the ship's intricate sensor web, Riiser inspecting the tactical systems, and Khlebnikova, as the XO, hovering over it all.

Khlebnikova reported: «XO: All systems operational // Standing by at departure stations // Awaiting orders / sir»

Frisch perceived the message not as spoken or written words but as raw thought. In the heat of combat, this thoughtwave channel was their time-optimized battle language. Frisch issued return commands by forming the desired thoughts, which the ship transcribed and transmitted back over the same medium:

«CO: Engines start / release EM moorings // Prepare to depart» The officers fired back confirmations as they finished, and Frisch was soon able to add, «CO: Thrusters ahead»

He switched to a piloting perspective to watch their departure. A swarm of dials and gauges appeared before him, providing a qualitative heft of the ship's status. As Evensen nudged them out, the readouts for engine thrust and fuel consumption flared, with those gauges magnifying themselves before the others to preen their spiking numbers.

After pulling away from the dock, they switched to their navigational engines and began working their way out along planetary traffic routes. Only once Gateway Station had shrunk to a speck in the surrounding dark did they go to their sub-light engines and truly begin defying the planet's grasp. Eagerly the ship responded to each command for more speed, climbing farther out of the gravity well and into wild, unclaimed space.

Once outside of Earth's restricted flight zone, they switched to their hyperdrive. And with that they disappeared from the universe proper and

began the super–light-speed portion of their
journey.

332

Chapter 37 - Buried

Peder had been hoping to arrive in Bergen quietly and skulk unnoticed about his business, but there was already a mob assembled to greet him from his first step off his jet. Fifty people had assembled chanting rhythmic denunciations and wearing holosigns that proclaimed, 'Corporates Out of Norway!', 'Murdering Foreign Scum!', and 'Remember Røros!' The only barrier that kept them from surging forward and tearing him apart was a wobbly string of airport security guards.

Peder paid them no attention as he deplaned by the jet's short staircase and strode across the tarmac. Walking into the secure international terminal momentarily squeegeed the mob off of him, but he was sure they would reacquire him later.

After passing through customs, Peder was greeted by a representative of the Bergen government. The man wore a plain suit and was only in his mid-twenties. Peon.

"Mister Kjaerstad?" he asked. "Welcome to Bergen, I'm Eivind Norum. I've been assigned as your attaché."

Peder shook hands and mumbled a greeting back. "Last I'd heard my meeting with the Mayor was approved, but I didn't have a time?" he asked.

"Yes, you'll be meeting with the Mayor tonight at his residence. After a private performance by the Bergen Quartet. A concert that the Mayor has also graciously invited you to attend."

"Oh," remarked Peder, surprised at so accommodating a move. "And when would that be?"

"Twenty hundred hours."

"I look forward to it."

***

Hanssen had received Mayor Laurantzson's message early that morning: Lindon wanted peace and was sending a 'Peder Kjaerstad' to Bergen to negotiate. Hanssen would have preferred that Lindon himself come as the contrite deal broker, but at least this Kjaerstad held the position of a corporate army CEO. So Hanssen had agreed to head to Bergen as well.

Yet he did not discount the possibility that these negotiations were really a ploy to lure the Home Guard's top brass out into the open. He advised Colonel Feiring to take precautions on traveling to Bergen, and for himself he had his jet plot a course that stayed well out to sea, away from any ambushes.

On arriving, Hanssen was directed—to this surprise—to the mayor's residence. He had expected they would meet Kjaerstad in one of the Ministry of Defence's imperious and intimidating conference rooms, but apparently Laurantzson had some ingratiating approach in mind. Then he discovered—to his far greater surprise—that there was to be a private concert beforehand, to which all the Home Guard commanders and even Kjaerstad were invited. But apparently Laurantzson had scheduled this concert months ago, and, when these negotiations had come up, he had simply conflated the two 'events.'

The mayor's household was thoroughly bedecked for the concert, with every surface buffed and polished, and the servants even breaking out their powdered wigs. A footman led Hanssen up to a second floor parlor where he was met by a lithe woman in a formal gown.

"Colonel Hanssen," she greeted him.

"Yes, Mizz ... ?"

"Ingrid Laurantzson, pleased to meet you."

From the angle in which she proffered her hand, Hanssen was obliged to kiss it. Been a while since I've done this, he thought.

"Thank you for coming tonight," Ingrid continued, leading him into the room. "My grandfather was so excited to have some new and unexpected guests."

So this was one of Laurantzson's granddaughters, he noted.

"The Mayor's invitation was most gracious."

"Have you been to Bergen before?"

"Yes," Hanssen replied. ... And he soon felt the awkward curtness of his answer. Had to flesh it out. "Your grandfather has ... kept this a wonderful city," he managed to add.

"Thank you. Allow me to introduce you to the rest of the guests ... "

Hanssen then became immensely glad that he had worn a dress uniform, because he was presented to two Norwegian mayors, three former members of the Storting, and three Bergenser councilors. They all congratulated him on the success of the campaign, though some had the mistaken impression that he was Colonel Brechts's subordinate, and that it had been Bergen's crucial pitching-in that had at last carried home Leknes's faltering campaign to a brilliant conclusion. The traces of Brechts's politicking showed on all of them like fingerprints on silver.

After he had made the rounds, Hanssen retreated to stand with Colonel Feiring and Major Heglund—a Home Guard officer from Lillehammer present as an observer. Brechts was also in attendance, but he was more at home with the politicians.

The next guest to arrive was Admiral Lene Willoch. Hanssen and the other officers snapped to attention. Willoch grinned and approached them first, opening with an,

"At ease, gentlemen." After she was introduced, she offered them her own congratulations: "I've been watching your campaign against the corporate army closely—excellent work. Especially you, Colonel," she said to Hanssen. "The whole country owes you a debt."

"Thank you, ma'am," he answered without bravado. Though he was glad to find someone who had not been infected with the Brechts-centric view of the campaign. Hanssen was not a vain man: he did not need acclaim for the part he had played. But that did not mean he was fine with someone else arrogating his share.

"It's a pleasure to meet you, Admiral," said Feiring. "Though I thought you were up on Gateway Station? ... "

"Almost all of the time, yes," Willoch answered with a weary lilt. "But every couple of months I check back in Earth-side. And Jakob usually arranges some memorable events during the time, that I might attend—such as these concerts."

Hanssen realized why Willoch was not another victim of the Brechts Deception: if she were always up on Gateway Station, then she was out of range of the Colonel's self-promotion.

"You and the Mayor are acquainted?" Heglund asked her, keying on Willoch's use of 'Jakob.'

"Oh yes. We have weekly meetings, discussing the country, coordinating personnel, managing the Navy's budget ... It's rather unofficial, but meeting with him makes it look like I have civilian oversight. The Eyes prefer it that way."

"Ahh," Feiring nodded in understanding. "Otherwise they might look at you like some rogue Soviet submarine commander. ... —Ma'am," he added after realizing Willoch might find that in poor humor.

But Willoch grinned at the characterization. "Actually that's about it. The Eyes aren't too happy about Norway's fleet being a detached military force. Of course they don't expect me to turn dictator, but they still feel better having a civilian looking over my shoulder."

Hanssen noted that, even though Willoch was the ranking officer of the Norwegian military, she essentially 'reported' to Laurantzson. This made the Mayor the closest thing to the country's leader. Hanssen had always respected the man, but this added a new stature to his person.

337

The final guest to arrive was Peder Kjaerstad. His entrance was greeted by every conversation trailing to a halt and all eyes riveting upon him. Yet this was only the man's latest cold reception of the day—and hardly the iciest—, so Kjaerstad merely nodded back.

Perversely, Ingrid led Kjaerstad over to the military officers first.

"Mister Kjaerstad," she said, "may I introduce Colonel Hanssen, Colonel Feiring—"

"Mister Kjaerstad, pleased to meet you," Brechts cut in stridently, walking over. "So you're one of the suits who gets all the damage reports once my boys have cleaned up." He refused to extend a handshake, and even gave a smug half-glance to the rest of the room.

Kjaerstad cleared his throat. "Yes, though accounting probably goes more into the numbers of that than myself."

He did not know what he had been trying to accomplish with that remark—if anything.

A three-count of awkward ensued.

Hanssen offered his hand and said, "Mister Kjaerstad." Brechts's uncouthness had triggered in Hanssen the ancient rule of 'enemy of my enemy."

"Colonel Hanssen, pleased to meet you," Kjaerstad replied, thankful for this switch in attention.

"You run the corporate army's … Third Lighted Brigade, yes?"

"… I do … " said Kjaerstad cautiously.

"Then I met one of your captains a while ago. A man named Mohr."

338

"Erik Mohr, yes," Kjaerstad nodded. "I recruited him. He's a good man."

"He has a mean punch."

Brechts shot Hanssen a look of extreme umbrage. It befitted General Patton having spied one of his staff making out with a Red Army chorine.

"If you would please excuse me," said Ingrid, bowing out.

A minute later she returned through the inner door on the arm of Mayor Laurantzson. The guests gave him a warm welcome. Laurantzson took a turn about the room to greet everyone individually. When he reached Hanssen and the other officers, he thanked them especially for drawing themselves away from their troops for the evening. Then he bade everyone move into the adjoining study for the concert.

**

After the Bergen Quartet's performance, Laurantzson begged the leave of his guests. He withdrew along with the Home Guard officers and Peder Kjaerstad, all of whom reconvened in a high-security conference room. There Kjaerstad outlined Lindon's offer, then left the Norwegians to their deliberations.

Laurantzson, Feiring, Heglund, and Hanssen were sitting at the conference table while Brechts was standing before the room's wall screen. This was displaying a political map of Norway that was overlaid with the 'before' and 'after' versions of the corporate army's territory.

"Kjaerstad's offer is a great deal," said Heglund. "They're giving back almost everything."

"Which is why I'm wary," said Laurantzson. "Even though they're essentially suing for peace, I still wouldn't have expected them to give up so much. And they would never offer us any deal unless it were in their interests."

"Kjaerstad at least explained that to my satisfaction," said Feiring. "All they really care about is their legal position, and before this they were just squatters. That was why they took over so much land—because they'd hoped it would make them look more legitimate. But, now that we're normalizing relations, it doesn't matter what they end up with so long as we recognize it. And that's what we're giving them. Oslo will be 'theirs' now. Practically that doesn't change much. But you can imagine how that would be a sore spot with the population."

"Yes, yes," said Brechts. "The press has spun this up into a campaign to drive the corporates out of Norway completely. So stopping anywhere short of that—and then giving them *Oslo* ... They'll consider it a desecration of holy ground."

"Of course we're not *giving* them Oslo," Heglund said. "The corporate army had it before all this even started. If anything, this will be putting Oslo back on the map. Before this it was just a graveyard, but now it'll be a major military base. It might start coming back to life."

"Still not the way I wanted to see it come back ... " Laurantzson mused.

There followed a long pause.

Once it had passed Hanssen's statute of limitations, he interjected with one of his swift verdicts:

"We have to accept their offer. Lindon won't give up his base in Oslo, and we can't kick him out of it. This is as far as we go."

Feiring and Heglund nodded.

"We've reached the culminating point, gentlemen," Brechts declared, ignoring Hanssen's verdict to announce his own, equivalent one. "Time to cash in the chips."

They relayed the positive outcome to Kjaerstad. Bureaucrats on both sides—Lindon Securities and the Home Guard—were allocated, and dates were penciled in to spindle out the particulars. A ceasefire was put into immediate effect, and Kjaerstad and the Home Guard commanders departed to begin their homeward journeys.

Except for Hanssen, whom Laurantzson had asked to join him and Admiral Willoch for a private discussion. He acceded, and the Mayor led them down to his ASAPR.

Unlike some modern mayoral residences that placed the ASAPR at the heart of a vault-like security complex, the ASAPR in Laurantzson's mansion was positioned in the basement as casually as a water heater. Walking past the wine cellar they suddenly came upon a torride door flush with the wall.

The Mayor's mansion had such a museum quality that Hanssen had expected that the ASAPR would be the one place in it allowed to flirt with modernity. Yet, after cycling through, he found that

341

the ASAPR was even more of an antique than the house. It was decorated with ornamented furniture carved out of dark woods; centuries-old paintings in centuries-older frames; arabesque rugs worn around their features; and the lamps were even the old bulb-and-shade models that cast their illumination in spotty, jaundice-colored islands. Here was the true inner sanctum of an aged intellect.

Inside Admiral Willoch was already waiting for them, seated at the coffee table. They joined her.

"So, Colonel," Laurantzson began plainly, "I asked you to stay because Lene and I have something more we wish to discuss with you. About Lindon and his corporate army. We may have just made peace with them, but there are more aspects to the problem they represent than just their military threat. In particular, there are some unresolved issues that go back to their founding. And this is what Lene and I wish to bring you in on."

Hanssen looked between his two hosts. "Me, sirs?" he had to ask.

"Yes. But don't think this is anything mysterious. It's just that here we have a civilian governor"—he indicated himself—"and the chief of the military"—he pointed to Willoch. "The missing link is a field commander. Someone who can take the policy we decide and act on it. Those are the three sides we need to address any threat. —And the corporate army is certainly that."

Hanssen thought this over. "I understand. Though … why isn't Colonel Brechts here in my place? He's senior, and he's Bergen's own field

342

commander." He tried to ask that without sounding ungrateful.

Laurantzson shifted in his seat. "I actually have read Colonel Brechts onto this before, but … his input since has not proven constructive."

Hanssen held back the smug reply, 'Ah, say no more.' He merely nodded.

"To begin," said Laurantzson, "let me recount briefly how the corporate army was established, and then you tell me whether this fits in with your own perception. … So, after the Singularity, Lindon's company went into Oslo to start excavating corporate and government property. As the city kept disintegrating and the security situation deteriorated, he brought in professional security contractors to protect his operation. Then, once Oslo was abandoned and his excavations were nearly complete, he had accumulated such a large force that he decided to turn it into an army-for-hire. They've had some deployments to Africa and Asia, and Lindon has continued building his infrastructure back here as their capabilities expanded. Does that sound right?"

Hanssen nodded.

"It seems plausible. But there are actually many contradictions. First, the whole idea of going back into Oslo after the Singularity to excavate property was absurd. The city's essential resource was data, not hardware. And, even if a company didn't keep backups of what they stored in Oslo, the only things they would have needed to salvage were a few kilos worth of drives. That's something you send in small

343

teams to accomplish, not armies of bulldozers and deconstructors.

"Second, the economics of it were preposterous. Lindon's excavations did pull out some high-end computing equipment, but it had to be refurbished to such a degree that he could only resell it at a loss. Only after two years—once the depression had retrograded the world economy enough—did he start to turn a profit. Maybe he just had the uncanny foresight to see this coming, but by then he had lost so much money in those first two years—and was making such a slim profit afterwards—that there was no way to recoup the costs.

"Third, his security force—the corporate army—was originally developed and maintained at great expense to support these excavations. Since these excavations were themselves a waste, that makes this army a double waste. Of course he has now turned them into a mercenary force, but, just as with the excavations, the jobs they get are so few that he'll never recover the original investment.

"All together, Lindon's Oslo operations—his army included—have incurred a bulk debt somewhere in the range of sixty billion credits. For a company with only twenty billion in gross revenues, that is nothing short of ruinous. Of course his company has many other successful ventures that are keeping it afloat, but it begs the question of why a company so shrewd in some areas would be so profligate in others.

"That is the background," Laurantzson concluded. "But now I must yield to Lene, as she will delve into classified information that she is much better versed in than I."

Hanssen suddenly felt the prickling expectation of a conspiracy theory—which seemed late in coming. This meeting had begun so casually that he had not been alarmed by Laurantzson's discussion of the corporate army's origins. But, now that Willoch was about to dispense 'classified information,' it seemed that Laurantzson might really have been laying the groundwork for some historical reinterpretation. Willoch was about to take the strange circumstances behind Lindon's corporate army and tie them into some theory that Jesus had really been a skinjob, or that prophecies stretching back a thousand years were about to be fulfilled. Hanssen brought up his guard ...

"What I have to discuss, Colonel," Willoch began delicately, "concerns the Singularity."

I knew it! Hanssen exclaimed. This set off an array of alarms, as there was no more fertile a breeding ground for conspiracy theories than the Singularity. The allotted speculation over every assassination, terrorist attack, and moon landing of the last hundred years was dwarfed by the storm that yet raged around that one event.

Still, it was odd to encounter conspiracy theorists so high up in the chain of command. And Hanssen found it hard to doubt the earnest faces of the Mayor and the Admiral. He narrowly decided to keep an open mind.

"There are many theories about what happened that day," Willoch continued softly, making determined eye contact with him. "In fact, the

345

speculation grew to be so outlandish that the public quickly fixed upon one explanation. Perhaps because they had no stomach to keep sifting through the ashes. So it was decided that Oslo was the site of a 'singularity'—some quirk outcome of too much technology in too unstable a configuration.

"But calling it a 'singularity' was not us finding the answer. It was just a collective, uninformed endorsement of one theory. A few pundits dropped the word on the nets, it was spun and recycled enough times, and eventually everyone accepted it as the truth. Maybe because deciding on such a vague cause made it easier to prevent such a tragedy from happening again. That way we didn't need to look closer and figure anything out, we just had to spurn technology, promote green parties—other desultory goals.

"But the Singularity was, by any measure, the most destructive and far-felt single event in Human history. We need to understand exactly why and how it happened. And our governments, our intelligence agencies, and the Lontans have been trying to do that for the last five years. So what I am about to tell you, I am *telling* you—this is not simply my own theory about that day. This is all collected fact from the ISSO, the Lontans, and other organizations.

"—And, as such, you are in no way cleared to know any of it," she added procedurally. "But this is my call. I only require that you not share or discuss this with anyone else. Do you accept those conditions?"

346

Hanssen stared back into Willoch's forthright eyes. "Yes, ma'am."

Willoch nodded. "So, we were discussing what happened in Oslo. The public perception was that it was a singularity, but singularities are not just random events. They're like earthquakes or tsunamis—definable, meterable disasters — only artificial rather than natural in cause. The Lontans define them as the event of an independent intelligence forming spontaneously within an infostructure. It is like ... the greater hurricane of technology suddenly manifesting an eye, a focal point, and from there it grows to sentience.

"But, because they are disasters, the Lontan Governate is always on a preventive 'singularity watch.' They're busy balancing our technologies and monitoring the infostructure to militate against such an occurrence. Up till 2040 they had actually done a very good job of this, and they rated us as only a distant singularity risk. So, when the disaster in Oslo happened and we all called it a singularity, the Lontans knew it was no such thing.

"They say that each singularity is unique because it depends upon exactly how a society has utilized technology to tie itself together. It comes down to the balance of wireless versus fiber communication; the levels and types of security usage; the preponderance of government, corporate, and personal data traffic; everything. But there is one quality that they all share, and that is 'madness.'

"Because the artificial mind born during a singularity is almost always insane. It experiences a traumatic birth into drastic abilities and awareness,

347

and it typically finds itself in a hostile world that is reacting violently to its presence. When an intelligence forms under those conditions, it is almost always mad. The Lontans can measure this instability, and then that essentially serves as the 'Richter scale' for singularities. The more insane the mind is, the more chaotic the event.

"Now, Oslo *was* the result of a conscious mind being released upon the nets—that certainly was what seized control of the planet's infostructure. But, when the Lontans ran this sanity test by observing the mind's actions, they found that it was orders of magnitude too stable to have been a true singularity intelligence. They drew the conclusion that it was a mind born earlier. One stable and methodical. In short, our 'Singularity' was nothing of the kind."

Hanssen had never held any firm beliefs about the Singularity, so there should have been no trouble in filling that void with what Willoch was telling him. Yet it was perhaps because of that old agnosticism that he found he had no purchase to give these new beliefs. The Singularity had loomed to him as the supreme act of God, so to try to attach any reasoning to it beseemed a sacrilege.

"The AI that caused our Singularity existed beforehand," Willoch continued. "It was built; it had a physical apparatus; it was stored somewhere. And building an AI is no small undertaking, so this project had to be the work of a large company or nation."

"You're sure of this?" asked Hanssen.

"Oh yes. We even know who built it."

Hanssen almost scoffed.

"Ever since First Contact, many companies were interested in creating AI. They saw it not only as a requisite goal for Humanity but something that would be a technological panacea. But the Lontans restricted related imports and progress was held back. Then, back in the thirties, there was a renewed push to make AI—or at least something approaching it—feasible in the near term.

"The idea was called 'surrogate AI.' Instead of trying to build a fully machine intelligence from scratch, they would take a Human subject—someone already with a developed consciousness—and try to replicate the functions of their brain on a technological device. If they could do that, and set the mind free to exercise the limits of its new substrate, then there would be little difference between this boosted Human mind and a true 'artificial intelligence.'

"One of the foremost researchers in the field was a man named Etienne Duchamp. He was a visible and revolutionary researcher up until '35 when he left his university post, taking a research position with an advanced cybernetics company named Norvig–Russell. You can guess where their main lab was."

Looking downwards, Hanssen said, "Oslo."

"Yes. Yet, even with all of the company's resources, apparently Duchamp couldn't make the project work. So they engaged in some smuggling: the company brought down a few alien tools with abilities above the Human state of the art. After this, they apparently enjoyed enhanced success. They could run their AI off of its artificial substrate for several seconds before its thought patterns dissipated. It wasn't a consciousness yet, merely a recording of one that could propagate forward briefly. But they were convinced that they were close to a breakthrough and finding the last key that would turn the recording fully aware, after which it could operate independently. This is what we believe happened on August 13th, and hence, the Singularity."

Hanssen was becoming agitated by all of this dry and scientific talk about the greatest tragedy in history—about the greatest tragedy of his own life, personally. His thoughts of 'sacrilege' were quickly becoming less of an allusion and more of a physical sensation.

"After Oslo, the company came clean," Willoch continued. "Those who hadn't been in the city cautiously approached the ISSO and the Norwegian government and divulged the activities of the lab. At the time no one was sure if that had been the cause, but, within a few months, we removed any doubt. There were several other AI projects active around the world at the time, but Norvig's was the only one close to achieving sentience on the scale required.

"But that still didn't answer all of the questions. Norvig gave us the design plans for their Oslo lab, and it was very secure. There was no way for the AI to breach the EM lockdown in place around it. And they had never even planned to give their AI direct access to the nets such as it would have needed. *And* there were many kill triggers in place around it to keep it from escaping the company's control. Whatever happened to disable all of these safeguards, we don't know.

"Yet their project would have produced the stable mind we observed in the Singularity. Despite the lingering questions, we still had the answer to what happened."

"Then *how* do you explain Oslo?" Hanssen cut in. The pressure had been building up in him from the first mention Willoch had made of that day, and he could contain it no longer. "We all saw the city afterwards—it was *destroyed*. Every arcology, every building, every—" he gestured wildly, angrily, "—everything had collapsed and boiled itself down. A million people were *buried* in a minute. Yet you're telling me that that was all the work of a stable, completely sane, *Human-born* mind? ...

"But it had *won!* It had taken over the entire world in hours. So why did it suddenly go crazy *then?*—At the very end?—When there was nothing left to attack it? Why did it decide to destroy itself and take an entire city along with it!"

Hanssen silenced himself and sat backwards, taking a deep breath. The memories were at last too strong, too long suppressed for him to turn from as he always did. He had to face them and ride through them once more, thinking back to that terrible day ...

He was lying sprawled on the barracks floor. He had been there for hours ever since his OHUD had been taken over, with nothing to do but stare into the whirling, hallucinatory stream that was

351

being forced into his eyes. To the superintelligence that had usurped the world, he and every other Human being was just another IP dead end—another axon to nowhere. What he was seeing was the dither at the end of that mind's nervous system, whatever it let leak onto the billions of vestigial connections it controlled. He had tried to crawl around or stand up, but he was blind and deaf—worse, because his senses were not just being denied but overridden. He had forgotten where he was and where he could even go for help. He could only lie there and wait for something to happen.

And then something did. It all stopped. The roar in his ears and the flashes of images ceased. He stood up and steadied himself against the wall. He looked around at the other men who were doing the same as him. They were all wondering why it had gone away, what had happened ... What would happen *next* ...

And then the sound. Tremors and rumbling coming from everywhere.

He ran outside, but saw nothing in their vicinity to explain it. He ran towards the landing strip, to the vantage point out on the bay. Everywhere people were joining him, running in the same direction, trying to find out what was happening. And with every second, that sound—that horrid, indescribable sound—growing louder; growing everywhere ...

When he finally got to where he could see, he staggered to his knees. He grabbed at his hair—he beat the sides of his head—he clenched his teeth till he tasted blood. At every point on the horizon, the city skyline was melting.

Oslo's arcologies had been swept up into rabid growth. They were sprouting with jagged towers and stubs, drawing the construction materials from their own structures. Some of the arcologies doubled in height; others fused with their neighbors; they morphed and flowed as if grasping outwards with simulated limbs. Knowing that there were people in those buildings made the mutations too terrible to watch—but they were too powerful to turn from.

But the skyline could only hold this new, impossible poise for a moment before the first arcologies began collapsing. With their supports eaten away by their own fantastic growth, the new-built extensions broke off and the structures folded inwards.

Every second saw the toppling of another one of those distant shards of glass, and for an eternity it went on. Hanssen had long ago buried his eyes and covered his ears, but nothing would keep out that sound—that cry of unsurvivable collapse. That prisoning demand that he be here, be witness to this.

Before it stopped, he had marshaled himself, stood up, and run for a car. Nothing mattered now: not going AWOL, getting discharged, getting killed. He had to get into the city, to get to them ...

***

Erlend and Kitano had taken Märtha to the opera that night as a treat. It was also a chance at sightseeing because the Leknes Opera House was located at the top of the Harald V Arcology. After the performance they went to stroll the roof gardens and behold the city suspended in miniature below.

353

During their walk, Erlend stopped them all and said, "Hey, Kitano, could you go powder something for a bit? I need to talk to Märtha alone."

Kitano narrowed her eyes.

"I won't have her *corrupted* in three minutes— would you just give us that?" he said, exasperated.

Kitano eyed him once more. She turned to leave, but she tapped her wrist as she did so—an antiquated gesture meaning she would be keeping time.

Once she was gone, Erlend turned squarely to Märtha and said, "Okay, I'm gonna try a little intervention on you. Most likely these words will just end up going on a sightseeing tour between your ears, but I figure you can't expect to hear this from anyone else. So here goes.

"Now, I and everybody else on the planet knows that you're hung up on Hanssen—don't deny it. You like the guy."

Märtha blushed.

"It's understandable. He did you a big favor once. And he hardly says a fucking word and whatnot. But I'm here to educate you. Now, I don't know how far along you are in 'Märtha's Romantic Fantasies'—probably up to season *five* or something by now. But Hanssen *can't* be interested in you. And—aside from all the legal and practical reasons—here's why:"

He sent a family picture to her OHUD: Hanssen and a brunette woman holding a baby. And Hanssen was smiling. Compared to the constant frown he wore, this was as incongruous as seeing a moustache on the Mona Lisa.

"Now don't go blabbing that I told you this," said Erlend, "but see her? That's Hanssen's wife."

Märtha felt a stab of hate.

"Well, ex-wife. —Err, 'former wife'—Well, whatever you call them when they're dead," he deftly corrected himself. "And that's their daughter. Dead, too. Both of them in Oslo, like your parents.

"See, Haze and I were stationed there during the Singularity. We were at our base out in the bay, so we were okay. But his family lived in the city. His wife had a real job and wouldn't live in military housing. Right after the … —Well, we both went into the city to try and get to them, but the details of that day are not for yours or any other ears. But suffice it to say that you can imagine how much you *can't* imagine how changed someone comes out from something like that.

"But I've known Hanssen a long time, and I saw it. He didn't just get knocked off his keel and someday he'll get set back to rights. He's a whole different person. And he's not waiting around for someone to come and melt his heart—make him feel love and shit all over again. —And, even if he was, he'd consider it too cliched to succumb to it when it actually happened. So that is Hanssen's life story.

"And what's the takeaway point for you? Just this: you *really* don't want to get yourself mixed up with some fractured widower twice your age. You may think that you do, but you don't. It is *unwise*. You're just *starting* to get things figured out, and you have no clue what's going on. So trust me, forget Hanssen. Go find yourself some strapping

Norwegian lad your own age and start things off right."

Märtha was staunchly looking off to the side, saying nothing.

"Now, I *know* exactly what you're thinking," said Erlend. "You're coming up with all these elaborate counterarguments and ninety-five theses rebutting what I've said. So why don't you just out with one. ... Come on, I won't make fun of you."

Märtha mustered her courage enough to look at him and say, "If that's true ... then why did he ask me to stay here in Leknes with him?"

"One, it wasn't *him* who wanted to ask. It was the Brigadier. Two, he didn't ask you to stay *with him*. It was to stay *with us*. You might've noticed how he immediately dumped you with Kitano and me to be your handlers. And three, he may have felt some impulse towards you, but it was purely a *fatherly* one. You don't have to be a psychiatrist to see how he might've thought that helping you out in the bay could have made up in some way for never saving his family. And I'm just trying to save you a lot of crying and Kleenexes and other sentimental bullshit."

Kitano reappeared from the other side of the lobby.

"Ahh, I see our time is up," said Erlend. "Thanks for listening. Now go fuck up your life."

Märtha's pent-up obloquy at last boiled over, and she stormed head-down—though tearlessly—out of the opera house.

Kitano shot Erlend an accusing glance.

"*What?*" he said.

Willoch and Laurantzson remained quiet, giving Hanssen his time. Everyone had lost someone in the Singularity, and from Hanssen's Home Guard file—and the two family deaths listed there—they knew who his casualties had been.

His record also showed that he had gone AWOL for three days after the event. When they had found him, he was working around the clock on the hopeless relief efforts: moving wreckage and pulling bodies out of the rubble, some of them alive, but most of them not. He was impressed back into his unit to help with its recovery work, but, when his commander ordered him to get some rest, Hanssen deserted again. They only found him a week later when he collapsed from exhaustion and ended up in the hospital himself.

Laurantzson, for as long as he had lived, knew he had never suffered anything like the man who sat before him.

Once Hanssen had collected himself, he said quietly, "I'm sorry—I ... "

"It's all right," said Willoch in a soothing tone.

"I'm okay." He avoided eye contact. "I— ... Please continue."

"... But you're right," Willoch proceeded softly. "The end was ... very much like a true singularity. We don't know why. Not even the Lontans do. Maybe the AI destabilized at the very end.

"But we do know that the AI itself was destroyed," she offered this as if it might bring some consolation. "When we went into Oslo to

357

investigate, we found that Norvig's lab was one of a handful of buildings in Sentrum Borough that had been atomically fused. Nothing inside could have survived. That's why we have no records of what exactly went wrong. Whatever was in that building was erased, along with the AI."

Hanssen finally looked back up. "Why are you telling me this? What does this have to do with Lindon's army?"

"That, too, we don't know for sure. But remember what Jakob said: that his army cannot be in Oslo for *only* the reasons they state. Economically, it makes no sense, so there has to be something more. And, considering what we know *really* happened in Oslo—and what may be concealed there ... The speculation can lead to nothing good."

"You think ... that Lindon knows about the AI?" said Hanssen. "That he might be searching for it?—for pieces of it?"

"Perhaps. We don't know. We don't even know *how* Lindon could know about the AI in the first place. The truth is very tightly controlled, and Lindon's company had no connections to Norvig–Russell, nor anything like its own surrogate AI project. Lindon may just be searching for his own clues as to what happened in the Singularity, which he doesn't know is already privy knowledge."

"We know very little," Laurantzson said, at last reentering the conversation, "and that's the problem. And that's also why you're here. If we should ever discover Lindon's true objectives, then that may bring us into conflict with him and his

358

army. So we need a field commander. Someone who knows the stakes as well as we, but who can act. And the recent campaign has proven to Lene and I that you are the man for the job."

Hanssen at last understood. And, despite the pains that this orientation had put him through, he was comfortable with the arrangement.

Nodding, he asked, "Is there anything you … need me to do?"

"Not for the moment," said Laurantzson. "We have a ceasefire with the corporate army, and the treaty negotiations will start shortly. For now, just think about what we've said. Get used to it. Should anything happen, you'll hear from us again."

Hanssen stood to go.

Only a few steps away he turned back.

"Thank you, sirs," he said solemnly. "For letting me know the truth. Sometimes I thought … that I didn't want to know. That I couldn't get anything from it. … But it helps. A little."

Interlude - Primer

Ever since the first sentient beings had gazed up at the stars, held the vastness of the universe up to measure against the speed of light, and realized how tediously *slow* the latter was, instantly had begun the search for any shortcuts. Wormholes, warp drives, instantaneous transport—there had to be something. The gods would not have left Creation with so shocking a design flaw. The Lontans, in particular, had spent the first 50,000 years of their stellar age chafing against the light speed limit, and the governing truth they had discovered was this: with scientific and engineering progress sustaining a rate far faster than its information could be propagated, only a handful of their core systems would ever matter. The rest of the universe was condemned to forever remain an exponentially stupider hinterland. The quest for FTL was on.

Yet, even for the Lontans, such a challenge could not be solved outright with just some concerted mobilization. A dim analogue for this may be the Human quest to turn base metals into gold, which started back in the Middle Ages under the banner of Alchemy. At first, whole centuries were wasted simply combining 'pinches of this' and 'elixirs of that,' putting mortar to pestle and firing the alembics, with everyone thinking they were just on the cusp of a breakthrough. Yet it would not be until the Scientific Revolution—a sea change in Human perception—that the alchemists would realize that everything they had been doing was wrong, but at least now they would be plodding down the right path. And then it would still take a further industrial revolution, a chemical revolution, three global wars, and the flight, atomic, and information ages back-to-back-to-back to finally get to where the whole base-metals-into-gold trick became a simple application of the 'Mr. Fusion.' And consider that no step of this process was actually undertaken in the hopes of turning lead into gold. Take the prerequisite of computers, which only came about because, way back when, some Germans had perfected an awfully efficient method of conquering Poland, France, huge tracts of Russia, and just about everywhere else. This behooved Britain—next on Germany's hit list—to develop some novel advantage. Meanwhile the Poles had had some success breaking the codes the Germans used to command their war machine, so, once they passed the torch to their British allies, this eventually led to Bletchley Park, Alan Turing, and the cryptologic *bombe*s used to crack Enigma. Thus the computer age was inaugurated not through the planned fulfillment of a long-sought academic goal, but from the wartime necessity of finding a way to blow up one's enemies cost-effectively. So even though the alchemists' goal was ultimately achievable, it still took hundreds of years of scientific and philosophical advancement before success arrived. And the discovered path ended up being thousands of steps long, with milestones in the vein of 'Invent calculus,' 'Discover radium,' 'Assassinate Archduke Franz Ferdinand,' etc.—a recipe wholly outside of what the alchemists might have expected. Likewise went the Lontans' crusade for FTL, and even their first efforts were just as blind and grasping as a mountebank's search for the *elixir vitae*.

But at last the Lontans discovered hyperspace. In hindsight, the physics of it made perfect sense—when using something as conceptually cartoonish as the Bohr model. Quantum mechanics said that everything was quantized, naturally. This included space, which lost resolution down below a Planck length. But obviously the value of this 'Planck length' was only the result of another quantization, like the discrete energy levels of the Hydrogen atom's electron; and so there should be other 'universes' exhibiting the other values. And indeed these existed: all spatially aligned with the plain old universe, but with their Planck lengths related by a geometric progression, the magic number being e.

The first step above the plain old universe—so-called 'A-band hyperspace'—had a Planck length exactly e times smaller. The next two bands, A♯ and B♭, had Planck lengths e^2 and e^3 times smaller, respectively; and so on, into apparent infinite. Thus, if it were possible to move an object into one of these bands, distances would contract. One could transit to A band, move a meter, transit back, and find that they had actually moved 2.718 meters in the plain old universe. Similarly, a meter-long trip in the A♯ band would advance one 7.34 meters. And, once all the way up in F♯ band, a single Human step was enough to take the entire Earth in a stride.

Via this tantalizing physical quirk, the Lontans saw made manifest the promise of faster-than-light travel. All that was required to exploit it was a way to transit objects between different universes, excite them to non-trivial velocities therein, and bring them back without the matter melting down in between. A tall order, but it *would* be achieved, the Lontans vowed. Shattering the light-speed barrier— or at least replacing it with another barrier that would not bother them for a couple million years— was top-priority. Whole planet-brains were allocated to the task to spin out cataclysmic volumes of thought. They developed a multitude of new disciplines and sciences, and extrapolated through a thousand revolutions a day. They digested and advanced the entirety of Lontan knowledge a million times over, doing anything they could to get the gears of progress turning faster.

Finally, at the long end of their toils, they had produced a prototype 'hyperdrive.' It let them transit objects up to A-band hyperspace, propel them, and bring them safely back. But sadly the low-order bands of hyperspace—everything from A up through E—were mostly useless. They contracted space significantly, but it took about twenty powers of *e* before interstellar travel started to look routine. Yet there was a geometric energy barrier preventing the Lontans from transiting up to a sufficiently high band of hyperspace.

So the titanic effort of inventing the hyperdrive was followed by a surpassingly titanic effort to improve it. Eons passed; seasons evolved and de-evolved; until the Lontans had developed another drive the size of a small moon that could transit to F♯ band and nudge itself along at the equivalent speed of 1.000 000 000 01 c. The light speed barrier was officially broken.

But this prototype was unsuitable for mass production, so the Lontans kept the champagne on ice and put their shoulders back to the mill. Yet it was barely another epoch later before they had an Ib-band hyperdrive that could cruise at 4,000 c. This was enough to do a circuit between Earth and Alpha Centauri inside of a day, and all at about one quadrillionth the energy cost of the previous methods. Here was the long-awaited Model T of hypertravel, and the next day they were simply rolling off the assembly line.

The only problem was that the Lontan Hyperdrive Consortium had released so few of its intermediate products that Lontan civilization was still sub-light, and so this finished product came as an unprecedented shock. When the new drive brought all the far-flung Lontan star systems online and up-to-date almost simultaneously, it precipitated not only the greatest economic explosion ever, but also a war that—even when measured against all later and better-equipped conflicts—still ranked as impressively destructive.

But Lieutenant Commander Frisch of the Royal Norwegian Navy was only dimly acquainted with these past eons of strife. He merely sat at the helm of his *KNM Jotunheim*, a Lontan-made destroyer that was the product of a thousand millennia of technological progress.

In tacspace, he commanded: «CO: Detransit»

The ship obeyed such low-order commands itself, no need for the nav officer to rubberstamp in between. The *Jotunheim* dropped out of hyperspace and appeared awash in star-filled eternity. Out here, in the inky depths of the Milky Way, each star shined to maximum brilliance.

«XO: Drop probe 157» commanded Khlebnikova, his executive officer.

Along the keel of the ship, a sphincter opened and closed, shuddering out the last of their sensor drones. This drone soon transited back to hyperspace under its own power and began its vigil.

«Wrap it up» said Frisch.

Khlebnikova: «XO: Retransit // Set course alpha rendezvous / speed: stealth +0.3»

«NAV: Aye» responded Kittelsen, and the hyperdrive kicked back to life. Their ship slipped back into hyperspace and took up a new course.

Frisch had always been disappointed with hyperspace from an aesthetic perspective. Most science fiction vids gave hypertravel some romantic depiction, whether it involved ships flying through glistening tunnels, or even the old screensaver route where stars streaked by like celestial lane markers. But hyperspace was a different universe, and so there was no way for instruments—or eyes—from Frisch's universe to observe it directly. All they could 'see' outside of the ship was the inside of the bubbular nothing that contained them. This appeared as Absolute Black—the 0 Kelvin of the color wheel. There were technologies that allowed indirect observation of the hyperverse, of course, but these were just million-year descendants of sonar, and all that evolution had not infused the practice of watching a radar screen with any more inherent drama.

With the ship back in hypertravel, Frisch's tacspace was filled with data from their indirect sensors. He saw slow-moving shockwaves expanding away from the *Jotunheim*—the turbulence caused by their transiting back and forth between the universe and hyperspace. Another feature was the great 'v'-shape of their wake, which flowed behind them along the direction of their earlier flight. This was another quirk of hyperspace: its 'quantum-fluidic' nature meant that a three-dimensional wake paid out behind moving ships.

Looking farther aft, Frisch saw the long litter of sensor drones they had deployed over the last few days. These were already whispering telemetry back to them via tight-band hyperspace transmissions. And some of them were even tracking enemy contacts. If the other Human ships were on schedule in deploying their own drones, then the entire sensor grid was now complete and hovering invisibly around them.

Their present mission accomplished, the *Jotunheim* turned towards its final waypoint and a rendezvous with the fleet.

THE END

366

www.ingramcontent.com/pod-product-compliance
Lightning Source LLC
Chambersburg PA
CBHW011457170626
46814CB00008B/2937